The End of Alice

A. M. Homes

GRANTA

Granta Publications, 12 Addison Avenue, London W11 4QR

This edition published in Great Britain by Granta Books 2013
Previous paperback edition published by Granta Books 2006
First published in Great Britain by Anchor, a division of
Transworld Publishers Ltd 1997

A CIP catalogue record for this book is available
from the British Library.

1 3 5 7 9 10 8 6 4 2

ISBN 978-1-84708-725-6

Printed and bound by CPI Group (UK) Ltd, CR0 4YY

A. M. HOMES is the author of the novels *May We Be Forgiven*, *This Book Will Save Your Life*, *Music for Torching*, *In a Country of Mothers* and *Jack*, two collections of short stories, *Things You Should Know* and The *Safety of Objects*, and the highly acclaimed memoir *The Mistress's Daughter*, as well as the travel memoir *Los Angeles: People, Places, and the Castle on the Hill*. She is a contributing editor to *Vanity Fair* and writes frequently on arts and culture for numerous magazines and newspapers. She lives in New York City.

'If the first major literary marker of the American dream of aspiration, potential and never-ending youth was F. Scott Fitzgerald's lyrical piece of doomed yearning, *The Great Gatsby*, its postmodern flipside [is] Homes's *The End of Alice*, whose paired literary voices made a grotesque harmony of two yearners after the dream of youth'
Ali Smith, *Guardian*

'Not all readers will want to see Homes's vision, but those who do will find themselves unmistakably in the presence of the Other'
TLS

'Chillingly precise and almost beautiful'
Will Self

'Undeniably shocking ... Superbly achieved by a writer who is a true artist in words'
Vogue

Also by A. M. Homes

Jack

The Safety of Objects

In a Country of Mothers

Music for Torching

Things You Should Know

This Book Will Save Your Life

Appendix A: An Elaboration on the Novel
'The End of Alice'

The Mistress's Daughter

Los Angeles: People, Places, and the Castle on the Hill

May We Be Forgiven

The End of Alice

For William

A stopped clock is right twice a day
                    – LEWIS CARROLL

Who is she that she should have this afflicted addiction, this oddly acquired taste for the freshest of flesh, to tell a story that will start some of you smirking and smiling, but that will leave others set afire determined this nightmare, this horror, must stop. Who is she? What will frighten you most is knowing she is either you or I, one of us. Surprise. Surprise.

And perhaps you wonder who am I to be running interference, to be acting as her translator and yours. Mine is the speech, the rhythm and rhyme of an old and peculiar man who has been locked away for too long, punished for pursuing a taste of his own.

Fair to say that I see in her the seeds of my youth and the memory of another girl I couldn't help but know.

Alice, I hand you her name gently, suggesting that if you hold it, carefully as I do, pressed close to the heart, you might at the end of this understand how confusing the beating of two such similar hearts can be and how one finally had to stop.

And by now, if you are anything at all, you know who I am – and find my disguise the silly childish senility of the long confined, of the good mind gone sour. But know, too, that as I tell you this, I feel like a contestant on *What's My Line;* before me is my tribunal, the three members of the panel, blindfolded – that detail should cause some excitement in a few of you. They ask me questions about my profession. The audience looks directly at me and recognizing my visage from its halftone reproductions is entirely atitter. I am the first pervert, the first lover of youth, they've had on the show. I am honored. I am touched. When I think no one is looking, I touch myself.

And let it be said that I have the utmost admiration and respect for the young woman to be discussed – for young women in general, the younger the better. Serving my sentence, I have become the chief correspondent, the conversant majora, in these matters. From near and far, by youth and beauty, and those not so fortunate, I am sought for my view, my sampling of these situations.

In the beginning, the words sent were often kept from me, the letters delivered opened and marked with long black passages, the jealous ink of my jailers' heavy hand. It bothered them that I had fans – and I still do – but at some point it was acknowledged, supported by research, that we are not a kind to operate in groups, tribes, or packs. We are not an organization, a political machine, we have no common goal and are therefore considered too diffuse, pathetic, and self-centered to cause a revolution. And so my mail began to arrive unencumbered, to simply be delivered, unopened, uninteresting. Then, too, over the course of time, my keepers have changed two, three, and four times, subject to varieties of administrations, the warming and cooling of the social climate, etc. And while I have largely been forgotten or dismissed by my keepers – no doubt due to my advancing age – the mail still arrives with astonishing regularity.

Unfortunately, I am not the correspondent I once was. I do read everything, but too often perhaps for some of you, I do not write back. I no longer feel that every question deserves an answer and can no longer afford to spend my pocket money on postage.

However, there are exceptions. What drew me to this particular offering, this large flat envelope – I find significance in the page not folded, the document of such value that it cannot be tampered with, altered to fit through the thin slot of a mailbox, that its contents are of such import that they need be taken by hand to the postmaster and left in his care for quickest delivery – what interested me about this well-typed tome was the willingness of its author to transcend, to flirt, outside her chosen category or group.

Among our kind what annoys me most is the unwillingness to explore, or even acknowledge, an attraction other than one's own. We – like the unafflicted – act as though our pleasure palace is superior, as though no other exists. This lack of appreciation for the larger world of activity causes a sadness in me that damn near ruins the whole thing. Why not celebrate the full range? That she, too, raised this question is perhaps near the root of my attraction to her – that and the fact of her attraction to him, attraction to telling me, the way she reminded me of my beloved Alice. And to be honest, I don't get much mail from girls. I immediately write back a short introductory note: 'Most interesting. Please do send a photograph of yourself as it would help me to understand better.'

She responds with a note of her own. 'Fuck photos. What are you, a pervert?'

Caught again. Returned to my humbleness, my place.

'Yes, dear,' I jot back on a plain white card.

I had hoped that in a photograph of her I might find some part I could enjoy, some piece still a child – there often is a little something left until one is well into the second or even third decade. Sometimes it's just the chin, a bit of the neck, or the lobe of the ear. Sometimes there is one perfect sliver that has thus far gone unmarked. From that, I am able to go on, focusing on that place, that segment of youth, filling in the rest, whatever is needed, from my memory of how it once was. But now I am getting ahead of myself.

Call me old-fashioned in that my concentration here is on an arrangement that according to many of my peers has long since passed. My fellow esthetes in this great colony of philes insist that I am a classicist. I am interested in the coupling that throughout history has propagated the human race. I realize that for many the real interest, the contemporary current, is in what some consider the greatest refinement, the linkage of related parties either by marriage, familial bonds, or the nearness and dearness of the same sex – the mind-bending adjustments, fascinating alterations, and gesticulations associated with the pairing of two like objects. But I ask that you bear with me, that you allow for this reconsideration of the more traditional of our species. All will not be lost.

She writes: *The way you talk is so peculiar – did you go to school in England? Or is it a speech impediment? One of my friends had to have a 'talking tutor' all the way through high school.*

I answer: University of Virginia, B.A., 1961. The speech impediment is an affectation.

Oh.

Before continuing I must also ask that you excuse the idiosyncrasies of my sound, of my thought, for I so rarely speak these days that all I do say seems to hurl itself forward, collecting references, attachments to both past and present as it goes. My access to society is limited, making what does filter through so much more dear, filled with import and meaning. I am often moved to tears, or worse, or more. Here, too, I could go on, I do go on, but it is best if we stick to the story at hand, that being hers not mine. Mine, all too familiar; mine, now a life of late nights in my room, cot against the wall, color television set – a gift from an anonymous admirer – on a distant chair, the spectral color wheel of light radiating across the white walls, throwing shadows into the stillness of night. Alone, I watch with the plug of a headphone pressed into my ear, and then sometimes I have company – I share my set with Clayton, a Princeton boy cum murderer, well adjusted, having taken the prison fantasy to heart. We have cable here, stolen in from a wire in the wall, working well when the winds are right. The volume is kept low, lest the keepers hear our groans, our howls, our tears, and take the toy away. We sit perched on the edge of the cot and watch: *Voyeur Vision, Nude Talk Show, Robyn Byrd*, ads for outcalls, Dial 970-Peee (the extra *e* stands for extra pee), Chicks With Dicks. And lest I sound like a hypocrite, I am horrified, breathless. For the first time I feel my age, as weak bones and heartbreak. But I am drawn to these things, that is the nature of my disease, to be drawn to far too many things. And I am horrified and I am sad.

Prison. The bell rings. Upstate New York – the cornerstone reads 1897. My room, housed in a wing known only as West, has not been redecorated for ninety-seven years. I've been up for hours. There is no rest. I make notes – beginning to feel that the clock is ticking faster, there's not much left for me. The bells – punctuation marks of the day. The bell rings and suddenly I am back. I am here, in prison, just as I was beginning to escape.

Morning count. I stand at the door, the gate to my cell.

Halfway down I begin to hear the names – some days I hear as far as Wilson, but more often the sound comes in at either Stole or Kleinman. I hear their names, I know their crimes. Some days I think Kleinman should have gotten fifteen to twenty, and other days it's five to ten. What makes me change my mind?

'Jerusalem Stole,' the sergeant calls – they are four doors down from me.

'It's a mistake – call me Jerry,' Jerusalem answers.

I tuck my shirt in and attempt to pull myself together.

'Frazier,' the sergeant calls, and Frazier, my next-door neighbor, answers, 'So what about it?'

I stand ready. When my own name is called, I review myself, my crimes, and am strangely silent.

Again, the sergeant calls my name. He presses his face to the bars of my cell and asks, 'Everything all right?'

I nod.

'How come you don't answer?'

I shrug.

'You got nothing to say?' His keys jingle. There are doors here, locks, that I believe serve no purpose at all. Trick doors. Fake doors, passageways that are roads to nowhere.

'What time is it?' I ask the sergeant.

Above the entrance to this place, and I saw it only once, twenty-three years ago, as I was coming in, above the entrance is a giant clock with only one hand.

'What time is it?'

'Ain't it a shame,' the sergeant says, fitting his keys into the lock and undoing me. 'It's breakfast time.'

Wet eggs. Dry toast. Little bowls of cereal. Milk.

The girl. She is home for the summer, returned to her people after sophomore year at a prominent girls' college, whose name

I will keep secret, to spare the institution the embarrassment or perhaps the pride, depending on which of the trustees you might ask. And while one can recognize the benefits of a single-sex education, the high pursuits of the few remaining such colleges, one rarely discusses the drawbacks, the demand that the body suspend its development, its inclinations, while the intellect is encouraged to grow. This lack of balance causes difficulties, a uniquely female disorder where the majority of physical evidence is displayed in strange postures (political, social, and sexual), a vicious and hostile lethargy, an attractive perplexity of the eye, and as has been reported a not entirely unpleasant kind of tingling sensation in the body's more yielding spots.

From her letter it is clear that she has been looking for years, searching out the places where all variety and versions of her chosen kind are on display, where one can browse, where it is easy to shop unnoticed. She goes to the public parks that dot every town in America, the baseball diamonds/soccer fields where they frolic in the uniforms of youth and league. They trounce and trample each other, jumping one atop the other, hurling their light flesh against that of their friends, slapping and smacking each other as though nothing else matters, as though no one is looking, or cares.

She sits on the sidelines, cheerfully applauding. 'Go, go, go,' she screams when the goal is made, when the bat strikes the ball and the player rounds third and heads for home.

She frequents those places where families congregate – zoos, circus performances, little puppet theaters – and watches them among their own, bickering over souvenirs and snacks, wrapping their plump palms and lips around fluffy spirals of falsely colored cotton candy, boxes of Cracker Jacks, helium balloons, felt pennants purchased for good little boys and girls. She can be found in amusement arcades and shopping malls where the fed-up, frustrated parents of these creatures deposit their offspring, as though this modern structure, this architecture of commerce and commercial intercourse, this building itself, were a well-trained baby-sitter.

In a case such as this where one has been looking so hard for so long, it is within the range of possibility that a buildup of ocular imaginings exaggerates the current draw so that the actual pressure within the eye from such frequent pupil dilation causes a discomfiture not unlike that found in other regions. At peak, it produces a kind of blindness – nearly classically hysterical – during which she does not see what she is doing, giving birth, so to speak, to the notion that her grabbing of his flesh is simply a hand reaching out for direction.

Perhaps quite differently from how it has previously been presented, perhaps in truth this boy is her guide rather than her demon. I have long suspected that youth knows far more than the sugar-glazed gap between mind and body allows it to articulate.

Spring semester sucked, two incompletes to finish by July, otherwise – academic probation! A paper to write, twenty to thirty pages on 'The Criminal Personality'? Dare me to submit my own journal?
   Wild with something, dunno what. Migraines. Aarrgghhh.
   What do you do for fun in that place anyway?

On the sixth day following her return, the previous days spent in a state of deep tranquilization, a close-to-comatose, chain-reactive, biochemically linked readjustment period replete with headaches severe enough to warrant the use of prescription medication, the stunning, stoning combination of Fiorinal and Percocet – pass the bottle, dear – and the development of a full series of symptoms fully related to the life of a female nineteen-year-old – anorexia, followed by gorging on mother's good cooking, a bloating feeling, four tempers played against declarations of love, nausea, strange dreams buried in the sound sleep of one's own bed, diarrhea – the closet cleaned and reorganized, still more of the unending supply of childhood remnants left in plastic bags at the end of the driveway for the Salvation Army to claim, purging.

'It's the water. The change of water never agrees with you,' her mother says.

On the seventh day, she rose anew and carefully washed and clothed herself: a floral-based bath-and-shower gel was used in the morning ritual along with fresh mint toothpaste, a talcy deodorant balanced for the acidity of a woman's sweat – she'll grow into it yet, damn her – and also a dab of mother's Chanel placed on the back of her spine just above the start of her ass crack. The minutiae of her ablutions not so much described as deduced by my own interpretation, my more personal understanding of her. I would also add that using a razor found in the shower, she did, taking care to lather first with mother's moisturizing soap, shave her legs, her armpits, and as though a gift to me, the few odd and not quite pubic hairs on her inner thigh. Thank God for the accuracy, the clean sweep, of the double blade. She then slipped into her disguise – a pair of oversize and out-of-style shorts and a shirt cast off by her father – went down to the morning meal, and then, costumed for obscurity, set out to find her man.

The amount of nervousness generated by these proceedings, these thoughts about to become deeds, was enormous. When her mother asked in a lovely and lilting voice, 'Where are you going?' breaking the concentration, disturbing the frequency of the daughter's thoughts, the obsessive-compulsive nature of her plan, her very movements, the child seemed to flicker and, for the portion of a second, to lose her mind entirely.

'Sweetie,' her mother repeated, following the still youthful one as she walked back and forth, a carnivore suddenly trapped, her mother's heels tap-dancing behind her. 'I asked you, where are you going?'

Our hero turned to her mater and bellowed, 'Out,' blowing the breath of ripe desire into her mother's face. The mother, overwhelmed, stepped back as the daughter went quickly out the door, slamming the heavy wooden bottle stop, the gate to the tomb, behind her.

Outside. The great wide Westchester open held the clarity of a late-May morning. The flowers through the earth, buds coming to bloom, the New York State sky, clear and bright, the air neither warm nor cold, but just right, and the silence of the suburban streets spread thick like a woolen blanket muffling whatever sound or impulse might lurk just beneath.

Down and around she wound, figuring to take the long way, the way that was no way at all, figuring to seem as though she had no objective. To walk directly to his home, to stand at the foot of the drive, binoculars pointed at his bedroom window, would be so painfully obvious, so pathetically boring, so terribly devoid of pathos, of anticipation, of all that creates mood and memory, that it was unthinkable. And thank God that it would not even occur to her. Thank God her mind was subtle and cunning enough to not even entertain such stupidity. Forgive me now for even having mentioned it.

Her heart is full as she rounds the corner. His father's castle is intact. The garage door stands open, she sees the toys – bicycles, sleds, skis, a canoe – the very props of the charade, laid up against the interior wall. For each she can construct a scenario, a scene and manner in which she'd like to see them used. She sees the family station wagon at rest, its bumpers clotted from the childish – hence uneven – application of what some might consider humor. If U Can Read This Then UR 2 Close; Drummers Do It to the Beat; Honk If You Like. . . . In a bustle of commotion, hurr and whir, the younger brother comes speeding down the drive on his 'Big Wheel' bike. Here I quote her directly, somewhat unsure of exactly what is described, but imagining something akin to a unicycle. She sees this little one but is neither amused nor interested – too wiggly. She knows from having done a semester's work in a nursery project, having zipped and unzipped, pulled down and up so many pairs of pants, having witnessed up close the peculiarities of infantile privates in plumpest form. She would have to say that, while it is sweet, while it is tender, it is simply not enough; nothing more than the stuff of a lovely brooch, a modern sculpture to be worn by the envious have-nots. The cherubic cock and balls, like so many other miniatures, like the bony baby bird, better observed than ordered, better taken in from across the room than taken on one's own plate. And so she stood on the sidewalk watching the small sibling until such time as he began to watch her back, and then she nodded and moved off down the street toward the school yard.

Her boy had been under observation for several years – he was of course not her first; there had been other, earlier experiments – but this was to be, she hoped, the first complete conquest. He had been discovered two years ago in the most old-fashioned way – on the playground behind the school. He was nine or ten and flanked by twin attendants, the assemblage of his ego, the entire entourage struggling to master the athletic form of the skateboard. The board was new and he on it was rather uncoordinated. All three boys were at that age of supreme softness where muscles waiting to bloom are coated in a medium-thick layer of flesh, highly squeezable. They were at the point where if someone were to take such a child, to roast or to bake him, he would be most flavorful. Our girl thought it a shame, a missed opportunity, that in the environs of Westchester and Dutchess Counties everyone not be treated to a taste of young flesh. She thought that perhaps, once or twice a year, as part of some great festival, one of each, boy and girl, should be prepared and the residents given a skewerful accompanied by lovely roasted onions, carrots, cherry tomatoes, peppers, the stuff of shish kebabs. But grudgingly she acknowledged that such a biannual event might result in a feeding frenzy, destroying the species, rendering it extinct. After all, for centuries it has been said that once certain animals taste meat, there is no going back, and for sure the pubescent boy and girl are of that most ripe, red, and succulent category that would cause such a reaction. Quite possibly just the scent of their juices spilling off the rack could start carnivores round the world salivating uncontrollably and charging the exits of national and international borders. Therefore in principle she agreed – although I am not so easily swayed – that while this massive public tasting was probably not in order, the denial of it encouraged, even begged for, a little nibbling at home.

She longs to sample him, but has waited, given him first a year and then a second summer of slow roasting, and now has returned, hoping to find him close to perfection, done. She drools.

The school yard is empty. Swings stand still. A woman with an empty stroller passes through, calling, 'Jeffrey, Jeffrey, I know you're here, come out, come out wherever you are.'

She marches on – our good soldier – quickly cutting across the painted playing surfaces, four squares and hopscotches, and crosses to the broader street leading toward town. Until now it hadn't occurred to her that it might take hours, days, to find him, that he might have been sent off somewhere for a summer's vacation. Panic dizzies her, blurs her vision, but the outline, the single-story skyline of town in the distance, keeps her to her goal.

If he is gone, all will be lost, all there ever was to be – after so much careful cultivation – was this one summer, this, the shining moment, the last rush of beauty and hope. By October her boy will be too bulky, brawny, full of himself. But here, now, there remains the fragile, the supple, the heat so close to the heart.

Camp. She hopes his clothing has not been anointed with iron-on identification tags, first-middle-last-name, has not been packed up in some hand-me-down canvas sack and tossed into a tall bus bound for the green hills, the blue mountains, the great glassy lakes of the upper Northeast. On a rampage, she imagines learning his exact location from the weekly required letters that the mailman unceremoniously stuffs into his parents' mailbox.

'Dear Mom and Dad, I'm playing lots of tennis, learning riflery, arts and crafts. Accidently hit a kid from Rhode Island with a golf club, he had to get stitches, but no one likes him anyway so it's okay. Send my goggles and some decent – not sugarless, definitely bubble – gum. Love.'

She will hunt him down, slither through the gates posing as a new member of the kitchen staff, and butcher knife in hand, will slip from cabin to cabin during the night sampling bits and pieces, a few in every bunk, until she finds him.

Camp. Evergreens. A mess hall of logs and mortar. Squat cabins dotting the acres. The air inside the cabin is dank, filled with the pungent meaty odor of boys. Not a clue that civilization is within rifle's range. Here they train, sending arrows through the sky, rigging masts and line, studying the identification marks of both spider and snake, embarking on evening expeditions, survival nights spent deep in the wood, skin painted with insect repellent, Six-Twelve, Cutter's, each camper equipped with a flashlight, Hershey bar, and Morse-code ring. She thinks of the five hundred boys, the excitement, the charge of their raunchy and rustic range as compared to her own memories of summers spent segregated, sent with a thousand girls to the hills of Pennsylvania. Swimming the dark and mossy lake, ankles kissed by slipper fish, feet taken by the mysterious murk at the bottom, the waterland, an unidentifiable mush forever threatening to open and swallow a plump young camper with a single gulp, a great burp bubbling to the surface. The sharp sting of the guardian's tin whistle beckons the little ones out of the water, back onto terra firma. From here, even with my obstructed view, I feel I can see them as though in the full light of day; the water beading on their skin, the nylon, the crocheted cotton of their suits, clinging. I see the outlines of thighs, plump and perfect buttocks, hard pin-headed nipples, the sloping, small, dainty V marking the smooth slit, the path to the queen's palace. I see them breast-stroking, sidestroking, crawling their way to health and good fortune, and God, I want one, any one would do. I want not so much to see her – that would be too much, would force too many comparisons – but to blind myself, to close my eyes and simply feel her. And perhaps, as though I were some crippled old man, she would take pity on me and lie next to me on this thin, narrow cot.

I hear a thousand female voices singing for their supper, crooning, 'Today while the blossoms still cling to the vine.'

I go with them to their cabin. The joint reeks of the endless variety of sprays and soaps they cream themselves with, leaving the cabin a hothouse, a nurseryman's nightmare of herbal intoxication, sure to make anyone with the slightest predilection to allergies wheeze, gasp, and grope for breath. I go with them into this temporary home and watch as they ready for bed, scurrying around the cabin taking turns at sinks, toilets, running wide brushes through their long locks. So many in motion, it is impossible to focus on any one. The action here is on the spin of the room, the tilt and whirl, so much clothing on and off. It goes on ten, fifteen minutes or more until all are finally washed, pajamaed, and orthodontically equipped for sleep. Like that, they gather round the table in the center of the room, and the counselors – themselves young and understanding women, just past prime – go through the evening prayer, the request to God that by daybreak each girl be so much wiser, more fulfilled, and generous with herself and others. Amen.

And then the twelve little girls form two fine lines, and one by one the counselors press their practiced lips to the centers of the mind, forehead square. Benediction made. The children, kissed good-night, usher themselves off to bed. Shhh, shhh, shhh, the counselors' last word. And the whispering is stopped. Shhh, shhh, shhh, and good-night. Lights out.

It is as though I am medicated, tranquilized. Calmed. Stilled. My respiration steady. I am in heaven, curled among the nymphic creatures: Courbet's red-nippled wonders; *Sleep,* touched; Rubens's *Jupiter and Callisto;* at one with the tittytweaking heroes of artistic endeavor; Second School of Fontainebleau, *Gabrille d'Estrées and the Duchesse de Villars.* I am strengthened, stiff from the presence of such pictures in my mind's eye, the ability of the senses to conjure. I wish only that the paintings were here so I might lay the canvases out along my bed and wipe my dry face over them, bury myself between the fluffy thighs of so many cherry girls. And perhaps, my dears, you do recognize that while pornography is prohibited from entering the compound – although be sure it does, disguised in the oddest ways; hidden in boxes of breakfast cereal, stapled into New York State tax forms – my interest is not in the clipped beavers of the 1970s or the overinflated bosom of the 1980s. As I have so often stressed, I am a classicist and I like my pictures the painterly and old-fashioned way. What art it is to remember, to cup the luminescence of the oils, the bulk and tang of its mix with the turp, to know the months it takes to dry, the propensity the paint has to slide, to move itself for greater comfort away from the artist's hand to a more suitable position. When in the heyday of this institution they offered courses of instruction, I took the art they gave, but when my still lifes became all too real, when I insisted on squeezing great gobs of paint through my hands and then turning the painted paw onto the primed paper, shaping out breasts and butts, gaping holes for the member made, I was led ever so gently out of the room, hands washed with the help of others in the big utility sink, and returned to quarters with no explanation. What hurt me most was that they kept my paintings, took them all. They came and cleaned out my room and I cried. I spent the night in a deep wallow, bellowing, 'But they're mine, they're mine,' and was not even offered a drug to quiet the forthright expression of such despair, even though I know for fact that my file says I am allowed such when perturbed. That night they let me suffer, the paint still damp under my nails, my cuticles and the flesh around the tips of my fingers semi-permanently stained. I sucked them, pulling in the pigment, the lead, hoping it would do me something, hoping the putrid flavor of such cheap compounds would draw me closer to some essential self.

———————————————————— 2

What do you do for fun anyway?

Two guards talk in the hallway. 'Best anniversary present I ever got her? This year – new boobs.'

'Big tits?'

'Yep. The perfect gift. She just got 'em put in. Cost me five thousand bucks.'

'How big are they?'

'Can't tell yet.'

'Isn't it amazing what medicine can do – like an oil change, you just take 'em in and they get big tits.'

'Unbelievable.'

'You bowling?'

'Not this week, did something to my back.'

'Twist it?'

'I dunno, something.'

'Get the wife to rub it with her big tits, you'll feel better soon,' the guard snickers.

'You're a card,' the other guard says. 'A real card.'

The decay is everywhere, inside and out. I stuff toilet paper into my ears and go back to her letter.

Camp. *My parents used to send me to camp, but the other girls were too queer, so I refused to go back.* She writes of the memory of one particular afternoon – or perhaps I write for her – her syntax, articulation, and understanding are still the stinted, stilted language of youth. The story is of coming into the cool of her cabin to collect her tennis racket and finding the two little girls from Louisville, Kentucky – the two who with greatest frequency received boxes of homemade chocolates – lying across the top bunk, head to toe, the brunette's narrow foot sweeping back and forth across the strawberry blonde's nipple, the blonde's jumpsuit unzipped and parted to the waist. When the lovebirds sighted the girl and smiled at her, there was a flash of light like an explosion, as the sun, reflecting off the brunette's metal tooth-braces – orthodontia – bounced round the room. And our girl, sour of stomach and spirit, gut rising in a retch, gathered her racket, her balls, and quickly hurried out.

'I thought I would puke,' she says. 'And they weren't tough like girls from Baltimore or Pittsburgh. They were from Louisville and wore long braids and pearl earrings.'

I wish to return to that camp with the young one, to witness through the gauzy screens of the curtainless cabin those two Southern girls taking each other high on the top bunk, the bed frame scraping the cement floor as they grind their flat fronts against each other, endlessly. The athleticism and stamina of youth should never go unappreciated. To go there with her and explain in greatest detail the goings-on, to suggest to her that perhaps the sickness she experiences, the nauseating turn, is her own internal structure cramped by the rise of a desire heretofore unknown. I would also suggest that the impulse to 'lose one's lunch,' to spill such rich and fine fare as the three or four peanut-butter and jelly sandwiches consumed under the elm by the canoe pond only an hour before, is not so much a mark of aversion as a pronouncement of attraction, the making room for greater possibility. As her guide, I direct her to watch the two experts from the Bluegrass State as they wrestle and writhe, and upon their collapse, I might give her shoulder a firm push and encourage her to join them for more. Then, there, outside the door, looking in on the three as they take to the floor – the bunk too narrowly thin, too precariously positioned for the synchronistic excursions of three – I'd get my thrill, my treat.

Something dashes by. A flash like the explosion of a photo cube. A blue dot left before one's eye. I see a girl in front of me. A girl. I blink. The girl is still there. I am being tempted, teased. Alice.

Slowly, the past comes back to me.

Again, as is my habit, my nervous tic, I have gotten away from the story at hand. And meanwhile, my new girl, my correspondent, waits for us alone and annoyed at the lunch counter in town, her only companion the gummy cheese sandwich she can't seem to make disappear.

'Take your plate?' the waitress finally asks.

'Please,' she says.

With nothing before her, she is free to pay the check, to wander slowly home. The exertion, her efforts, her concentration, has left her drained, dulled. She walks slowly, pathetically, home, tripping over occasional cracks in the sidewalk. Safe behind the doors of the family fort, she lays herself out across the living room sofa, swallows the start of a good cry, and hopes to sleep.

'Bored already?' I imagine her mother asking as she sweeps from room to room, arranging and rearranging the objects that are their lives. 'You know, I have a hair appointment at two – you could come with me. I could have you squeezed in and highlighted. Maybe that would perk you up?'

The daughter doesn't answer. The image of her head capped with plastic bag, strands of hair pulled through premade punctures by a practiced hand, is far too frightening.

'You know,' the mother says, beginning the second sentence of her streak with the same phrase.

'Why say "you know" when clearly I don't?' the daughter asks.

'I was going to say, you're not a girl anymore, you should start dressing more like a woman. I could take you to Saks in White Plains and have Mrs Gretsky find you a few new things. We haven't gone shopping together in years.'

The daughter imagines herself in a knitted suit with a pillbox hat perched on her highlighted head, chunky gold jewelry like a dog collar wrapped round her neck and a small alligator purse over one arm, still snapping.

'I thought there was a court order against our shopping together. All the screaming, the swearing.'

'You're older now and hopefully more grown-up.'

'I doubt it.'

'You know, I'll never know exactly what it was I did to make you so angry, will I?'

'No,' the daughter says, pulling a creamy cashmere blanket up over her shoulders and turning her face in toward the pillows.

'Then rest,' the mother says. 'You sound crabby, you must still be overtired. I'll see you later. Nap, but don't drool.'

*   *   *

In my memory it is always summer, a certain summer.

Morning in June. Breakfast. I go downstairs and find my grandmother in my mother's place, my grandmother hovering over my mother's stove.

'Over easy or sunny side up?'

'Up,' I say, forever an optimist.

My mother's absence is not mentioned. And I'm sadly sure that this day is a repeat of the day two years before when I woke to find that while I'd slept, my father had died. My father, a true giant, seven feet eleven inches, had died while I was dreaming, and as I slept, five men eased him down the stairwell, lowered him like a piano with a rope tied around his chest, his body too long and slowly going stiff to carry around the corners.

'Where's Ma,' I finally spit at supper.

'Charlottesville,' my grandmother says, waiting to speak until after dessert is served. 'Charlottesville,' she says, as if the name of a certain small Southern town will tell me what I need to know. 'The asylum.'

'How long will she be there?'

'Well, that depends now, doesn't it?'

My bags are packed. I'm removed from my own life and taken to live at my grandmother's house. In my memory it is always summer. I have a yellow toy truck with real rubber tires. I love the tires.

She writes: *Sometimes I have the weirdest dreams. . . .*

Boys. Boys from before, ghosts, come back to visit her. One in particular, sixth grade. The tag end of the elementary years, a four-foot-eight-inch transplant from Minnesota. First noticed when she caught his eyes on the figures at the bottom of her

31

page, copying answers to the math test. In the coatroom, her thick whisper threatening to turn him in had him fast begging for mercy, for leniency, for her pardon. She offered closely supervised parole. He accepted.

When he felt her up, all he got were the puffy protrusions that promised greater future swellings, and when she felt him down, all she found was the narrow little nightstick that might with patience grow to a cop's thick billy club. Like that they played, equals, bald in all the same places.

And perhaps in the guise of making new friends faster, perhaps not knowing the disillusion it would cause – one so willingly makes excuses for the young – at the first boy/girl parties of their lives, before her very eyes, he took up with other girls. All of them, one right after another, if only for a single kiss, a five-minute ride on the swings. She often caught him, lips pressed to the evening's hostess, to the girl whose desk abutted hers, the one with the blondest hair, biggest boobs, him and whomever, rustling in the bushes beyond the patio. Hers was the divorced heart, but she carried on, sure – or nearly sure – that none of the others did the things she did with him. On the floor of her mother's walk-in closet, she gagged his mouth with a suede Dior belt; behind the cinder-block retaining wall, she employed a railroad tie to hold his legs spread. Deep in the furnace room, hidden among the spare tires and Flexible Flyers, she repetitiously wrapped him with kite string and extra electrical cords, tying him to the hot-water heater, his puny ass burning a bright and cheery pink as heat seeped through the thin insulation. She pushed him past his limit, drove his sweet *Schwanstück* backward and forward, slamming him from drive to reverse. Stripped, she slid her naked body over his, sweeping the rubbery tips of her tits across his fine and sensitive skin from neck to nuts, making him twist and turn, trying to pull away from the heater, the heater itself making a groaning sound and him begging, 'Put it in, put it in.' She'd pull away, smile, take herself in hand, and do a little dance around that furnace room, hairless body, narrow hips pumping the oily air until finally with the smallest shudder she'd stand suddenly stone still, like someone struck dead. And when she recovered, she'd go to him, pull his underwear up over it and put her mouth down on it, sucking him off, the thick BVDs a kind of prophylactic cheesecloth. In the end, she'd untie him, turn him round, and spit onto his hot buns, licking his bright red ass, soothing the sore flesh with the water of her tongue. And he'd thank her profusely, bowing to her honor, 'Thank you, thank you, thank you.' She'd shrug it off, moving on to the next thing – the teaching of luxury, of smoke and drink. She'd hand him a Winston filched from the cleaning lady, a stolen bottle of her father's whiskey, bartered marijuana in a corncob pipe. Days and nights they spent together, inseparable. 'Sweet,' both sets of parents said about the twinness of their children, so charmed. Playmates.

Slowly, steadily, he fell in love, never losing the fear that she would turn on him, direct her anger at the five inches of difference between them and once and for all take it from him – though there is no way he could have told me this, I can swear it is true, remembering it from my own experience, from my grandmother's helper girl who once came at me with a paring knife. If you don't believe me, I invite you to my room, where I am free to raise my shirt, lower my pants, and show the white scar it made, tracing down from just below the inverted stump of my umbilicus, through the matted down, and on into the nether regions stopping not a breath away from the veiny cord that is my manhood. Scarred forever.

Summer. Her boy went to camp – the recurrence of this theme being explanation for her worry about the new boy being lost to those woods. There was a long, slow good-bye in the trunk of his father's Ford – the tire jack like an extra member nearly taking her up the ass – followed two weeks later by a strange late-afternoon phone call and her mother coming quietly into the den, whispering, 'Lightning on a ballfield.' And the girl, being the closest companion, the best friend, was offered his toys, his collections – buffalo nickels and tumbled rocks – his cassettes and stereo as parting gifts.

Prison. Between the bells. I am lost in memory.

My yellow truck is not allowed on the table.

'It's a dining room, not a parking lot,' my grandmother says. She squeezes orange juice. My grandmother squeezes the blood of an orange into a glass and sets it before me, thick with the meat of the fruit, with seeds. I am afraid to drink, to swallow, for fear an orange grove will grow inside me, reach its branches up from my stomach and into the back of my throat, tickling me.

'No seeds,' my mother always said. 'Spit the seeds.'

'Swallow it,' my grandmother says. 'No one wants to see you spitting at the table.'

A little girl from down the street presses her nose against the screen door. 'Can he come out and play?' she asks my grandmother.

'Go on,' my grandmother says, 'out from under my skirt.'

My mother is in the asylum. The little girl likes my yellow truck. I love my rubber tires.

No letter. For several days now, I have had no word. I imagine she has been pulled away from her correspondence by a high school chum who, in late-night session, bordering on exorcism, has brought low this girl's senses, encouraged her to get a summer job, to take a college-level course and fulfill her foreign-language requirement, has, in her excitement at discovering her friend could be so bold, taken the sick thrill to heart. Aren't you afraid to write him? Don't you worry that he does something strange to the paper, implants it, impregnates it, fills it with some of whatever it is that makes him that way? I wouldn't be able to touch it, I'd have to wear rubber dish gloves and open the envelope with a steak knife. And do they let him write to anyone he wants? Doesn't the envelope say, 'Caution, insanity enclosed'? Just his words, the things he says, could get inside your head and do something to you.

I fear she has been taken from me before I could win her, before I could make her believe that what is between us is ever so much closer to the core of things, to her true nature, and that a summer spent temping in the attorney's office or learning German will, in the end, bring little to her life, but a summer swapping trickery with me would change her forever. As one day turns to two, panic takes over and I curse myself, damn, damn, and damn. I will never answer a letter again. I will not allow myself to be put in this position, this begging pose. They have no idea of how important they are to us, they do not feel the power we allow them, do not recognize that with so small a gesture they are in our lives. No one realizes how little there is.

Henry, hawking his wares in the hallway, breaks my concentration. Like a proper peddler he goes door-to-door, cell-to-cell, taking the pulse of the place, establishing himself as an ersatz psychopharmacologist, whipping up between-meal snacks, supplements, little things to lighten the mood. A man of the mouth, formerly the most oral of surgeons, Henry had the habit of giving his lady patients laughing gas, putting them out, then fiercely fucking them, while tugging on their wisdom teeth. His getting caught was a slip of the tongue, so to speak. While he was buried deep in a muff, some sharp thing slipped, and his prize patient, Mrs Mavis Gilette, woke to find a harpoon hole through her cheek and her lost licker languishing on the floor. And not only that, but her blouse was buttoned all wrong. Upon incarceration, plagued by the need to assuage his guilt, Henry developed another kind of habit, and to better cater to his own needs became a kind of pharmacist, mixing his own elegant elixirs, etcetera, etcetera.

He is at my door. 'What'll it be?' he asks.

'Peace,' I say, eager to get on with my work, this awkward explanation, 'and quiet.'

'May your dream be your reward.'

'What time is it?' I ask as he's walking away.

'Past time,' he says, and moves on.

Memorial Day. A slackening of the custodial services is evident over the long weekend. Someone throws up in the hall, and for hours the puddle lies there, its stink ripening and seeming to slide down the hall, closer and closer.

'That your stink?' Frazier, my next-door neighbor, asks.

'No,' I say, thinking of how much Frazier annoys me, how the echo of his snoring keeps me up nights.

'If I find out who did it, I'm gonna make him eat it,' Frazier says.

'Ummm,' I say, responding only to keep relations neighborly.

Our keepers play with their families and come in late,

hungover, faces baked from too many hours standing over the barbecue. And since they trust us not with fire and frankfurters, we are given cold sandwiches for lunch and dinner on Sunday and on Monday, a potentially poisonous picnic supper. The chilled chicken leg included is so thoroughly petrified one would wonder if it had not first been stored in formaldehyde, if it were not some fetal dinosaur never quite born or the quartered remains of an exhibit at the forensic institute down the Northway.

Two new guards talk in the hallway – it seems as though every week there are new guards, fresh recruits, no one lasts long. 'Took my kid to the petting zoo,' one says.

'Shhh,' the other says, 'don't talk about it here, they jerk off to what we say.'

I stand on my bed and look out the single sealed pane of glass someone has nerve enough to call a window. If I raise up on the tips of my toes, I can see a little piece of the outside gate. Tourists are pressed to the gates, slipping the lenses of their Nikons between the wrought-iron bars that wrap this architecturally unsound palace. The prison was designed by a now famous gentleman who went on to build great museums and Long Island estates. But this, a monument from his youth, was suggested by a judge who clearly had the young draftsman's future in mind, offering him a choice, time on the inside for yet another mishap under the influence, one in which a whole family of merchants was killed, William Morehood and Sons no more – or time out to design this convoluted construction. And so our ceilings sag, the walls bleed water on a schedule more regular than a woman's monthly cycle, and in the summer the floors swell a good inch or two so that under the right circumstances one has the feeling of walking on air. And tourists come.

Prison. A bell rings. Lunch. Ham. Cheese. Green Jell-O.

*   *   *

I reread her first letter. *One of my reasons for writing – and there are lots! – is to let you have a look at my life. I thought you might be curious to see what someone like me is really like. I'm crazy to learn more about your life and hope you'll tell me all about prison. It sounds very exciting. Do you make license plates?*

I respond. Today, I have a small headache of my own, an annoying frontal jab that indicates a piece of glass working its way to the surface. In that combining of fates and forces, in what's most often referred to as an accident, my head once met a windshield, and in that split second, the two became sufficiently intimate that I took away with me great sections of fine and fragile glass. And despite the careful dissection under magnified glass in a local hospital, pieces continually come to the fore, introducing themselves as sharp little stingers below the surface. I earned my initial rank here by removing a rather large sliver before an audience; it went off like the popping of a great pimple. I squeezed and out it came, coated in a pinkish, watery fluid that seemed precious being that it flowed so freely and close to the brain. The shard was then passed around the room and ultimately pronounced authentic by one who tested the extrusion upon himself, scraping his skin. The ease with which the splinter drew blood was taken by the witnesses to be evidence of its high quality. I can feel it now, another piece will soon be coming through. When I raise my brow, it scratches; when I rub my fingers across my forehead, the tips are pricked.

It will be a long day. There are many of those, moments between sunrise and sleep that stretch into centuries. I daydream, soothing myself with memories and imaginary games. I force myself to conjure. Clutching my pillow, I pretend the pillowcase is skin. I touch the sheet bunched at the bottom of the bed and think of the bones of Alice's ankles. Beauty. I have loved. I think of the clean white sheets on my grandmother's clothesline. I think of the little neighbor girl who liked my truck, I give myself history lessons.

Alice; naked by the lake is how she found me. She is there on the beach, standing between me and my clothing. I turn away, overcome with false modesty. She watches. She wears war paint and carries a bow and a quiver filled with white arrows ending in blue suction cups. She giggles. She points to my shriveled self hanging down below.

She finds me amusing.

Her amusement I find humiliating, arousing.

I instantly want to do something – to silence that stupid giggling.

Alice collapses, beside herself with glee.

Visitor. Two guards I've never seen before come to my door.

'Surprise, surprise,' they say, 'long time no see.'

'Have we ever met?'

'You have a guest.'

I've not had a visitor in years, can't imagine who it might be, but know better than to ask. The guards wait with leg irons and a belly chain. I take a moment and change into one of my two good shirts; it literally cracks as I unwrap it. I comb my hair, take a leak, and make sure everything is put away.

'Always important to make a good appearance, you never know who you'll meet,' I say as the guards fit me into the various cuffs and chains.

'Big day on main street,' Kleinman says, watching them lead me away. 'Good to see you getting out of the house, and wearing something decent. I wasn't going to say anything, but you were starting to look frumpy.'

My chains rattle, the guards' keys jingle. The great steel gates roll open.

I am taken to the visitors' center – led through the maze on a route that is new to me. Even if my visitor is some door-to-door salesman, a fucking Fuller Brush man, I am grateful for the outing.

'I'm lost,' I tell the guards. 'Didn't the visiting room used to be off to the right?'

'It's been reconfigured,' the guard says.

'Two years ago,' the second one adds.

'I don't get out much,' I say.

They have no response. The men of West are not the most popular in this facility; scariest of the scary, our crimes the most criminal of them all – we are kept in a special section for the sexuals. Car thieves, petty larcenists, and common murderers will have nothing to do with us, and so, to keep the calm, the cool, we are kept entirely apart and are therefore all too easily forgotten. The visitors' center is the crossroads; East meets West, North meets South, and you can tell who's who by the jewelry they wear. North and South are minimalists, unadorned, low security, petty criminals really. Easterners are kept handcuffed, and all Westerners are bound at both wrist and foot. People stare.

A small room in a series of small rooms, a glass door, high glass walls, and a narrow counter – like a phone booth without a phone. Cut into the glass is a small pattern of holes, a place to speak. The lighting is harsh, fluorescent. I squint. Suddenly self-conscious, I look down at myself. My shirt is yellow, stained although I remember it being clean, new. I stare at the stains. I try to rest my hands on the counter. There is no natural position.

An old man steps into the booth.

'How are you, Chappy?' he says loudly, using my childhood nickname, a reference to a perhaps extreme affection for the product Chap Stick.

Frightened by his familiarity, I am suddenly sure that despite the glass that's supposed to protect him from me, at any moment he'll do something that will finish me – I imagine being shot, the bullet shattering the glass. I slump in anticipation of the impact.

'It's me, Burt, you ass. My God, you're awful. It didn't occur to me that you'd be this far gone. Sit up,' he says, dusting the chair on his side of the booth with a handkerchief and then sitting down. 'Jefferson Warburturn Marx.' He gives the name of my grandmother's sister's son, who as far as I know has been dead for years. 'The third,' he adds.

My cousin, my second cousin. 'You used to be younger,' I say.

'So did you. Perhaps I should have called ahead. It didn't occur to me. I didn't think you'd be going anywhere.'

'When did I last see you?'

'Uncle Richard's wedding. You were in junior high, I was a freshman at Dartmouth. I got you drunk and made you eat a lot of wedding cake. I thought it would absorb the alcohol.'

'I was sick for days.'

'And how are you now?'

'Better.'

'Good,' he says. 'I was worried.'

In the booth to my left a couple is kissing through the glass, tongues and all, steaming up the booth. The guard makes them stop.

Burt continues, 'We got to talking about you. It still comes up, you know, and there was some wondering how you're getting along. I was elected to investigate.'

'Curiosity killed the cat?'

'Something like that. So,' he says, clapping his hands together. 'How are you getting along in here, are you adjusting?'

'It's been twenty-three years,' I say, intending it to sound more like a reminder than a reprimand.

'Well, yes, I know. I'm sorry to have been so out of touch, it's just that, well, the whole thing was very upsetting, scared a lot of people. Frankly, I was never frightened, just hesitant to get involved. Actually, it was more my wife. . . . Anyway, I've been awful busy, just retired last year.'

'What time is it?'

'Haven't you got a watch?' he asks, looking at his own, taking it off, motioning as if to hand it to me, as if I could reach through the glass and take it from him.

'Sir,' the guard says, interrupting him. 'You'll have to put that back on.'

'But I'd like to give it as a gift.'

The guard shakes his head.

'Is there a clock?' I ask. 'Out front, above the entrance, a clock with one hand?'

'I didn't notice,' Burt says, strapping the watch back on.

'Do me a favor. When you leave, look up and see if there's a clock, let me know if it's working.'

Burt changes the subject. 'Do they offer you any treatment, any hope?'

I suppress the urge to tell Burt the truth, that their idea of treatment was encouraging me to jerk off while watching porno movies with something called a plethysmograph strapped to my penis measuring my hard-on – and with them watching me through a one-way mirror, no doubt doing a little handiwork of their own. I have the urge to tell him that quite clearly my treatment was for their entertainment, but I don't think he'd take it well.

He goes on. 'Has it been a learning experience? I mean, you wouldn't do it again, would you?'

I shake my head.

'Well, that's good. And it's a decent place? They don't pick on you? There's not a problem with the other men?'

'No problem.'

'I admire you. For toughing it out.' He blots his forehead with his handkerchief. 'My reason for coming is that there were some boxes. They must have gone from your mother's house to grandmother's and then off to my father's, and somehow they ended up with me. Anyway, we were cleaning out and came upon them, mostly things from your childhood, old clothes, mildewed books, rusty toys, a couple of your mother's pie plates that you made into tambourines, that kind of thing. Long story short, they were in the basement, we thought about having a big garage sale but didn't, and then a letter came from a new museum, the Museum of Criminal Culture?' he says, his voice going up on the end of the word *culture*, as though he's checking to see if I've heard of it. 'They're opening in Cincinnati?' he says, again his voice rising, curling into a question mark.

I shake my head. 'So?'

'Well, they wrote asking if we had anything of yours, and well, I wanted you to know. I didn't want you to find out from someone else – that would be cruel. We sold your things. The curator himself came to pick up the boxes – very pleased with the haul. And, he assures me that they'll be well cared for. And, should you ever be released, they'd love for you to come and tell them a bit about some of the items – you are up for parole or reconsideration or whatever it is very soon, aren't you?'

I nod.

'Well, I just wanted you to know.'

'Should I feel honored?' I ask, stalling, wondering if there's a way to get at what I really want to know – how much they got for me.

'Up to you,' Burt says, standing. He takes his card out from his wallet and, unable to actually hand it to me, holds it pressed to the glass for a minute so that I might memorize it. 'Keep in touch,' he says, stepping out of the booth.

A fat old man has disturbed my day, coming to tell me that he has sold my childhood to a museum in Cincinnati.

I stand, and despite all my metallica, my chain-link fencing, I am able to pick up the chair I've been sitting on and hurl it at the glass. Plexy, it bounces off, bounces back and hits me in the head. The guards are on me, tackling me from behind.

Burt turns. 'Good to see you,' he calls as they're hauling me off. 'And take care of yourself.'

Unchained. Tossed into my cell. The door is locked.

A while later Henry comes and whispers through the slot. 'Do something for you? A tiny taste?'

'Why not,' I say, succumbing after a lifetime of abstinence. 'Just a taste.'

He slips a packet of powder under the door and instructs me to rub it into my gums. I sleep like a baby.

My yellow truck has gone to Cincinnati.

4

Sorry for the silence. My parents made me go with them to Washington for the long weekend. Would have written from there, but there wasn't anything to say. We missed the cherry blossoms, I looked up Abe Lincoln's nose – it's chipped – they're fixing it, paddle-boated around the Tidal Basin, went to National Archives for the Nixon tapes, bought you the enclosed.

Inside the envelope is a vellum copy of the Declaration of Independence. Cruel child. For the first time I have the idea that she might be playing with me, but am quickly distracted by the uneven ink of a note scrawled at the bottom of the page.

P.S. Got 'em! And I wasn't even looking! Went to the store to get correct-its for the typewriter, and there they were. More soon!

Hallelujah. She has found her man. He is with friends in the five-and-ten, piling bags of chips, comic books, and candy bars onto the cashier's counter. She hides behind the rack of panty hose and takes him in – her man with his men.

Her boy slips an extra and unpaid-for candy bar into his pocket and her knees weaken. She falls against the rack, knocking sandal-toes to the floor. The boys pay for their loot and leave.

She follows them with the exactitude of a bloodhound. Outside, on the sidewalk, in the spotlight of late afternoon, they work hands, teeth, and jaws, tearing at the layers of foil and plastic that keep them from their prizes. Thinking herself a pro, a watcher extraordinaire, she walks right past them, ignoring them. She goes to the corner, and when the white-flashing man in motion beckons her across the street – walk, walk, walk – she crosses. On the other side, she positions herself near the bank, half-hidden by a leafy tree. From this vantage point, she can see it all, and no one would ever know, suspect, the nature of her interest.

Across the street, the feral pack joyously jams fistfuls of fried, dried, potato, corn frizzle-drizzle doo into their pubescent – hence ever-hungry – chops, cramming the orifice with far more than it can possibly hold. Chunks, giant crumbs of half-chewed food, fall over them like hail, like snow – the phenomena of weather – lodging in the folds of their clothing, using the high absorbency of T-shirts to stain, to permanently mark them with this foul evidence, proof. The boys step backward as if repulsed slightly, then tilt forward, leaning over the tips of their Nikes, their Reeboks, making room for the foul matter, the remains, to fall free. They use the sidewalk as their napkin, their plate, their trough, their ground. They trade materials, passing cans and bottles of soda between them as if mixing the ingredients, preparing equal measures of some serious solvent, drinkable Drano – one part diet Coke, one part Mountain Dew, and a drip of Orange Crush. They swap items, taking a bite, a swig, a handful, and passing it on. They dig deeper into their brown bags and bring out the smaller, sweeter objects, cubes and flats of chocolate, with nuts, with Krispies, crackers, wafers sandwiched in between further layers of chocolate with caramel, with nougat, whipped tufts of fluff.

The feast, the ravagement, the savage hoarding of the tribal reward, goes on until there is nothing left. The bags are empty, the last salty crumbs licked from the wrappers. Garbage, plastic and paper and aluminum foil, is collectively smushed, mushed, compacted in on itself, stuffed into a single brown bag, balled up, crushed, shaped, and formed until it is a bullet, a bomb, a basketball. And then the tall one, the one with the beak, fires it in a swift and daring shot toward the trash can on the corner. Hitting its mark with greater force than anticipated, the bag knocks the top layer of garbage out of the can and onto the sidewalk. Humiliation drives the tall one toward the can, toward community service. He takes a few hurried and embarrassed moments to straighten up the area as several of the town's residents, who have seen the shot, have seen its failure, the sprayed garbage, walk around with their heads shaking and their glottals clucking. The other two members of the group, unable to support the beaked one in his failure, which they take to be their collective failure, stand to one side, shuffling their feet, the weight of mischance heavy on their shoulders.

'Going home,' one finally says. 'Almost dinner. Later, man.' They slap hands and shoulders, butt heads, and kick each other, ending their slapstick routines with long, loud, multisyllabic belches that turn heads up and down the block. 'Wondrous,' they say, 'Unbelievable,' and then they take off in different directions for the shelter of home.

Ecstasy!

Sometimes I wish she would just stop. Not with me; with them. Sometimes I am so frustrated, so bored, so annoyed at how easily she is taken in, turned on, how she unabashedly sucks up this juvenile grotesque. This is not true child's play, it has none of the charm of that. The gluttonous, consumptive moods of these boys to men, their constant testing of the limits, how much one can take, is so baldly adolescent, so pathetically pubescent, that it sends me up the walls. How can she be so blind?

I jot the shortest of postcards. Everything! Does not! Require an exclamation mark!

She is not stupid (I hope). She should want more, she should want the very best. I want the best for her. But it is a telling picture, the portrait of her across the street from them, her khaki shorts from last summer now snug in the derriere and in the thigh – she is, unfortunately, no longer just a girl, but also a woman, the body already dissolving from the tenderness of youth to the buttery bulk and sway, the free-flowing flesh of the fullest female. The notion of her crotch being heated, dampened, made warm and wet, by these boys disgusts me. I want it to require something more, something younger, something older, some greater mystery. I hate it when she is so damn obvious. Hate it to no end. I want to shake her, to slide my own gnarled, hairy, and arthritic five thick fingers between her legs and feel the heat, the high humidity, evaluate it for myself, and then bring her to her senses.

Cursing her openly, I'd slide my hand up that sleeve of khaki, whilst grabbing the flesh of her face between my teeth. Finger-fucking her, I'd bite her cheek, piercing it. I'd give her a sizable piece of my mind. I can afford it. God, they are so annoying when they believe they can think for themselves.

My yellow truck is lost. I am suspicious, thinking that perhaps my grandmother has stolen it, jealous.

'Where is my truck?'

'Who knows,' my grandmother says.

'I can't find it.'

'That's what happens when you drive all over town; maybe your little meter maid knows where it is.'

'I want my truck.'

She doesn't answer.

'When's Mama coming home?'

'Your guess is as good as mine.'

My yellow truck has gone to Cincinnati. When I am released, sprung from this rat trap, I'll visit that museum and tell them the story of how my grandmother kept it hidden from me, kept it for weeks parked in the back of her closet.

Had I not been so distracted, diverted, I think by now I should have been a congressman, an inventor, or at least a novelist. If I could have contained my feeling, if I could have channeled my libido into my career – although I suppose I did that in a sense – if I could have given myself a more familiar and well-accepted career, as many wonderful men have done, if I could have guided my prick instead of having been guided by it, I could have been a leader of men, a molder of morals. Who do you think gives us missiles and fighter planes? Frigates? Certainly not some fur-trapped pussy, that much is clear – they have no interest. Cock and balls, that's what it's all about, everyone knows. Why don't the candidates just go ahead and drop their shorts so we can see for ourselves what they've got, who's the bigger, better man. Elect big dick, he's calm, he's collected, he's the winner all around. You know it. But because we can't see it, because we're so gullible, the shrively dick always wins. Why? Because he fights, he overcompensates, he competes because it all means so damn much to him.

War is a circle jerk.

*　　*　　*

It pisses me off that they can have so much and I have to starve.

It's surprising, I write back, how much we have in common.

Again, she has found them, the sweaty threesome in which her mark is buried. They are in the luncheonette, en booth. He is protected, bounded by his mascots, his sycophants, his small cadre – one with a nose so large it can hardly accommodate his even larger, thick-framed glasses; the other so rotund, front and back, that there is a gap, one or two inches of unbearably white, Crisco-soft lard, between the bottom of his T-shirt and the top of his pants. And he, in the middle, average in every way but, surrounded by such freakage, seeming to her like a demigod. He notices nothing outside of himself, the entirety of his focus is internally directed. His oblivion may be his greatest attribute.

Thoroughly spaced.

Ten times in fifteen minutes he loses his place in the conversation. With all the frequency and regularity of breathing, he says, 'Huh?' and his friends willingly fill in the blanks. Far from stupid – according to her – but forever catching up, he radiates the preoccupation of a boy for whom history holds great things.

She sits at the far end of the counter, hunched over a plate of cottage cheese and cling peaches, watching them in their booth, mesmerized by the consumption, which so far she has counted as four plates of french fries, two club sandwiches, four Cokes, and three milk shakes. When the last drops of spit/milky chocolate shake are sucked up through the straws with great fanfare and gurgle, the silence that follows is almost instantly filled with the by now trademark series of ragged bellowy belches that echo through the establishment. The boys smile and rub their stomachs, proud of their gastronomic gluttony and the resonance of the displaced gases. Upon encouragement from the owners the threesome pay their check and leave.

The tennis racket belonging to our boy remains in the booth. Shaking her head, the waitress plucks it from the corner, and before she turns around, it is snatched from her hand.

'I'll catch him,' my girl says. She races out of the restaurant and, looking right and left, spies the three down the block, window-shopping the music store. 'Hey,' she calls, 'hey,' hurrying happily toward them in what is almost a childlike skip, waving the racket as though it were a flag. 'Your racket, your racket.' Finally he catches on, looking at her as she extends the racket (and herself) toward him, thrusting the ball-beater back into his possession. 'Oh, yeah,' he says, taking it from her with one hand and rubbing his chest with the other, his expression that of someone performing a complicated trick, a sophisticated display of coordination. And in the rubbing, he seems for a second to give his own left tit a tiny tweak. 'I forgot.'

Noticing the tit through the T-shirt, she smiles and wishes to tweak it herself with her two front teeth. He notices nothing about her. To him she is an object of little interest. Too old, too ready and able to wonder aloud what his mother would say if she knew he'd left the racket behind – What's the matter with you? Don't you take anything seriously? You would if you had to work for it. He looks at his shoes, bracing himself for her verbal assault. Because the moment is unanticipated, because her action, her fast-forwarding of the process, has caught her unawares, she is without words. She fumbles, blushes, averts her eyes, and seems much more like a little girl, a dainty doe, than the brazen hussy we know her to be. The picture of her so unsure – so drunkenly filled with the destabilizing flush of adrenaline and whore-moans – warms my heart. And it is possible that this rickety path, this rocky start, only helped her. Had she been cooler, more calculated, she might have come off as distant, unapproachable, a bitch. But here, like this, she is, for the moment, no better, no worse, no less than he.

'Maybe we should play,' she says. 'I was on the team in high school, but I'm really out of practice.'

Head hunkered down, still stupidly waiting for the strike, he glances at her, eyes rolling up and around like loose eggs.

'I'd pay you for your time. Five dollars an hour? Think about it,' she says, not at all knowing what she is doing, with no idea of what will come next, pushing forward only because she is desperate not to leave empty-handed – she must realize some profit, some tangible progress, from this encounter. Unwilling to let the moment fade, she pulls a pen from her pocket – the habit of keeping a writing utensil handy comes from college, but the point of having paper, too, has thus far escaped her. 'Here's my number,' she says, taking his limp hand and scrawling the details on the soft flesh of his palm.

'Should I give you mine?' he asks. She nods and prepares to tattoo his numbers onto her skin – even though she already knows them, having found the family name first on the mailbox at the end of the drive and then in the phone book. It's so easy to spy when no one thinks you're looking.

He closes his eyes as if to conjure a photographic replica of the seven digits that phone home – that ring the bell, that fetch the maid, who finds the boy and tells him that someone, somewhere, wishes to speak with him. There, on the street, she feels she can see through the boy. Through his thin white T-shirt, she begins to examine him, the occasional holes in the cotton like guiding points, reference marks. Taking a step back to sharpen her focus, she breaks him down into sections that can be reviewed, called back again and again at will. She divides him up as though there's too much of him, as though he can't be filed whole.

Shoulders, out from the neck in an even line across the top of the torso, a T square of knobby bone protrusions, prehistoric finds marking the development of man. The torso itself is still reed thin, the pecs barely rounded; she suspects his nipples are like flat, pale dimes, and near the hips there is the faintest ring of baby fat about to stretch into a man's wide rope of muscle. He is twelve and a half and on the verge, ripe. His chin is smooth and clean, cheeks barely fuzzed, and his hair falls in odd locks down to his eyebrows, which are coming in nicely, firm and steady. His eyes are green and slightly unfocused.

'What's your name?' she asks. Until now, this has never mattered, and even now it only gives title to something. It's the decorative and crowning touch, like the little plastic clown heads a baker's assistant sticks on cupcakes. In situations like this when you finally have the name, you have the heart, the soul. Without ever touching, she is exploring him, feeling things, seeing how he will lie against her, gauging his weight, the sharpness of his bones.

'Matthew,' he says. 'Matthew,' he repeats, as if to be sure he's gotten it right.

So many virginities to lose.

5

Prison. Clayton comes, in a strangely good mood. Mostly his countenance is that of a miserable soul, someone so sorry that he can hardly walk or talk. Now, he comes smiling – behind him, Henry hovers in the doorway. They are both smiling, smelling of sweet smoke, stoned.

Henry sees me working and laughs. 'A regular writer,' he says. 'Fiction or non? Memoir? Am I in it?'

'Crossed out,' I say, and he goes off down the hall calling, 'Caps for sale, caps for sale.'

Clayton fills the room, his muscles swollen, heated from his hours with the weights, his shoulders, back, and neck hard and hot – and more than anyone has a right to ask for. He smiles, face breaking into the thin lines that define his dimples, his this and that. I see the Princeton boy, the glamour-puss. I smile back.

He fixes a makeshift curtain over the door.

I am on the bed.

'There, like that,' he says, although I haven't moved.

Upon my arrest, I immediately began to prepare myself for events such as these. In the holding cell, I forced myself to think of the interior, of penetration, of what it feels like to pierce the cavity, to plunge, to plow, to be held at the center of things. Awaiting legal counsel, awaiting the announcement of the arrival of my fate, I continued to prepare myself, again and again, never sure what would happen, when it would happen, but convinced that it would happen, that it was an inevitable element, a piece of my punishment. Fucked. My fingers toyed with the rough edge of my asshole; there was none of the slippery warmth, the buried angle, of a girl's hole – only a puckered drop of dung hung unceremoniously fixed behind my balls. I tried to push the finger through because it seemed one should practice, one should be prepared. I met with full resistance, but continued. The body rejected and simultaneously wrapped itself around the first inch of my finger; the nail scratched and I withdrew the digit and brought it to my mouth. The taste was hearty, rich, surprising because it was so unlike the flavor of my jailers' food. One would have half-expected the strange bleached-white absence of flavor, texture, essence. I sucked the finger to soften the nail, then bit it down to the pink, wet it good, and reinserted it, this time getting to the knuckle.

I thought of my girls and their unsuspecting parts. Surprised, temporarily taken aback, horrified by my inspection, but always beneath the gentility of my touch, the firmness of my hand, my tongue, my member, they surrendered. Slowly, they allowed themselves to be laid out, spread. They responded with detachment, separated from themselves. It took months of careful cultivation to get them to engage in the repartee – to have them voluntarily hook their legs around my back, to have them not pull away as I slide my hand up and under their little dresses, curling my fingers into their underpants. There was one who was reaching for me within two weeks. She would lower my zipper as we sped along the interstates, putting her mouth over me – little snake charmer. I soon left her by the side of the road with the sick and frightening feeling of having created a monster, worried for the life of the unsuspecting trucker who would likely pick up the hitchhiking and precocious nymph. Cunnus Diaboli.

I am on the bed, my knees bent into a desk, a book against my thighs. Clayton takes the book and thoughtfully closes it so that the dust jacket marks my place. He puts a hand on each of my knees and leans forward as though he is about to perform a circus trick, a balancing act, flying on my knees like the airplane rides we all give each other as children. But as I am at that age where the distinct and hard pressing of interest, impatience, and passion comes across more as pain than excitement, I pull away. He leans and tries to kiss me. I turn my head. The kiss lands on the side of my cheek near my ear. He tries again. It is against the rules (our rules) that Clayton kiss me, he knows that, but because he is in such a rare and good mood, I don't say anything – a good mood is such a fragile thing. Already by turning away, I'm sure I've challenged it, but I couldn't not turn, it would have been too out of the ordinary, it would give away my own sad state of mind.

Clayton is kissing my face and neck, at first tenderly and then harder and wetter; all of it causes me to draw back, to pull up inside myself. If it were a single kiss, I think I might be able to enjoy it, but these, too furious and frequent, are filled with a strange and hurried panic. He is kissing and kissing me, lapping at me and now kicking my knees out from under so that he is firmly on top of me. I feel his length, his weight. I feel his care in trying not to crush me and take it to be a gesture toward my years – my soon-to-be infirmity. I raise my hips off the bed as he unzips my trousers and pulls them down. He does the same with my underwear, everything to the ankles, and then reaches back and takes my shoes off. They drop to the floor, two heavy clunks; the echo I'm sure is an announcement up and down the hall that I'm being had again. Clayton pulls his T-shirt off, the muscles ripple. His left nipple is pierced and through it he wears his leaf from the Ivy Club, his Princeton dining affiliation. He stands, takes his pants down, and lays them out carefully on the floor. This is a man who can't be read, can't be understood, a man who if he were so inclined could kill me in a split second – a feature that undoubtedly adds an unarticulated element of excitement. He is three-quarters hard. Even though I thought I wouldn't – could never – I do enjoy looking at him. It is like seeing one's self, like seeing one's self with a certain sense of remove. He takes a tube of (bartered) jelly from his pocket and spreads my legs; his hands on the insides of my thighs, prying, pulling until my legs unlock – this is something still difficult to do voluntarily, without help, encouragement. He squirts jelly onto his fingers, rubs it for a moment to warm it, then slides one or two digits into my ass, greasing the path; sometimes his other hand is on my belly when he does this, sometimes he is pulling on my cock, but today he jiggles my balls and laughs. I see him getting harder. This is not exactly punishment; it is not torture. It is an experience I deserve (need). I am the woman. I lie here and he fits himself into me. In order to survive I must relax. I feel him inside. I feel him against my entrails and am, as always, most impressed. I think of the ones I have been in – the flash of terror as the nine-by-two-inch wonder wand is about to be crammed into the half-inch hole. I breathe. I feel Clayton's weight and understand both the comfort and fear of suffocation. I feel my cavity fill with his fluid and know that for hours it will slowly run out of me; it will mix with shit and leak out a milky brown, soft suede. I will feel him in me longer than he will feel me around him. He will zip up and walk off and I will still lie here split in half. I will have to roll over and take matters in hand. I am the pussy and I take it to heart. I know what it means to be the wife and am so glad to have this horrible moment, this degradation, under my skin.

I check myself in the mirror. I am old, so old. My youth, my beauty, has been lost to this place, that is what they've stripped me of – my finest years. As a young man there was a notable fineness to my features: clear eyes, a thick head of hair, even my chest tresses evoked a certain mystery – there was a mystical spin, a magical weave, to the pattern of that thatch. It swirled like a hypnotist's spiral, round and round. And look at me now. The skin that every summer broke out in freckles is awash in liver spots. The mat on my chest has gone silver, spare, wiry like steel wool. It is the wiring of death, my own wiring breaking through the skin. My body is softening, spilling out over the edges. Everything attractive has disappeared. The fine cap of hair that crowned my pate has receded into thin gray strands – I grow them long and carefully sweep them back. When my teeth go into a jar, that will be all, the end. I'll file the damn dentures sharp and bite my own jugular.

On turning fifty in this criminal hothouse, as the institution's gift the cook baked a dozen of my beloved cuppy cakes – the finished product was leaden like Civil War ammunition, coated with a heavy brown frosting that had less flavor, less firmness, than shit.

'Thanks,' I said to the cook. 'Thanks very much.'

'Happy birthday,' he said.

'And many more,' the sergeant added.

6

He called! My mother answered the phone!

Obviously she hasn't received my latest missive yet, the post-card that explains the proper time and place for exclamation marks!

His voice cracked! Tennis date, tomorrow! Can't wait!

Tennis. They meet at the courts. He arrives early and stands by the fence, swinging his racket, the Wilson wonder wand, back and forth through the grass as though it were not the accoutrement of activity, the measure of athletic prowess, not a sporty bit of equipment but that most modern whip, the freshest fetishistic toy for playing out the empire's old relation between homeowner and his lawn, a weed whacker.

She arrives, says not hello, but are you ready?

Hello is a word that comes with a blush, a flush of shyness.

It is not absolutely necessary, and so it is dropped. She is dying – half-dying – not having known until now that he would be so willing, so easy.

They step onto the courts. Quickly, she goes to the far side. Her T-shirt catches the breeze, fills with air, billows like a sail – catches my eye, catches my breath, my full attention. With only the slightest effort, she could fly.

For his part, the boy wears the vestments of virgin, white tennis shorts and a proper white T-shirt. The shorts are too snug, the shirt too large – his father's. His effort displays his desire to please, the seriousness with which he has taken the job, his vulnerability.

She smiles.

With the exception of two women in tennis togs at the far end, the courts are empty. The women are volleying, taking great care to avoid the baby carriage parked midcourt by the sidelines under the shade of a maple tree.

To catch his attention, she holds a bright green ball up in the air.

He crouches, readies – the crotch of his shorts bunches up. She loves playing tennis. He hits, she hits, they hit. She plays him well, but rarely allows herself to win. She compliments him, but not too much, not too often. She does not make him work excessively hard nor does she make the game too easy. There is time for that. The ultimate move, the great reach out and touch someone, must come from him. He must initiate otherwise he will be too shy, he will feel put upon. She will wait until it is his idea, until it is something he wants, knows he must have. Until then, they will just play.

The ball escapes and flies into the far court, into the ladies' game. He indicates that he will retrieve it. She looks at the two women, looks at her boy looking at them. They are in short white dresses with frilly white panties, like diaper covers, over their underwear. When the boy comes toward them, one of the women bends to pick up his ball. Bent, the full fluff of her upper, inner thigh is flashed in his face along with the sparsely haired turkey skin that surrounds the extended pubic region. That the hole is hidden, swathed, only makes things worse – that it, too, isn't flashed in his face heightens the suspense, hints that something more special is buried there, makes everything seem better than it is, than it ever could be. The baby begins to cry and the woman leaves him for the carriage. The boy returns with a rise in his shorts. From across the court, she sees the distension, the bulge, bloom. The fat bitch has given him a hard-on. Will mysteries never cease?

I am Casper here, the friendly, fondling ghost. I walk out onto the court, stand behind her, and take her arm as she pulls it back to swing. I touch her. There is the high hum, the holy harmonia, as if to touch, to tickle, were the highest, most sophisticated of all tantric exercises.

Even though she is well past age, even though not quite so fine as something brand spanking new, I am stirred by the feel of her flesh. Is it because I have been deprived, have gone without for so long? Is it possible that as my age advances, the acceptable limit of their years also rises? The idea that if I live to be eighty, I will find forty-year-olds attractive, will think them babes, is a thought that should I ever think it, I hope will be seconded by the impulse toward suicide. That I might find charm and sustenance in fully flowered – past ripe, nearly sour – endowments, that a grown woman's warm welcome of my intrusions, protrusions, my wicked weapon, might someday appeal, is far, far beyond what I am willing to allow my imagination to conjure. They say women peak sexually much later than men – I have witnessed though not sampled such; a willingness to experiment, wife-swapping, doing it with the dog, with the bisexual daughter of the couple next door, etc., and frankly it scares me half to death.

Her. It is urgent that I take her in my hold and encourage her to step into the ball, pivot, rotate fully, to arch her back when serving. I need to stand pressed against her, spread her legs, then ask her to check her balance, her position. I want to slightly humiliate her in her game, to rub myself against her, and through this loving, gentle guidance separate her from him, that she should play with only me. I want to lick her lips, to spit in her eyes, and spray her with what is mine.

Can't wait!

And when their hour is past, when their hearts are pounding and sebaceous glands pouring sweat, she makes the gesture of checking her watch, an unspoken but undeniable signal that their time is up. He comes to the net. 'Great,' she says, blotting her nose. She has a propensity to sweat, to produce water bubbles like blisters that cover her shnoz – good pores, effective but not too large. 'Yeah, great,' he says, echoing her sound, imitating her blotting with a wider gesture, wiping his whole face with the shoulder of his father's shirt. She reaches into her pocket, pulls out a ten, and he starts to hesitate, to actually back away, to pretend that he's not going to take her money. But she holds steady; the bill remains, extended, curled in the air between them. He takes the money. 'We're pretty well matched,' he says.

She nods. 'Again tomorrow?'

'Sure, why not,' he says, waving the ten through the air before he pockets it and walks off.

I am here, taking it up the ass, and she is out there, roaming the hills, the valleys, of Scarsdale, Larchmont, Mamaroneck, in a post-acquisition high, a moment of tranquillity, of pseudo-satiation. And in that flash of release, she has relaxed her vigilance. Upon returning home, balancing her electrolytes with Lay's potato chips and Orange Crush, she allows herself to be cajoled into Mummy's car and led to the shopping mall. She is there now, trying on tennis togs, having her racket restrung, shopping for the supplies her fantasy demands.

That she is so clever, manipulative, as to have both him and me engaged is something that were I younger, I would feel the need to take to heart. Taking matters in hand, I would remind her that though I am caged, I remain viable – a man. I would dilly myself, shoot onto the page, leave it to dry, then fold the crusty wad into even sections and slip it into an envelope, mailing it to her for reconstitution. In the comfort and privacy of her room, she would collect in her mouth a fine blue loogie, a big ball of spit, and drop it down onto my page and, then with either the tip of a pencil or her pinky finger, would swirl the two together. And then as if applying a plaster, a medical paste, she would collect the material on her finger or perhaps raise the page itself, pull down her panties, and rub it against herself. Like that, we would be together. And I, in my cell, connected to my fluid as though it were my faith, would shudder and ripple as she worked the paper back and forth until our wetnesses mixed and the thin blue lines that rule were all worn off, until the paper itself was just a sliver, thin as a pathologist's cross section. Finished, she would drop this page onto the floor by the bed, and later in the afternoon she'd slide it – still not quite dry – back into the envelope, tape the seal, and with a red pen mark it *Return to Sender*.

'Been opened,' the postman would say, squeezing the damp, the lumpy. 'Can't return to sender if it's been opened.'

'Didn't open it,' she'd say. 'Came that way.'

And because she is sweet, and because she is young, and because she looks like his sister the Carmelite nun, he'd accept her letter and drop it in the great box bound for upstate.

7

Prison. Bells. Commotion in the corridor. I wake from my dream, rise from the fugue, and pull to the surface.

'He bit me. Broke the skin. Sick fuck took a chunk out of my arm.' A guard is crying.

The Special Tactics team has Appfelbaum, the abortionist with the habit of snacking on the fetuses he scraped, cornered, pushed back into his cell.

'Broke the skin. Sick fuck. Does he have rabies? Tetanus? Something worse? Do I have to get tested? Do I have to get shots? I hate this place, fucking zoo.'

Appfelbaum's door slams closed; the click of the lock falling into place echoes down the hall.

'I ain't gonna lie,' Frazier says. 'No point pretending. Just is the way it is. No surprise.'

How does the watched pot boil? How to let it steam,

simmer, froth, without them knowing? If it spills out and over, they will put it down fast and furiously. I know. I have been shackled to this cot and left to twist and turn for days and nights, the shackles so biting my flesh that I required stitches. I have been left alone and awry in a dark bed, a wretched wet stink. I have been swaddled, stuffed into a straitjacket pulled so tight that my ribs broke and my breath slipped away from me in a thin, high whistle. Trapped and tied and left for days, involuntarily paralyzed. I'm too old for that now – not too old for them to do it, they have no limit, but too old to have it done. I haven't the stamina. In my blood, in my muscle and veins, there still lurks the impulse, the urge, the coursing poison of rage. But in my effort to contain it, to spare myself the humiliation of an explosion – imagine how much more forceful an explosion is in a confined space, how much more hazardous – I turn this poison on myself. I maim myself in order to stay the line, in order to go unnoticed. I pain myself so deeply, so thoroughly, that when I am through, I have no ability, no interest, in paining others – or so one might think. But if you are smart, you must know that as I hurt myself – and I feel I am hurting myself for you – as I assume the burden and beat you to the punch, I loathe you all the more. It is too much to keep inside. If I were able to relieve myself, to simply piss it out, it would hiss and foam a thick black and inky line. The body is not the proper capsule for such poison. And my contempt for what I am made to do to myself mounts, so, when you are not looking, and be sure that at some point you will blink, your mind will wander, I'll slip this blade that I carry stealthily, silently into your heart.

My poison is my vigilance.

The bells ring. Order is restored. Everything is as it was.

What time is it? I wonder, but there's no one to ask – Frazier doesn't wear a watch.

Clayton is in the doorway. '*Edge of Night,*' he says. '*Edge of Night,* can I?' I nod. He turns on the television and fits himself onto the cot next to me. The episode is well under way. I want to fall into someone, collapse upon her/him and have the walls of my skin, the container of my vessel, dissolve so that their embrace becomes me, envelops and swallows me. She is strong enough to take it. I can tell. She has the stamina, the muscle of youth. I look at Clayton, the beautiful boy, and wonder what he sees in me – father figure, I fear – what our relationship really is. That someone should climb in and voluntarily curl so close fills me with a sense of success and disbelief, repulsion and love. And with Clayton, that I have done nothing to deserve this fortune, that I have made no seduction, no grand overture, is my gift and my punishment.

I run out of the room, even though running indoors is prohibited. Up and down the hall, always stopping halfway, stopping before the end. I cannot come up against the metal wall, the immobile door. To touch, to even accidentally brush against it will compel me to hurl myself, forcibly butt my head against it again and again until my skull cracks, until it bleeds, until I am senseless and no longer know where I am, until I cannot see, stand, or speak, until I no longer know where the wall is, until I am truly powerless, until my heart actually stops.

I think of you, your picket fences, flower beds, holly bushes, your life measured by the alarm clock's tick, the car-pool rotation. You claim to be a prisoner, but until you suffer the anxiety raised by the uselessness of decision, of desire, you are free. As I mentioned before, there is little need to control oneself here, except that it is degrading not to; if you don't do it yourself, they will do it for you, that much is proven, and it will not be pleasant, that too is promised, guaranteed. You long to break out but comfort yourself with the structure you rebel against. You encircle the goods you are hoarding, all that you own, those damned privet-hedge definitions of what is yours and what is mine; your houses, cars, wives, children. That is why you are there and I am here. They say I have trouble with boundaries. How close can I get? How far can I go? I have a populist's streak that says all for one and one for all. I am not a stingy man, but then, the sum total of my possessions would fit neatly into two cardboard boxes. Who has more? Argument could be made, could be won, saying that by having nothing, no actual object, I have everything. I am neither defined nor bounded by what I own. Truth be told, I am jealous of you, hungry to touch, to feel, to hold each item in your drawers: steak knives and potato peelers, twenty-five pairs of socks nestled nicely against your wife's brassieres. Your gold cuff links and her good jewelry buried under your boxer shorts, the family jewels.

Am I being too presumptuous, claiming to know who you are, when just as easily you could be someone else, a bum, or someone surprisingly like me?

Clayton bunches up my pillow and fits it under his head. *As the World Turns* is spinning as Evan finds out that James never had a vasectomy, which means that Edwina has been lying. Shocking! I forbid myself to gaze at this radiant tube during daylight hours – it is the cheapest drug, the lazy man's way out. And when I do watch, I have rules for my viewing: a firm avoidance of the networks, and never, ever, do I turn to the local channels during the news hour. Nothing is more tortuous than the stilted elocutions of a half-brained, half-baked, ugly Rather be Brokaw attempting to bring me the goings-on beyond these – be they ever so – humble gates.

Unforgivable.

I can't allow myself to think that daylilies are blooming not a quarter mile from my cage. People at this very moment or the next are deciding what to have for dinner, whether or not to mix a second drink, open another can of smoked almonds; perhaps they're deciding to skip the meal altogether and take the wife upstairs, fuck her until she's blue, humping to the slap, slapping sound of Johnny in the driveway bouncing his ball, grinding to the dry hum of Sally downstairs playing with her toy vacuum cleaner.

I don't want Wendel the Weatherman to tell me what time the sun will rise and set on these near hills because, here, on this side of the wall, the weather is different, it's a whole other front, time passes on its own schedule. The clock is broken, has only one hand, and an hour can be a year, a minute, or a month, and the little square of daylight that drifts across the yard, over the floor, can come and go in a second.

It's not the world I live in, it's not mine.

I collect the headlines, keep them in my various files. What one might find in this tiny town, this near city, frightens me. The untamed environs, the suburban subdivisions, the hazards of the garbage disposal, trash compactor, and radar range are much more violent, more dangerous, than what you imagine happens in these hallowed halls. Your capitol dome and bureaucratic bulges, gubernatorial pitches for reform, coupled with the grisly grit of who was killed, who was maimed, and what twelve-year-old child was mowed down on his way home from school, stun and stone me. I am here. The criminal element is contained – held under lock and key – and still it happens. How could it go on without me (us) – is that too narcissistic a mind? What I'm getting at is that, with so many of us locked up, you'd think it would stop. That it continues means that it is you and not me. Tell me about your day, your routine, and what you did at the drugstore when the dumb little girl charged you five cents instead of five dollars. Did you speak up? Are you all so lily-white? The harder it gets to be safe and secure, to trust, to find love and understanding – the more you feel entitled, allowed, even encouraged, to cheat, to lie, to steal, and then later, even to kill. That you are just beginning to feel it now only means you have been lucky for too long.

And while you might think I'd find it heartening that such accidents do happen to others, that in all this random sense-lessness we are all of us caught in a kind of forced criminality – you are in error. You are breaking your promise, the very terms of our agreement – the one that puts me in here and lets you stay out there – if I commit the crimes for you, you must be good for me. You and I, we're in this together, best not to forget.

Clayton is on the bed, he has kicked off his shoes. The perfume of his nether digits, his toe jam, permeates the room. I breathe deeply, the damn sock and sweaty sneaker have the hint, the vague reminiscence, of popcorn, buttered. *As the World Turns* has turned into *The Guiding Light*; Bridget gives birth to a boy. David, who assisted, agrees to keep quiet about the whole thing. Clayton could lie here all day. I hate him for his ability to do nothing, to be unoccupied. I turn off the tube and plant myself in front of him, wiggling my hips in his face, slipping my fingers through my belt loops, hiking my pants higher, highlighting the bulge.

I could stand to have my cock sucked, but Clayton does not think it is his job; as far as he's concerned, it is a favor, a rare treat reserved for birthdays and similarly special occasions. He ignores my crotch and looks beyond me out the window. 'Sun's out,' he says. I nod.

Out of my room we go, descending the narrow back stair-case, the dark pit that leads to the tunnel, past the laundry, the boiler room and morgue, and into the chute. There are only certain paths available. In steel cages mounted in the ceiling there are cameras (circa 1978) with bulletproof lens caps. They are watching, recording every move. Were we to do something strange, something unexpected, they would be upon us, would appear from out of nowhere and remind us that we are not alone.

'Chartres. I'm thinking of Chartres,' Clayton says. 'I've been pretending I'm there.' He pauses. There is always the problem of having an Ivy League boyfriend – in truth no one else wants him, no one knows what the hell he's talking about, they think he's crazy. 'The Virgin Mary's robe is buried beneath the apse.'

I say nothing.

I wonder if Clayton should be taking antidepressants, an official prescription instead of smoking and sniffing Henry's concoctions. He is ahead of me, opening the door to the yard. The opening, the letting in of light, the letting out of oneself, is a great release.

Out. The screen door slams. Flowers, red, orange, purple, circle the house. 'Boy,' my grandmother calls. 'Boy.' I run into the light. I hide behind the sheets hanging off the clothesline. 'Boy,' she calls again. A bee, a butterfly, a bird in the distance. The air is warm and thick. I sit on the grass, splitting blades of greenery. Brighter than bright. Blue sky, cloudless. I lie back and fall asleep with the laundry – sheets, shirts, and my grandmother's housedresses and underpants – billowing above me.

'Fool,' my grandmother says when she finds me, bee-bitten, sunburned, smiling. 'You and your mama. One and the same.'

I miss Mama and am glad to hear her name. 'When's Mama coming home?'

'I told you before, she got to collect her marbles before she can come back.'

'Good,' I say, thinking that can't take long.

* * *

'I'm going back,' Clayton says. 'I'm going to Chartres and hang myself from the high North Spire.'

Again I don't speak. There is nothing to say.

Clayton walks adjusting and readjusting his crotch. I think of the popcorn scent of his feet and imagine the heady, perfumy, pissy flavor at the front of his underwear. I think of him in his Jockeys and am reminded of the thick cotton of kiddie panties, the ultra-absorbent weave that holds the scents, the drippings, that slowly steams the full flavors until they reach a nearly toxic, almost lethal fruition.

The prison yard is a square, fenced kennel, human doggie run, a playpen for criminals bounded by stone walls and reams of razor wire. Around the inside perimeter, there is a well-worn footpath, a kind of ring around the collar for men who go round and round as though eventually at some surprising moment the circle itself will split open, unfold into a long flat line, an open road, and they'll just walk straight on out of here.

There are days when one should avoid going out, when it does no good, when it only makes matters worse. On such occasions, one should feel free – perhaps a poor word choice – to hide in or under the bed until the feeling passes, until things have the potential to seem good again, until something can be gotten from lying on the ground, staring up at the sky, knowing that at least the clouds are unfettered, free, and you can be in them if you choose.

There's an odd charge in the air, I felt it right away, but at first thought it was just me. Or us, Clayton and I. Clayton finally responding to my request, my interest in having my cock sucked, me responding to the subsequent image of her sucking my cock with Clayton looking on, her watching Clayton fucking me. No, I don't want her to see that, don't want anyone to see Clayton fucking me. Too embarrassing. I fear they would think less of me if they knew what I let

Clayton do. I've gone too far, trespassed. I backtrack.

In the yard everyone moves with an urgency typically absent. The men on the path are walking as if racing, pumping their arms back and forth through the air, faster, faster. Smokers are smoking, puffing and pulling, blowing billowing clouds of nicotine into the air. Faster. Faster. Time is spinning out of order, calling attention to itself. A guard comes out onto the catwalk, the terrace that surrounds his turret, raises his binoculars to his turd face, and scans the yard. Not yet.

I'm the first to notice. Jerusalem at the wall.

He touches it, puts his hands up against the stones as if he can read them with his fingers, with his eyes closed, in braille. The story of a man. One foot inches up and catches on a stone in the wall, his weight shifts and the second foot leaves the ground. His fingers clutch the edges of the stones, digging into the mortar. He is five feet into the air. In the turd tower a guard pulls the cord and the farting foghorn of a siren begins to bleat. A warning. The walkers, the men on the path, freeze and then begin to dart back and forth, unable to make their rounds, to cross beneath the climbing Jerusalem. Instead – and as though this were the predetermined emergency plan – they go back and forth, up and down, pacing the length of the yard. Jerusalem is shirtless, Wonder-bread white. The flesh on his belly and back wriggles. He struggles to find his footing, get his grip. Twenty feet into the air. Rifle in hand, a guard comes out of the tower and stands on the catwalk, whispering into a walkie-talkie.

Clayton turns to me and says, 'Wedding day,' in my ear.

'What?'

'Daughter Debbie's wedding day. Doesn't want to be late for church.'

I remember Jerusalem showing me the invitation: The honor of your presence. Deborah, Darling Daughter of Emma and Jerusalem, to Keith Quick. Eighteenth day of June.

Christ Church, Poughkeepsie. Reception to follow.

And now Jerusalem is on the wall. The turret terraces are full of guards with their guns drawn. Shoot to kill. They have the authority. The farting horn bleats every thirty seconds. Excruciating. They hold their fire, allowing us the illusion that someone can get up and over. They humiliate us and Jerusalem by letting him play out the fantasy. Their refusal to shoot represents their unwillingness to participate, to even dignify our desire. The pressure is too much, we are being simultaneously scrutinized and ignored. We begin to slowly crack. The men, responding to the intensity of the focus, the sudden flood of chemicals through their delicate systems, develop involuntary spasms, twitches – Jerusalem's climbing disease. He is on the wall, working his arms and legs like an insect, desperate, trapped. There is a roar, a growing growl, as the energy, the impulse, overwhelms, as the inmates come undone. They howl and bay at the guards, they claw and tear at themselves and each other.

Clayton looks at the guards in the towers, the guns, opens his arms, and holds them above his head. 'Ready,' he screams. I step away. 'I'm ready now,' he yells. He spins, showing himself to them. 'Now would be nice.' He takes off his shirt and bangs against his chest, his heart. 'Here. Here would be good.' They ignore him. 'Do it,' he screams. 'Do it already.' And still there is nothing. 'Please,' he begs. 'Please, I can't anymore.' And when the guards continue to ignore the men below, Clayton hurls himself through the air, throwing his body like a punch, landing in the mud puddle from yesterday's thunderstorm. He hits the muck with a slapping sound. I am embarrassed by his display. I move farther away, toward the door leading back inside. Men cower there. The door is locked. They are keeping us in the yard, in this antique stadium. Jerusalem is ten feet from the top; his breath, the gallop of his heart, plays off the stones, echoing over the yard. He moves carefully. His hand is on top, over the edge. He starts to pull himself up. His legs are pedaling the wall, finding their footing. He leans forward without thinking. I see him do it. I know as he does it, there will be trouble. His shoulder snags on the wire; he turns, twists, and pulls his legs up. His shoulder is in the wire, it digs into him, pulling at his flesh as he moves. He dips down, as if by going lower he will release himself. His face is down. The more he fights, the more tangled he becomes. Wrapped, trapped, buried. He moves as if he's swimming in place. The guards lower their guns. We are fifty feet down, looking up. Five minutes, ten minutes pass, and the assembly of guards seems to be dissipating as each goes on about his business irrespective of the fact that a man hangs like a piece of laundry.

'Pyramid.' Word sweeps through the yard. 'Seven, then six, five, four, three, and two.'

Clayton pulls himself out of the puddle and positions himself on the bottom. The men stack themselves on each other's shoulders, six men high. The guards return, cocking their rifles. They step into position. Reinforcements magically appear, administration men in dark suits draw their .38s and aim them at the dull spots between our eyes. The two inmates on top wrap wads of shirting around their hands and arms and reach into the wire. They separate Jerusalem from the steel, plucking him out, leaving pieces like samples, small strips of skin set out to cure. His limbs stay bent as they bring him down. They carry him across the yard – his back is the only part uncut. Blood drips from him onto their heads and into their eyes, trickles down to their chins and splashes the ground. They lay him down; Frazier goes first, kicking him hard in the ribs. 'Useless,' he screams. 'What were you thinking?' Then Wilson hauls off and gets him in the gut. 'Idiot.' Embarrassed, humiliated by Jerusalem's display, Kleinman swings his leg, tapping

Jerry under the chin. And Frazier goes again, this time for the groin. 'McNuggets.' Clayton kicks him solidly in the back. I am horrified. Jerusalem curls protectively and someone else kicks, and then Frazier is taking another turn and it's going around again. The guards stand watching, and soon we're spent, bored. Jerusalem is still. Seeing that we're done, the guards open the door. Clayton and I are the last ones in the yard; we peel Jerusalem up and drag him to his cell.

Henry comes and pokes the man, checking for broken bones. 'Superficial,' Henry says, pressing his ear to the chest, listening for cracks, pops, wheezes. He gives him a shot, a 'low dose of my new analgesic,' and leaves.

I lean forward, dipping my tongue into the blood on Jerusalem's chest. Clayton looks at me. 'There's red on your nose,' he says. 'A hint of pink on your cheek.' He smiles, laughs, and licks the blood off my face.

'The flavor of life,' I say.

We lean forward and lick Jerusalem's wounds, teasing the scraps of flesh with our teeth and our tongues. And as we lick Jerusalem, cleaning and drinking him like crazy cats, he begins to moan. He weeps at the sting of our saliva, the flick of our tongues.

'Jerusalem,' we say.

'It's a mistake,' he says. 'Just call me Jerry.'

Finally the siren stops. The bells ring. Dinner. A second set of bells. Lockdown. Room service. We bid Jerusalem good-night and go back to our cells. We don't eat. We have already feasted and for now are sated.

8

Do they let you have silverware in there or do you just eat with a spoon?

Beloved, by now I would have thought you'd know the etymology of the expression *finger-licking good.*

His mother calls and invites her to dinner. His mother calls and speaks to her mother. It's the way these things are done. All the while the lively leprechaun lolls in the background, pretending to be infantata, too small to reach the telephone, to let the touch-tone language of love link her.

Instead, she makes her mummie do it.

Like good witches in fairy tales these mothers are near-sighted, afflicted with an astigmatism of affection. They are brainless-bat-full in the belfry, the last lost generation of homemakers, trained to be deaf, dumb, and blind. They stay in the house, floating from room to room, cans of Endust and Lemon Pledge in hand, palms pumiced into soft cloths, seeping polish from the pores. Whatever they caress is transformed, the tarnish lifted. Surfaces gleaming. And when they are done – and they are never really done – but when they sit down to rest, they regress. Like little girls they play at the great game of keeping house. They chat it up on the telephone, whilst working the emery board forward and back, dipping the thin brush into the red lacquer and sweeping it over their nails. They chat it up as though the telephone were not the crown jewel of communication culture but a set of empty orange-juice cans strung together with string, stretched from house to house. Receivers tucked under their chins, they move through their kitchens making the sandwiches, stirring the sauce, frosting and defrosting their freezers and fridges, constantly keeping the curly cord wrapped around their neck – it's a wonder more don't strangle themselves.

'I don't think we've ever met,' one says to the other.

'No, I don't think we have.'

What does it matter. They're all the same, all on the same boat, the same sinking ship.

'How lovely,' her mother says, hanging up the phone. 'That was the mother of the boy you're giving lessons to, inviting you for dinner. It's so nice, you made yourself a little job. You never tell me anything anymore. Where is he in school, St Andrew's? A lot of the boys go to St Andrew's.'

Babbling in the background.

Our girl lies on the sofa, eyes closed, listening to her mother's orchestrations, the *Symphony of the Emptying of the Dishwasher;* a cacophony of china, ringing glasses, the percussive rumble of the silverware bin and the lyrics of her litany. 'You know, you could help me in here.'

'When's dinner?' the girl asks.

'Six-thirty.'

'Tonight?'

'Is that a problem?'

She is horrified. As though she would need weeks of warning. Truth be told, for the young one, the one who is not so practiced, there is little need for planning. Things here are best served by moving forward without delay.

Daydreaming, she lies on the sofa, pinching her nipples, testing them, sensitizing them for future use. Her open palm rubs up and down her front. She spreads her legs. Her mother comes in – but doesn't notice at first.

'Sweetie, what are you doing?' the mother finally asks.

'Scratching.'

'If something is irritating you, why don't you go upstairs, take your clothing off, and run a nice bath. Put a little corn-starch in it. A good soak is always a relief.'

'That's an idea,' the girl says, stopping her work, but remaining on the sofa.

'Where are all your friends this summer? You used to have so many friends.'

The girl doesn't answer.

Six-thirty p.m. Fast approaching his house. Out the kitchen window slips a thin curl of black smoke. It rises. She charges up the back steps, hurls herself against the back door, which pops open as if it were a prop. The toaster oven is engulfed in flames. She snatches an open box of baking soda that just happens to be on the counter and throws the contents over the fire. The flames subside.

The mother of the house rushes into the room. 'I smelled something burning.'

'It's out,' the girl says, shaking the empty box of Arm & Hammer like a rattle.

The mother takes the girl's head between both hands, fitting her fingers into the depressions, the dents behind the ears, the place where forceps went, a reminder of birth. 'Precious,' she says, kissing the girl full on the lips, slipping her tongue in and out. 'Precious, thank you.'

Six-thirty p.m. Fast approaching. The father works on the car. He is shirtless. He is wearing gym shorts. He is covered in grease.

'Is there anything I can do to help?' she asks, coming up the driveway.

He sighs, rubs his blackened arm across his forehead, leaving an oily streak, filling in the blank between his eyebrows. 'Stand over me when I go under,' he says. 'When I ask for it, give me what I need.'

She nods.

He lies back on the dolly and inserts himself headfirst under the automobile. He's in up to the waist. She squats over his knees.

'Higher,' he says.

She slides up.

He bends his knees, trapping her on top of his crotch. Each time she bends to hand him a tool, she rubs against him. He's hard. He's calling out: 'One-half inch. Allen wrench, screwdriver. Phillips head. Awl. Awl.' He drops his tools, holds her by the hips, and grinds against her, marking her with streaks of grease. He moans. When he's finished, he slides out from under the car and wipes himself off with an old T-shirt, a cum rag. 'Thanks,' he says. 'Thanks for your help. It's just not something you can do with only two hands.'

Six-thirty p.m. In front of the house, in the turtle-shaped kiddie pool, the littlest one lies facedown. She plucks him from the water and lays him out, rhythmically pressing his chest with her hands. Bending low over him, she blows air in and pumps water out. He sputters and puffs. Hearing his coughs, his racked choking, the family dashes out of the house. They are all over her, offering her everything, anything she desires, their firstborn son?

They reprimand the little one for being so stupid as to nearly drown himself.

'I thought I was a goldfish,' he says.

'You're not.'

Six-fifteen p.m. The first real day of summer, she departs her doorstep, showered, shaved, conditioned to conquer. Minutes later she is at his driveway, exhibiting serious symptoms of heat and humidity – huffing, puffing, red-faced. She's unaware that she did not walk here, but truly trotted, fast flew over the green grass and the neighbors' privet hedges. She is sweating, discharging salty rivulets down her chest and into her brassiere where they pool betwixt her breasts. She wishes she hadn't eaten all those desserts. The fifteen mysterious pounds absent-mindedly assembled during the school year are at once fully present and accounted for. Her shorts have worked their way high into her crotch. Her thighs, like clamps, hold them bunched up so the flesh is free to rub against itself, twin thighs trading smacky wet kisses back and forth until they erupt in a pimply rash.

She thinks of turning around and going home, trying again. She could take another shower, change her clothes, and borrow the car. After all, she is old enough to drive.

At the bottom of his driveway, she rests, brings her head to her knees, blood runs to her brain. Slowly straightening up, she blots her forehead with the sleeve of her blouse and waddles up the flagstone path to the front door – twice pausing to pluck the shorts from her crotch.

She raises the brass knocker and raps.

Inside the house, the mother is yelling, 'Did you feed the dog? It's your dog. You're the one who wanted a dog. I thought you loved the dog. Why don't you feed the dog?'

She raises the knocker again and puts her ear to the door. There is the inane sound track of a certain cartoon character, an anthropomorphized animated duck with a lisp. Again, she raises the knocker, banging as hard as she can against the door.

She stands waiting. And waiting.

One. Five. Seven minutes. There is the shift of mood that comes with waiting. Her sweat cools. Anxious to angry. Annoyed to exhausted. Disheartened. Did this dinner not mean anything to anyone but her? Of course not, but she doesn't understand that, yet.

Wasps. Residents of the nest above the door are returning home, wrapping up a day's work. They buzz around her head, and before she realizes what they are, she swats at them. Stung. Her eye. She cries out. She stumbles, falling back against the doorframe. Her elbow hits a heretofore unnoticed doorbell. Chimes echo through the house.

'Door, door, door,' a voice calls, translating.

The clunk of a dead bolt retracting. The door is opened. Kitchen towel over her shoulder, the mother is there with a can of frozen pink lemonade sweating in her hand.

The girl's hand is over her eye. She is pressing against it as though she can make the swelling go down.

'I got stung,' she says.

'Are you allergic?' the mother asks.

'I don't think so.'

'Can you breathe?'

'Yes.'

The mother ushers the girl into the kitchen, her office, her great laboratory, and makes an ice pack out of the dishrag.

'Should I call your mother?'

Deeply humiliated, the girl shakes her head, not realizing that this accident will work in her favor. She is a little dumb, with none of the cunning and lithe charm of a true temptress, who would see fortune here.

'I'll get you some Benadryl.'

'What's for dinner?' an anonymous voice screams.

There is no answer.

The boy, her boy, Matthew, a gift of the Lord, comes into the kitchen. The sight of her beloved sends an almost unbearable flash of nearly nucleic heat through her. Every vessel is dilated. Breathless, she bows her head – a gesture of respect, a peasant tipping to royalty. He wears madras shorts, and an untucked, crookedly buttoned blue oxford-cloth shirt – several sizes too large. His feet are bare. It is the first time she's seen his toes. It's all she can do not to fall onto her hands and knees and lap at them.

'Were you, like, in a fight?' he asks.

She shakes her head. The mother comes back into the room and stands before her ready to dispense the medication in the child's liquid form. Momentarily distracted from her boy by the teaspoon being pushed toward her lips, she swallows the stuff. It's not nearly as good as sucking toes.

'Isn't it two spoons if you're over twelve?' the girl asks.

The mother reads the back of the bottle and pours her a refill.

'If you'd like,' the mother says, 'I could take you home.'

The girl shakes her head. 'I'm fine.'

'What's for dinner,' the boy says.

'Turkey burgers.'

While my intention is not to interrupt the proceedings, you should be aware that I have no idea of what they're talking about. I've never heard of a turkey burger and can not quite imagine such a thing. Perhaps I have been away for far too long, perhaps this item says something about these people, something I'm not quite picking up on – therefore, I leave it to you to understand its connotations. But in case you are as baffled as I am, let me add that according to the girl, the item is one that requires the combining of many ingredients into a huge bowl, the use of a frying pan, a sprayed or pumped vegetable-oil lubricant, and there are bread crumbs involved. I myself abhor bread crumbs – they are a kind of softened sawdust, an extender used in efforts to make something out of nothing.

'I hope I won't have to feed the three of you first,' the mother says continuously from six forty-five until seven-fifteen when the father, damp and disheveled, arrives home.

'Car still in the shop?' the mother asks.

The father nods. 'No taxis at the station. I walked. Hot out.' The mother pours him a cold glass of pink lemonade, which he appears to swallow in a single gulp. She pours him another, which he consumes almost as quickly. He holds out the glass for another refill.

'This is all there is,' she says, holding the pitcher close to her breast. 'I made it for the children.'

The father goes to the sink and fills his glass with water. He splashes his head and face and reaches for a dish towel.

'We have three bathrooms if you'd like to wash up.'

'Is that my shirt?' the father asks his eldest son.

Matthew shrugs.

'You know I don't like it when you wear my clothing.'

The boy shrugs again.

'You get funny little spots on my things, spots too small for your mother to see. She pretends they aren't there, but I see them and they don't come out. So what about that?'

Our girl watches the father and son. They seem to be in competition with each other, vying for something the boy has yet to figure out. The father is intent, well-focused on pulling the rug out from under if only to taunt, to tease, to trip the young one up. For the moment her boy has forgotten her, but she doesn't worry. She recognizes that she must leave him alone, must learn to spend time with him that is unremarkable – that will be her way in, the seeming ordinariness of things. For now, she is content to simply watch, to witness. And although it seems strange – they have all forgotten she is there.

So far, the father, the pater of her dear one, has not so much as spotted her sitting at his kitchen table, ice pack pressed to the right side of her face, dripping chilly water onto the linoleum floor. To keep from jumping out of her skin, from jumping up and running out of the house, bellowing, 'You don't want me, you aren't even paying attention,' she talks to the dog.

'Oh, you're a good dog, a pretty dog, a lucky dog. Did you have your dinner? Was it a good dinner?' She rubs the un-damaged side of her face against the dog's muzzle. He licks her.

After pulling plates from the cupboard, the mother decorates them with artful arrangements: beds of lettuce, piles of potato salad, rings of onion, and tomato wedges. She hurries back and forth from kitchen to dining room, laying the table, flipping the burgers, fetching the ketchup, mustard, and mayonnaise. No one helps her. Her servitude is unspoken and predeter-mined. She does it all herself. The girl could help. She has taken home economics and is well-educated in these matters, but knows that to act would divide the room into male and female, waitress and waited upon, would separate her from what she wants. Instead the girl scratches the dog's ears. He sniffs her crotch and attempts to mount her leg.

'Wallace,' the mother says, grabbing the dog by the collar, jerking his neck. 'Stop.'

The two boys wrestle in the hallway, the little one screaming joyously for help as his bigger brother flips and flops him, braiding his limbs like a soft pretzel. The father has for the moment disappeared, excused himself to make a phone call from somewhere quiet, somewhere where he can think, where he can talk and be heard.

Burgers are piled onto a platter. 'Dinner is served,' the mother announces. 'Dinner,' she repeats. And the troops are assembled. A guest, a guest. It is as if rumor of the girl's attendance is only now circulating as family members find themselves ushered into the dining room and not the kitchen, as they find the napkins are cloth and the glasses crystal. No plastic or paper. Surprise. Surprise. The mother takes the ice pack from our girl and leads her to her place, next to the little one, across from her boy and close to the father. Our girl smiles. 'Nice,' she says.

'This is Matty's tennis teacher,' the mother says, formally introducing the girl to the father, who takes one look at her and then excuses himself to mix another drink. 'I was on the team at Penn, nationally seeded,' he calls in from the living room, before returning to the table vodka tonic in hand, but smelling of Scotch.

'Ice maker's on the fritz,' he tells his wife as he steals ice cubes from his children's glasses, stirring his drink with his index finger, which all too recently could have been up the bum of an office boy or sliding in and out of the slippery slit of a secretary. He pulls his finger out of his drink, licks it, then begins to pick at his dinner.

'We're going to need a new fridge any minute now, I've been telling you for months,' the mother says.

'I don't want to know about it,' the father replies, attending only to his drink. He wishes to be oblivious, wishes all parts of his spread to be wondrous and beautiful. Beyond that, he could care less, so long as it doesn't set him back. And it is exactly that, the sensation of being set back, kept against his will, held hostage by the ice maker, the garbage disposal, the old copper pipes, his wife and children, that fouls his mood. The father is a bitter and stingy man.

'What year are you?' he asks the girl.

'Junior,' she says.

'And your field?'

'Psychology and literature.'

'Is Freud still part of the program?'

She nods.

'Ah,' the father says, excusing himself to mix another drink.

'Isn't it enough?' the mother asks. The father doesn't answer. He returns to the table with half a glass of vodka, this time mixing his poison with the last of the pink lemonade. He tilts his head back, closes his eyes, and sips. The burger on his plate remains untouched.

He turns to his son. 'That's my shirt isn't it? Did I ask you that before?'

The boy shrugs.

'You know I don't like it and still you do it,' the father says, shaking his head. 'Ketchup,' he says, without pausing for breath, and the bottle of Heinz is slapped into his hand. With a farting sound a clot puffs out the top, splashing his fingers. The father, disgusted, wipes it off. 'Clean napkin,' he says. And his wife slips one onto his lap.

'I'm so happy you're giving Matt lessons,' she says, picking up the slack, keeping things moving, smacking the wrist of the youngest one, who's playing peculiar games with his food. 'Fifteen dollars an hour, that's a deal. At our club it's thirty, and the pros haven't played in twenty years. And you're on a team, that's wonderful.' She pauses. 'It's funny. Last month I wanted to sign Matt up for group lessons and he refused. But private lessons. Fifteen dollars an hour. We feel very lucky.'

The kid is making money, fifteen from the mother, ten from the girl, pocketing twenty-five a pop, fifty to seventy-five a week – raking it in. She is pleased. He's not as dumb as you'd think. She looks at him across the table. He's fidgeting. She winks, but because one eye is already closed, it looks more like an extended blink. He's rolling in dough. He's got plans. She is all the more excited.

'What do you aspire to?' the father asks. It is clear from the tone of his question that she shouldn't try to answer. 'When I was young,' he says, 'it was a certain success, a career, a wife, a child, and after that a club, a boat, a country home, a better wife.'

'Let's leave it for now.' The mother stands and begins to clear the table even though they're still eating.

Her eye, her swollen blindness, her sluggish, drugged state have impeded her coordination. She has dropped food on herself. By meal's end she is dotted with samples of everything served – a piece of corn hangs in her collar. Wallace, the family dog, is working in tight circles, licking the floor beneath her, nosing into her lap, getting what he can.

'We used to play with real balls, white balls, none of this neon green, flaming magenta crap,' the father says. 'It was a civilized sport, a good game.'

'My serve's harder than yours,' Matt says to his father.

'No doubt,' the mother says, patting her son on the head, running her fingers through his hair, remembering when . . .

The old man opens his eyes and looks first at his son and then at the girl. 'I hope you teach him good,' he says, and then turns back to his son. 'I'll play you this weekend. I'll kill you.'

'I have balls,' the little one says, although no one (but me) is paying attention.

* * *

A pie. Mama makes a pie. Before she loses her marbles, she makes me something to eat. She goes into the kitchen, takes out her mixing bowls, and starts adding things: flour, salt, baking soda. With her bare hand she scoops Crisco out of the can.

'Peel,' she says, giving me a knife.

With her hands she mixes the things in the bowl, throwing in more flour, an extra pinch of salt. She takes my apples, chops them, sprinkles them with sugar, cinnamon, and a splash of orange juice. She moves fast, frenetically.

'Don't you need instructions, a card with the rules written on it?'

She taps her head. 'Memory,' she says, rolling out the crust.

She is baking as though it's a game, as though everything is make-believe.

I want to tell her that in order for it to work, it has to be done a certain way. I want to say something but don't.

The pie goes into the oven. It begins to smell, the smell of apples melting. It begins to smoke.

'Fire,' I cry. 'Fire.'

'It's just the juice,' she says, not even checking. 'The juice burning off.'

The pie is gone. I make a tambourine out of the tin, punch it full of holes and hang bottle caps off it. Mama dances around the yard while I bang my tambourine.

Mother is gone – the tambourine has been sold to the Museum in Cincinnati. Burt told me as much.

Is there still a chance I could have some pie?

Back at the house, dinner has come to a standstill, a serious impasse as my characters have stopped eating and speaking and are now sitting, staring at their plates daydreaming for five minutes or more. The terrible trance is broken by the jingle of bells, distant down the block.

'Good Humor,' the littlest one shouts, slapping his hands on the table. He rushes to the door. 'Good Humor,' he cries, unable to get the latch. Again there is the tinkle of the treat wagon, and Matthew and the girl are just behind him, all three quickly out the door.

A position held by many I've known, one I myself turned down on numerous occasions. It is, simply put, too complicated, rather hazardous, what with all the driving, the serving of the cones, the continuous and unrelenting need to pull the cord that jingles the bell, and all the while trying to do one's own work. No doubt I would have wrecked the wagon on my very first day. But for those who are more surely coordinated, less inclined to spin the head around and crane backward while moving forward, straining to get one last glimpse, for those who can handle such, it is a wonderful job. A true calling. And there is an ease to the operation: one simply rings a bell beckoning the young ones to submit themselves for inspection. Veritable herds to choose from, and if one doesn't like the choice, one simply drives to another hamlet, the Middlesex of one's choice.

The jingle of bells and all the children, our girl included, are caught in a Pavlovian response. They are out of the house and down the flagstone path before the mother makes it to the doorway, shouting, 'Do you need money?'

'We have money,' the kids scream back as though this is the least of their worries.

'Get me something,' she cries out. 'Something good. And you better get Dad one, too, or he'll eat yours.'

They wave her away and race down the street. It is early evening, not yet twilight; the sky is a deep blue, the air holding the heat of the afternoon. The ice cream truck is ahead of them. They run, overcome with apprehension, the fear that the truck will drive off before they arrive – they've seen it happen before. Just as they come upon it, the driver lets out the brake and rolls away, a-jingle. And the fact is, the drivers do it on purpose, especially where fat little kiddies are concerned. As the chubby child nears, the truck pulls a few hundred feet farther down the street and pauses. As the hefty hefalump again closes in, the truck eases another two to three hundred feet down the road – a teasing tug-of-war repeated several times before the driver grows bored, pulling away entirely, causing tubby to turn homeward, to deepen his depression. Or the driver, if given to a kind of sadomasochistic sympathy, will tease and taunt and then stop, ultimately letting the obese infant have his reward, figuring to have made him work for it, to have made the ice cream better than good, a treat actually earned.

Like precocious playmates, proper pals, our girl follows her boy up the sacred staircase to the family's private quarters. Good Humor in hand, they are temporarily returned to a world of childhood, of make-believe where all is goodness and nice. And in his room, his cramped but special cell, they circle each other, spinning, turning the tension tighter as they struggle to keep a space between them, as they dance in rings around each other, like dogs sniffing.

She is the teacher, he is the pupil. She is the girl, he is the boy. She is older, he is younger. She has the power, he has the power. Neither knows what they are doing. It is a tie, a dead heat; they spin and spin and suck on their melting ice cream sticks. They circle until they slowly settle, until they are dizzy and nauseated from the duck, duck, goosing version of musical chairs, until she is left sitting at his desk and he on his bed, each hiding behind the melting bricks of ice cream that hang precariously off their wooden sticks. He finishes first, leaving a chocolaty ring, an outline and guide around his mouth. Again and again, she wipes at her lips, craving to keep them clean. But it is impossible to stay untouched, untainted, in such a situation, and without noticing she drips onto her shirt.

They look at each other but don't smile.

His room is like that of any boy, decorated with furniture of his parents' choosing, augmented with sporting equipment and dirty clothing. On the bedstead is a clock radio, a pile of sticky Popsicle sticks, and a large wad of hardened green gum. Low on the wall, down behind the bed, where no one but an expert, an archaeologist of greatest experience, would think to look, are gray-green smears, chunky crumbles, fragments of discharge, the nose picked and smeared, boogers. His sheets, thoroughly visible due to the unmade nature of the bed, are well-worn, thoroughly loved Batman sheets. For the boy, they are a source of power. Putting him to sleep in this bed is like slipping him into a battery recharger for the night. Head positive, feet negative, and with eight hours of solid charge each night, he glows, positively shines by morning.

What to do? What to do? What do these children do? Talk about? After all, they have never really spoken before. Nothing that one could consider a conversation has passed between them, and now they are alone, like this. What will happen next? My heart races. I am watching with my hands over my eyes. I want to know and yet I don't want to know. The suspense is killing me. If you haven't noticed it, you are a fool. This is the beginning, the true start of things, the time when, without speaking, they simultaneously acknowledge the real reason for their meeting. Sometimes you are such a fool that I wonder what you are doing here, playing these pages. Perhaps you would be better off with the *World Book*, a nice quiet encyclopedia.

'Wanna see my stuff?' he asks.

She nods.

He gets up and moves to whip out his things, his collection of cards – baseball, football, etc. He shows her the cards and talks about how he is a generalist, specializing in nothing, dabbling here and there, sampling this and that, sure that someday, some piece of it will be of enormous value, which piece he can't quite be sure.

'Know what else I've got?' he says, peeling back the closet door, pulling the light chain. 'Records. I have all my father's old records. I'm building a collection. Used to love the Beatles, but now I like Jimi. Jimi Hendrix?' He begins to play air guitar and dance around the room. He comes close to her. She is reeling. He jerks open a desk drawer and flashes a succession of neatly ordered boxes.

'And candy,' he says. 'I collect candy. Theme candy. Java Jaws. Pandemonium Puffs. And glasses. I have a small collection of gas-station glasses. They're downstairs. Every time there's a new glass, I make my dad fill up or get an oil change, whatever it takes.' He falls silent and rummages through the drawers. There are things from school: ruler, compass, calculator, pencils and pens, metal fragments, pieces of this and that, spare parts.

'There's another collection, something I make myself,' he says, taking a small white cardboard jewelry box out of the drawer. 'Promise not to get grossed out. I mean, I know you will, but like, swear not to hold it against me or anything.'

'I'd never hold anything against you,' she says.

He seems hesitant, suddenly shy.

'I swear.'

Still dubious.

'Show me. I want to see.'

He opens the box, lifts out the cotton, and tilts it in her direction. In the corner she sees a few small raisiny, shrively things.

'Scabs,' he finally says. 'I pick my scabs and save them. Dried out they're crispy, kind of chewy. The flavor changes depending on what generation it is, whether it's blood-based or peroxide. It's kind of complicated, a science, knowing how, when to harvest. But they're good. I pick them, put them in this box, and then every now and then grind one up between my teeth. Am I the strangest guy you ever met?'

She shakes her head. 'No, but you're very sweet.'

The boy looks at her as if she hasn't heard a word he's said, as if she's entirely missed the point. 'And you're cute,' she says. 'And I bet you taste great.'

He blushes and starts to rattle his box. 'Want one?'

She nods. 'Fresh,' she says, pointing to his knee.

There is a thick crustation across the mid-kneecap, dark and heavy, close to mature. The edges poke up slightly.

'A little accident on the gravel about a week ago,' he says, flicking it with his fingernail.

She drops to her knees and crawls across the floor toward him, kicking the door closed along the way. He scoots to the edge of the bed. His legs are hanging over. She licks the knee, the scab, to soften it, to wash and ready it. The flavor is a wondrous rich mix of dirt, sweat, and blood. She licks slowly and then, with the long nail of her index finger, pries, peeling the scab up. It comes away slowly, painfully, leaving a pink well that quickly fills with blood. She presses her tongue to the coming blood and draws it away. The well refills and then overflows the wound, running down his leg. She holds the scab to the light of the Luxo lamp on the desk.

'A good one?' she asks.

'The best,' the boy says, still breathless from his surgery.

She slips the scab into her mouth. He shudders. She is eating him. He's never seen anything like it. His eyes roll up into his head; he falls back onto the bed.

Fainted. Out for the night.

Without a word, with only the smallest smacking sound of her sucking the scab, she goes to his desk, opens his notebook to a blank page, and scrawls, *Tomorrow at three*, her words going out of the thin blue lines. And then she goes downstairs to the living room, taking care to tuck her treat between cheek and gum so as not to lose it, not to swallow too soon. She stops to thank his mother and father for their hospitality. 'Thank you,' she says. 'Thank you so much.'

'You're welcome, dear. It was a pleasure having you. I'm sure the boys really enjoyed it.'

The girl nods and moves toward the door. The mother shows her out. 'Your eye is going down,' she says. 'That's a good thing. In the morning you'll forget it ever happened.'

The girl doesn't speak. She works her teeth back and forth over the lump of flesh, the piece of their boy between her bicuspids.

'You know,' the mother says, stopping her at the door, 'you probably don't do this kind of thing, but if you're ever inclined, I'm always looking for a baby-sitter. Don't say anything now, but think on it.'

'Again, thank you,' the girl mumbles, taking great care not to lose the bit between her teeth. 'And good-night.'

9

Prison. A sour old mop and bucket. Bleachy smelling salts of Clorox lift me from my thoughts. The man mops with a mixture so strong that if the job is well done – the way it should be done – when he is finished, we will be thoroughly scrubbed; our floors will be clean, our lungs will be clean, and our thoughts will be clean. I wish him all the luck. The bucket sloshes as he comes toward me. The gray tentacles of his mop dip into my cell. 'Wash?' he asks.

'Sure, why not?' I say, lifting my feet from the floor. He makes a quick sweep of the place and is gone. I sit watching the water evaporate, the smell of his stale mop curdling, becoming high and thin like milk that has turned.

'Let me see it again,' Alice says.

'I know what she is referring to and instantly blush.

'Oh, don't be a dolt, show me,' Alice says. 'I just need to see it.'

Clayton, the pathetic fuck, shuffles into my room, feet scraping the floor as if he's sanding himself down, the scrape, scraping of his soles like two sheets of sandpaper mounted on wooden blocks, like the noise we used to make in elementary school under the guise of music and drama. He sits on the edge of my bed. Speechless. Whatever he might want to say would mean nothing, all words and deeds are useless. He knows that, but as a shark keeps swimming, a man keeps talking.

The Guiding Light is over. Josh has returned to Springfield for the wedding even though he's upset that there's a new man in Harley's life. As Julie repeats her vows, Bridget arrives and starts reading her the riot act.

All too much. The television is off.

'I'm thinking of piercing my dick,' Clayton finally says. 'Putting a nut and bolt through it, so I can fuck you like a truck.'

'Only the finest for you,' I say, tweaking the ivy leaf that hangs off his left titty.

He twists away.

'How about a lip plate; that way when you're pouting, it won't be so obvious.'

Fishwife. Nelly. Tired old queen. My surprise at myself, my horror, quiets me.

We stew. There is no point in getting up and running out. There is nowhere to go; his cell, my cell, what difference does it make?

'Do you want your mail?' he asks.

'If you wouldn't mind.'

As usual there's plenty for me, none for him. Requests on university letterhead for an interview, an extensive study, a few questions to be answered, research papers, a book.

I respond politely. For someone with a reputation such as mine, it is important to behave oneself, to be mannered and kind. At least on paper.

Dear Monsieur or Madam,

Thank you for your kind letter. I am hardly the fellow you think me to be. I am shy, hesitant to involve myself in studies such as the one you describe, although I am sure it will be insightful and entirely original – a work of great value. But I, being who I am and things being what they are, beg to be excused from this round. However, if you are open to suggestion, I would wholeheartedly recommend several men here, in particular my buddy Clayton, who allegedly – and more than once – fucked men on the Christopher Street pier and then pushed them into the Hudson River where they drowned.

To hear Clayton tell it – and he rarely does tell it – the men he fucked were so taken with the events, so absorbed with the back and forth of the in and out, that when it stopped, when Clayton breathed a sigh of deep relief and shot high into their asses, the men surged forward, flinging themselves into the water. And Clayton, so suddenly drained, so recently depleted and a nonswimmer himself, would go to the edge and simply scream, howl at the water, at the night, offering his arm, his hand, his fist, to the men, who were already dipping under, flailing far from Clayton's reach.

Again, thank you for your interest and good luck with the project.

All best—

Mail. There is a letter from her. I do my little Gene Kelly, tapping my toes, counting the pat-patter of my heart, my hands, my feet, the echo of the tapping, the metronome of movement, the keystrokes of her Smith-Corona. She is tapping the keys, tapping to tell, and I am tapping my toes, titillated, ready to receive. I save her for last, hoping Clayton will grow bored with the habits of my correspondence. I answer each as I open it, defending myself against the heavily writ tomes of maniacs and wanna-bes, the romantic rhymes of curious widows, and occasional outbursts from the parents of my old girls – you'd think these would be censored, that the same protection that keeps me from them would keep them from me. 'I don't know what kind of man you are,' they say. But of course you do, that's why you deign to write. I answer everything, to everyone I have something to say, today more than usual. I write for hours, hoping Clayton will tire and take leave of his own accord, leave and allow me to enjoy my girl, alone, as I must. He plays with a pad and pen, drawing perspective boxes within boxes, heavy black lines. The doodles of a depressed man.

I can wait no longer. I have dealt with the details. All has been answered, sealed, stamped, and rests on the desk awaiting return to its rightful recipients.

Her envelope is thick, heavy, too promising to put off. I tear at it.

Hi. How are you? What's new? It's July. I'm sweating. There's an air alert. The cleaning lady fainted yesterday and I had to drive her back into the city. Chinatown. Took Matt and co. with me. Everything is sticky.

A ride. Her boy and his friends. I'm jealous. She's buoyant, breezy, too caught up in the events to elaborate, to do more than list the dates and locations, the briefest documentation of her deeds.

Greenwich Village. Eighth Street.

I quote directly, too overwhelmed to paraphrase. My heart speeds. Unbeknownst to me, in these few quiet days, between communications, my feeling for her has grown. My girl. My girl – sweetest thing out on a summer adventure, with this boy, her toy, the practice playmate. So much has changed and she doesn't know it yet. Mine, all mine – I myself am just catching on. In these letters, and how quickly I have come to look forward to them, cannot live without them, am, in fact, living on them, in them; it is as though I am her, she is me, and we are in this together, doing this twisted tantric tango. If only she were a lezzy, a lady licker, the experience would be more satisfying, more mutually agreeable. The talk of boys, of little men, is fine, but when it comes down to it, when we get to the great and gritty, she'll have me fucking the boy, essentially fucking myself, which is all too familiar, slightly degrading, and hardly enough fun. Except for special occasions, my incarceration being one, I like pussies not pricks, it's as simple as that.

Love. It's only come to me now, in this moment. Love. I am in love. Don't tell her. Don't tell anyone. I'm telling you, only you. Never tell them, or rarely. It's the kind of thing, the exact thing, one doesn't want them to know. They take advantage. To admit it is to let on that one is weak, vulnerable, ready for the wound.

I am stunned. This unexpected rush of fine feeling, this revelation, has come as news to me. Clearly I suffer from a kind of internal blindness – so much of my life, my feelings occur unbeknownst to me.

The letter. The letter is still in my hands. I try to read it but can't. It appears not to be in English. I struggle with the language, a pidgin-twisted tongue – the anxiety of my awakening has crippled me.

I beg you, translate for me.

Matt bought Doc Martens. Took Matt to Tower. Wash Sq. Pk. Ate falafel, baba ganoush. Matt had an egg cream.

Matt. Matt. What is this Matt, like a door-mat, like a thing

I should wipe my feet on, a thing I should walk over to get through to her?

She must be on drugs. Her language, the words she uses are brainless, convey nothing. They come with no pictures, no complement. That, or she is retarded – with pathetic eating habits, like those of some third-world villager. A poor correspondent; I have given her so much and she fails me. Nearly every time she fails me. I am close to hysterical with confusion. My breath is short. I don't understand what she is saying except that she let the boy cajole her into being his chauffeur. She's taken the boy and his friends into the city on some sort of medicinal (Doc Martens?) shopping spree instead of doing what she ought.

Riled. Despite my flash of fine feeling for her. This girl is a fool.

'Ink worm,' Clayton says while I furiously scrawl back the first draft of my reply. It often takes several tries before I get it right. 'Ink worm.'

I continue to write. I write faster and faster and more furiously.

In the back of my head, I hear Clayton singing to me. 'Inchworm. Inchworm. Measuring the marigolds. You and your arithmetic will probably go far. Inchworm.'

'Ink worm,' he says again. I shake my head as if to brush him from my thoughts. 'You're getting into something you won't be able to get out of.'

Fuck off, I think, but am too busy crafting my reply to say it.

'You're in too deep.'

Ink worm.

He's jealous. I'm glad. It is a test. If he were really as indifferent as he pretends to be, I'd worry. That I continue to evoke emotion is heartening after all these years. After all, jealousy is but another form of arousal, and some people will do anything to get a stiffy.

He puts his arms around me. My movement is restricted. I can no longer work the pen across the full line of the paper. I am writing in short columns – four words wide. Clayton squeezes my arms tighter.

'Stop,' he says. 'Stop.' He pins me down. I cannot write anymore. He wants my comfort. I offer none.

He goes for my zipper. I allow it. Paper and pen fall to the floor. I have no will. I will always allow it – who can pass up the opportunity to be serviced, especially when service is such a rare occurrence? Clearly, Clayton is trying to get on my good side. I close my eyes, ignore him, and think about my girls, all my girls, all that has come before, will come again. I am aroused. I am hard. It is Clayton. I know it is Clayton, and yet where it counts, I think it is someone else, some exceptionally talented member of the junior committee.

The silky slipper of a mouth swallows me whole.

I pray he doesn't talk. Not now. I am not interested in the lurid lullaby of an innocent man. We are all innocent men. Our innocence is our crime.

My pants are down. I am erect in my breezeless cell. His mouth, his most experienced organ, is upon me, and despite how he thinks of himself, Clayton is best at sucking. He is on me, indefatigably dipping up and down on my cock. And all I can think of is that he is a she, a ten-year-old frisky filly with a long brown mane that I yank to make her whinny and neigh.

I shoot. Clayton swallows my milk, a thirsty babe, a starving suckler, choking for a half-second, inhaling his enthusiasm and then drinking it down. And while I'm still pumping out empty but deep relief, he rolls me over. As I'm turning, I see his face, the stubble of his beard, and am disgusted: a man. How unlikely, how rude and raw. How could I have come to such a thing? What has happened to me? What has happened? He turns me over, I assume to take his turn, to beat and bugger and remind me of who I am. This is the price I pay for my age, my desire, my experience. I expect to be fucked, but instead there is the heart-stopping tickle of a tongue between my legs, coming at me from the back, licking the long hairs, teasing the tops of my thighs, tonguing me in places a man is rarely touched. He is kissing my ass, licking my loving piles. He parts my cheeks, my white moony mounds, and his mouth is there, tonguing my tushy hole. Too much. Too good. I am too old for something so new. I shake, rattle, tremble, and begin to fill again with blood. This has not happened in a long time, a very long time. I am flush with youth, fresh with possibility, am literally overcome – frightened and repulsed from whence it comes and where it goes. It is one thing to fuck it, to lose oneself in that way, but quite another to kiss it, to tenderly poke one's tongue around the ruffled edges of the darkest, foulest mouth. The more interesting it is, the better it feels, the less I think of Clayton. To have a head down there, two eyes in such a place, is not the right thing. In his desperate depression he is making himself be what he thinks I want him to be – a lover.

I am an old man, set in my ways. I will kill Clayton before I let him do this again.

I squirt onto my stomach, staining myself, my belly hairs.

Wordless, with shit on his tongue, Clayton leaves.

In this late life, the genitalia hang thick, puckered, and nearly nude. The skin – brown, dark, deep with wrinkles and flappy turkey toughness – is dotted with coarse and crispy hairs, follicles of negritude that burst through the surface, further ruining it. The budding breasts that are so arresting on a twelve-year-old are suddenly one's own, bulging out of the former flat like fatty tumors; the exposed pink dot of nip spreads out, glowing like a baboon's red butt. Spare tire, not the graceful rounds of a Rubens or now a Balthus, mine is the Michelin man, white circles of cheap lard, Crisco – hard but soft – the Pillsbury doughboy personified. And the greatest part, our private giantess, begins to droop, to hang low; it begins to behave erratically like a sulky monkey, slow to respond, slow to begin the long climb, the rise to attention, sometimes entirely a refusenik. The internal walnut, the ring-o-prostate, clamps down demanding to piss constantly, further humiliating the tired old owner by forcing him to stand at the pissoir surrounded by boys and their hoses, their high-volume water pumps, while he squirts in short, uneven streams. An article – written by a woman no less – tells us that we never learned to pee right: we press and push when we should relax, that it is not about forcing it out, but about letting go. And so we go and go and go.

That Clayton finds this attractive, something he can put himself close to, is the final straw. I have no feeling for him but the worst.

We of great seniority, awaiting our senility, the complete forgetfulness of the sensual, live with the memory of softness, of impossible tenderness – something far too subtle for our weathered fingertips to comprehend were we even to come upon it now in this deteriorated condition. Although, I wonder. I wonder if I would not feel more deeply upon the alteration of several layers of finger skin. Perhaps things could be improved upon. I think that now before I would try again, I would make certain preparations. In advance, I would boil my hands until they were puffy and pink, open to sensation. I would warm them over the fire of a stove, the flame of a Bunsen burner, the heat of a candle, a match, until they were ripe and ready. And when they were so parboiled, when they were abuzz, tingling, then and only then would I touch the girl. My hot hand cupped over her mound, my fingers prepared to play her like the best Knabe, my baby grand, I'll tickle her ivory. I hold her under my thumb and feel the shock, the recoil of recognition, as she realizes that she is in fact being brushed by a stranger for purposes not entirely necessary. These are the touches that aren't quite touches. There is a quiver, a waver during which time it is important that the hand does not move, ground must be held. A short breath is drawn and we are past the initial surprise. She coats herself with greasy goo. With a second finger, I part that curtain and begin my investigation in earnest.

The letter. I go back to the letter. I will always go back to the letter. She is there, waiting for me, waiting with something to tell me, needing me. Without me she is nothing.

What do you like about girls? she writes.
    Their secrets.

Blueberries. She's been out picking berries and has sent me the stained white sheets, eight and a half by eleven, marked with purple juice, the would-be wine or vinegar, a special pot of jam, pressed into the pages. Thinking of you, always thinking of you.
    I imagine she has sent me these pages so that we may lie together in the fields among the beetles and bees, lie together on the cricket floor at the height of day, heat of noon, in the full force of God's light, and have it done – blessed with the necessary relief of an urgency that couldn't wait. Our personal swellings so engorged, nearly anaphylactic in their shock, that they could not be ignored, and so we'd hump, bump, frig, and

fuck, and just in the nick of time, I'd remove myself, spraying my fertilizer, my own dangerous DDT, into the fields while her own quiet passion nectar slowly trickles out. She has mailed me such so that we might be together and enjoy the day.

I bring her pages to my nose, smell the out-of-doors, the curious honey of a fruit field, the uncaged air, the scent of her envelope, her paper, her fingers – Lord knows where they've been. I breathe, grateful that at least my olfactories are intact. Once, long ago, I saw a wooden board, a sign that said FREE WIND TAKE SOME. Her letter is like that, filled with so much. I breathe. Breathe and touch.

Matt's mom took us picking in Fairfield County. We had a contest to see who could pick most, fastest, etc. I kept dreaming of pie, steaming hot with a lump of vanilla ice cream across the top. Matt picked most and fastest and kept throwing berries at me so I punched him, hard. I think he liked it.

Take note and notice, I am old, more concerned with what is wasted, what fruit falls to the ground and is trampled upon than the intent of their game. Foreplay. Affection expressed. She tells me these things and then adds as if an endnote, an after-thought, *And then we did it.*

Did what? What did you do? Did it. Done it. What does that mean? Why does no one tell me anything anymore?

I cannot forgive her the imbecilic nature of her communication. There are people who perpetually drool, who cannot hold their head up straight, cannot unfurl their hands well enough to grip a pen, who have a better command of the language than she with her university years seems to display.

How do you even know what you're doing? You are so back-ward that your idea of 'doing it' might be to pull down your pants and bump butts the way Sissy Hobson and I did as children. We slid our shorts down, had our heinies kiss, and got the greatest thrill.

Is that what she's getting at — some kind of game? Or did they really do it? Did she stake a claim and steal his slippery stream? Did his minute member grace her saintly shrine? Did he even know what was happening? Did he ask for it, beg, get down on his hands and knees and pant, 'Can I? Can I?' And did she simply say 'do' and it was done? What happened?

We did it. So she says.

Slut. Whore. Fucking cunt. Does she think I am immune to her musings? Does she not see that I am drawn still further in, that I am to share her with no one else? Does she think that because I am here, because I have been here for so long, that I've gone queer? Does she assume that because I am so old, I have no interest?

What do I care that she plays with the boy, learns a trick or two off him? What do I care? I must be crazy, half-gone. I must be. It matters. It matters so much to me.

Shut eyes. Clench jaw. Hold tight. The din, the warble. Roar. Screaming siren. I will not be awake. I will not stay for this.

More soon.

10

Prison. Night. My gut burns in the bottom of my belly. Searing, deep, starting on the right and spreading left. A smoldering fire is buried in me. Toss. Turn. It is worse lying down, worse yet on my side. I bring my knees to my chest.

'Boy,' my grandmother calls, and I run. Apple pie. Mother is back. She comes out of the door and stands in the yard, white and gold, porcelain and milky glass. Everything is good and right. She smiles. She laughs. So fragile, so cracked. She is the former Tomato Queen. Queen for a day in Morgan County, in the tiny town of Bath, of Berkeley Springs, buried in the Mountain State, West Virginia.

'You and I,' she says a few days after she's back – we're still staying at my grandmother's house. 'We'll take a little trip. We'll go back to see where I was raised.'

My grandmother, bent over the oranges, elbow bearing down, shakes her head.

'It's not up for discussion,' my mother says.

Somewhere near the Fourth of July, the Tomato Queen returns to her hometown. She drives slowly, pausing on the outskirts to brush her hair, freshen her lipstick, to suck in the long deep breath that will glue her together. She eases her Chevrolet into town, holding herself as if she expects the streets to be lined with well-wishers waving, a band of trombones and tubas waiting to play a certain pomp and circumstance, as if she is still the Tomato Queen and this is still her day.

'A bath,' she says to the attendant at the old Roman baths. 'A great big bath.'

The woman leads us down the hall to a room with a heavy wooden door. 'You have an hour,' she says, turning on the tub. Mama ushers me into the narrow room. The water is running.

'How much does it hold?' I ask.

'A thousand gallons,' Mama says.

As wide as the tub and only a little longer, the room has a small space for the steps that lead into the water. There is a narrow chair and a thin cot dressed in a clean white sheet, and that's all.

'Sometimes, it's just too hard, it's just too much,' she says, sitting on the narrow chair, taking off her shoes, reaching up under her dress and rolling down her stockings.

I sit on the cot watching.

She smiles.

I'm watching Mama, more than watching, looking.

'I'm so glad to be home. Missed you,' she says, unzipping her dress, sliding it off her shoulders. 'Thought about you three times a day.'

She escapes her underthings and I look away. I've been

looking too hard, looking instead of watching, looking instead of not noticing.

Her body continuously unfolds, a voluminous and voluptuous twisting, turning monument to the possibilities of shape, to the forms flesh can take. A body. A real body.

'Are you getting shy?' she asks. 'Getting too old for your ma?'

My face goes blank, all feeling falls out of it. She reaches over and starts to unbutton my summer shirt, the one my grandmother has starched and pressed so stiff that it's sharp, painful in places. I raise my hand and take over the unbuttoning. I undress with the awkwardness of a stranger, wondering if this is the way things are supposed to be, if this is simply how it is done, wondering if my discomfort is my own peculiarity. I have no way of knowing.

Mama turns off the tub.

At dawn I call for the guard. I am doubled over, bent in on myself. 'The doctor, the doctor,' I say.

In shackles. That's how they do it, how they move us from place to place. Guards and guns, flanked front, back, and sides. Arms and legs in steel shackles.

You'd think I was an ax murderer.

I am led through chambers, twisting paths, through doors that must be locked behind me before the one in front of me is released. I am held for several minutes in what feels like a vapor lock, in what could be a gas chamber. I listen for the hiss of pellets, sure they would be willing to sacrifice the guards as well, if only they thought it could be done with no complaint.

'Eyes front,' the guard at my back says, poking me with a billy club.

Due to renovation work, the infirmary has temporarily been relocated to the main building, the administration area, where the corridors are wide and free people, employees of the state, secretaries and civil servants, pass by. They stare. I growl. That is the voice I have left. The cool wand of the billy club taps my shoulder and then brushes against my ear. My head twitches. 'Don't push it,' the guard says.

In pain. My gut.

In the examination room someone screams. My keepers yank my chains. The doctor, blood-splattered, steps into the hall, followed by an inmate. The back of his head shaved. I take note of the long, thick line of stitches running across the rear of his skull.

'Slipped in the shower,' the doctor says, chuckling. Everyone laughs.

The inmate is led past me, shaking, drenched in his drying blood.

My stomach, my weak stomach, my sensitive intestines, curl tighter. I am taken in. A male nurse asks my complaint, and while I'm still shackled, my shirt is unbuttoned, my pants are pulled down, trousers and boxer shorts bunched around the steel at my ankles.

The doctor enters. He is a short, pig-faced man, pink not red, too pink like a runt still struggling to stay alive. What makes a man become a prison doctor? A sentence of his own, the payback of a certain debt? A bad loan? A good doctor does not put himself behind bars, does not give up the nice bums and pretty titties of the upper classes for the privilege of serving the poor, the pathetic, the perverted.

I am rolled onto my side.

'Bend your knees,' the male nurse hisses in my ear, his breath tickling the short hairs.

I do what I can. The metal around my ankles clanks.

'Ever had a rectal?' the doctor asks, jamming a jellied finger into my blind orifice, my toothless mouth, under my tangled tongue and up.

I suffer the indignity of a man in chains, his pants pulled down, privates probed by a putz, while a male nurse, major homo, looks on with great approval.

'Have you ever engaged in homosexual activity?'

Mama pulls her blond hair back, piles it high on her head, and pins it there where it won't get wet. Strays trail down her neck. Her neck is damp, perspiration mixed with perfume, a sweet fruit, a strong liquor, the place you want to bury yourself, to drink. I kiss her neck and, with my lips still pressed to her skin, inhale. Her neck seeps sweat. Teardrops afraid to escape her eyes sneak out the back, slipping down her spine only to find her ass and be sucked back in.

Slowly, she descends the steps into the water. Her body, round, truly a pear, a plum and then some. The most beautiful woman, front and back. Still the Tomato Queen.

She sighs, sweeps her arms wide, and splashes. 'Heaven,' she says.

I slip out of my underwear, leave everything folded on the chair, and sit for a minute on the cot; naked, totally naked, so naked.

Mama smiles. 'You know, this town is where I met your father. Right here in this park, at a party for the Strawberry Festival. He towered like a tree.'

She's back. We will go home to our house and summer will start again. In my memory it is always summer. None of this will ever have happened. The bath will wash us, will clean us, erase everything, and we will begin again.

I plunge in and swim to my mother.

'Your father loved it here. This was the one tub he could fit into. From the time he was ten or twelve he was just too big. He loved baths. Liked to soak.'

She leaves the bath, pulls a bottle from her purse, and pours herself a glass. 'Bathtub gin,' she says, carrying the glass back into the water.

In the water, she turns pink, she turns red. She lies back clutching the bar that goes the whole way around, and like a ballet dancer doing her exercises, she opens and closes her legs. She teases me, making waves.

'Did I ever show you what having you did to me?'

I shake my head.

She shows me her breasts. 'I'm bagged out,' she says, cupping them, holding them up, pointing them, aiming them at me like missiles. 'Bombs away,' she says. 'You stretched me all out.'

'Sorry,' I say, horrified.

'Nothing to apologize for. It's my own damn fault.'

She reaches for the bottle she's left by the side of the tub, refills her glass, and drinks quickly.

'Have you ever engaged in homosexual activity?' the doctor asks.

'Yes,' I say, naively thinking that something about the way my butt hole hangs will tell him anyway, thinking that even if I don't say it, he'll know.

'Do you have a regular partner or more than one partner?'

I don't answer.

'Who is your partner?' he asks, wiggling his finger high into my gut.

Again, I don't answer and he doesn't ask again. He pulls his hand out, snaps the glove off, and throws it across the room toward the trash can. It lands on the floor. Who will pick it up? Surely not the doctor, not the nurse, and not me. Who then?

'Blood in your stool?'

'No.'

'Pain on urination?'

'No.'

'Burning? Frequency?'

'No.'

'Impotence?'

'I'm frightened,' she suddenly says. Her face has lost its color, she goes white, deathly white. 'Give me a hug.'

I go to her. Swim there. She pulls me against her. My cheek, my mouth, is at her breast. She flattens me against it and sees my embarrassment rise under the water.

'Impotence?'

I shake my head. 'No.'

Mama smiles and hugs me hard, looking down at my rise through the water.

'Go ahead,' she says, holding my head in her hands, turning it so that my mouth is at her nipple. 'If it belongs to anyone, it belongs to you.' She moves my head back and forth over it. The softest skin, not skin but a strange fabric, a rare silk. My lips are sealed.

She rubs her finger over my mouth. 'Open,' she says. 'Open up. It's only me, it's your mama. Taste, just taste.'

Like butter, only it doesn't melt. A tender saucer that pulls tight under my tongue, ridges and goose bumps.

She reaches for my hand. I try to pull away.

'No.'

'Yes,' she says, pulling harder on the arm, leading it toward the place between her legs.

'No,' I say more desperately.

My hand goes through a dark curtain, parting velvet drapes. My fingers slip between the lips of a secret mouth. My mother makes a sound, a guttural *ahhh*. I try to pull my hand out, but she pushes it back in. Pushes it in and then pulls it out, pushes and pulls, in and out, in, out.

'It's your home,' she says, one hand at the back of my neck, holding my head against her still, the other on my hand, keeping me there, her leg wrapped around my leg.

'It's your home,' she says again. 'You lived there, before you lived anywhere else. You're not afraid of going home, are you?'

It grows slick, greasy with something wetter than water. My hand is inside my mother, in a place I never knew was there. Deeper. She takes three fingers and threads them into her. Perfume and juices, the cavern grows. She moves the hand in and out. My fingers are swallowed.

She grabs my arm at the wrist. 'Fist,' she says. 'Make a fist, curl your paw.' It doesn't go at first. Too large. 'Push,' she says. And I do. 'Harder.' My knuckles round the edge of the bone and pop in. My fist is inside her. My fist, like I'm angry. I turn it around, screwdriver, drill. I feel the walls, the meat she's made of, dark and thick. My fist is in and almost out and then in again. Her fingers dig into my biceps, she is controlling me. 'Go,' she says deeply, desperately. 'Go. More.' She is pushing and pulling. I'm rocking, fighting. Buried in my mother, I'm boxing. Boxing Mama, punching her out, afraid my hand will come off, afraid the contractions of her womb will amputate me at the wrist. My shoulder is stretching, nearly popping out, and I can't stop. That much is clear. Whatever I do, I can't stop. She is filled with fury and frustration and there is no way of saying no.

She keeps my mouth at her breast. 'Suck,' she says. 'Bite it. It's yours.' Harder and harder. Never enough.

And then with no warning, the teeth of this strange second mouth bite my hand. Her head goes back and she bellows like I've killed her, and I cry out, too, because she's hurting me and I don't know what's happening. I'm scared and I want my hand back and I want my mother back and I want to be out of this place.

* * *

The anal exam is over. I am returned to my back, legs laid out straight. I give the doctor the gory details of all my comings and goings. Hesitantly, he presses my belly – they are loath to touch us, as though the criminal mind will seep out through the pores and poison them. The doctor feels his way around. What once was stiff has gone roly-poly.

Silence. The false solemnity of the occasion eats at me. A long time has passed since I've spoken to a man without a sentence, a man without a gun.

'So how is it?' I ask.

He doesn't answer. I attempt conversation. I speak as though I've forgotten that they are reluctant to treat our melancholia. If we're sad and suffering, they are pleased; legally if not morally, they're obligated by their mothers and wives, sons and daughters, to rub it in. They have done their jobs, the punishment is working.

I mention my concern about Clayton, his poor mood.

'I don't do couples therapy,' the doctor says curtly.

He picks up my chart and scribbles simultaneously with his speech. 'Gas,' he says, writing it down. 'You've got bad gas.'

Wonder bread. The damned Wonder bread, they've never heard of wheat or rye.

'At your age,' he says, and then without finishing the thought, he turns away, digs deep into a steel cabinet, and pulls out a large canister of orange-flavored Metamucil. He hands it over as though he's making a large and luxurious gift.

'Thanks,' I say. 'Thank you very much. Thanks from the bottom of my heart, which just so happens to be located at the top of my bowels.'

The nurse eases me down off the table, all too experienced with the range of movement, the ins and outs of men in shackles. He bends and brings up my boxers, my trousers. I am allowed to zip myself.

As I shuffle out under heavy guard, the doctor taps the canister of Metamucil. 'Two teaspoons in a glass of water every morning,' he says. 'And you'll be good as new.'

It's over. As suddenly as it started, Mama holds up a hand. 'Stop,' she says. 'Stop,' she whispers in my ear. 'It's enough.' She puts her hand on my shoulder and tries to push me away, but my fist is still inside her. Suddenly, I am an intruder, a thief. I am doing something wrong. It takes me a minute, more than a minute. I've gone deaf, I don't catch on right away, I keep pulling and pushing, boxing her insides, going the rounds, giving it my best. I'm doing my job, doing all I can.

'Stop,' she says again loudly; the echo off the tile makes it sound like a shot.

I stop.

She reaches between her legs, plucks my hand out, and lets it drop like some discarded thing. I've failed. I turn full front toward her and begin to rub her, to poke at her with my skinny stub. She laughs and pushes me away. 'Now you're just all excited. All riled up.' She laughs as though it's so funny. She gives me a kiss and climbs out of the tub, wrapping a towel around herself. She lies back on the cot, hand over her eyes, and sighs, breathes heavily, deeply.

I'm staring, wondering what I've done wrong.

'Don't ogle,' she says without even looking at me. 'Swim some, get your flippers wet.'

I am still so small a boy that for me this tub is a pool. I take off, circling, turning laps and somersaults. I make myself relax, loose the cat-o'-nine-tails that stood between us.

A knock at the door. 'Hour's up.'

Shriveled, I climb out of the water. My mother wraps me in a towel and lets me sit on the edge of the cot, resting while she dresses. I suck water from the towel and try not to look while she loads herself back into her costume.

'Don't worry,' she says. 'It's not to worry about. It's not you. It's not new.'

Mama is home.

'No,' I say.

Mama insists.

11

You seem so impatient. How can someone who's been in jail for twenty-three years be so impatient. Isn't it bad for your blood pressure? How many girls did you go with? Was it ten, fifty, or a hundred? Were you a voracious pedophile? Do you mind when I call you that? My mother says I'm too honest, is there such a thing? Back to you — Did you always know you were like this? I guess I'm like you, but you'd never know it just looking at me, everyone thinks I'm shy, a little depressed, a late bloomer. Do you think I'm unusual?

Today she drives me further in. She drives me to know things about myself, things I already know too well. Goddamn. Goddamn. I am wild. I am trapped. Appfelbaum knocks on my door and asks if I'd play him in checkers, if I'd crown his king. Today, I'd just as soon knock his head off with a baseball bat.

I want something else – to see and to hear something entirely different. I want to escape myself.

That she is out there, unleashed, untamed and untrained, free to wander, to feed freely, to satisfy her desire, her whim. That she can pursue her fantasy, her silly summer's delight, infuriates me. And that I, a true connoisseur, a talent unparalleled – okay, okay, not oft paralleled, lest you think me egomaniacal – that I am kept down, restrained like this, is beyond my comprehension, my sense of justice, of all things right and wrong, good and evil. I am a good boy and she is such a bad girl.

Alice is beside herself with glee. She has found me naked by the lake. I say something sharp like, 'Quiet, you little fool.' And then follow this interdiction with, 'Have you no manners? When you come upon someone in their nakedness, you should pretend you have seen no such thing. You act as if you have come upon someone dressed in white tails. And if you are compelled to comment, you address the person by saying something along the lines of, "My, you're looking well today."'

'You're my captive, my prisoner,' she says, still half-laughing. She points to a hearty oak tree. 'I must tie you up,' she says. 'Will you go easily?'

'You mustn't come so close,' I say as she steps toward me. 'Perhaps on my person I have a hidden gun, you might get shot, wounded by my release.'

'Then that's the price I pay,' she says, yanking my arms behind my back, exposing me. She produces a coil of rope; the tickling touch of her small, clammy hands causes blood to rush from my head. My knees buckle beneath me.

'Your totem pole rises,' she says, referring to the state of my nakedness. I am thawing from the freeze.

She jerks my arms tighter behind my back, showing herself

to be surprisingly strong and quite adept, if not practiced, at the art of knot tying.

'Is this the way you win your friends?' I ask.

'Yes.'

'Well, then, I take it you're quite popular?'

She looks at me. 'Have you anything you might buy your freedom with?'

I shake my head. 'No.'

A letter. An interruption. She is the one who sent me into this world, this excavation of my experience, and now I resent her intrusion. I am in my thoughts with my beloved, with Alice, and she has come barging in – a poor substitute. In my less lucid moments, I might confuse them, conflate the two – maybe adding a little of this and that, dashes and hints of other, less significant girls. But in my heart of hearts I know the difference. Today, I hate her, I wish she were someone else. There is no comparison.

She writes: *His mother begged me. 'Would you, could you, just this once, please, pretty please. The regular sitter has the flu. I know you don't like doing it, but could you make a special exception? For me? For Matt?' Can you believe? I'm sitting there, thinking, what to do, what to do, and my mother is yakking in the background, going, 'Who is it? Who is on the phone? Is the call for me?'*

'Would you, could you?' his mother asks.

The girl pretends to ponder, to think. Time alone with the boy, her toy – her heart leaps. The girl agrees. 'Sure,' she says.

'Thank you so much. Thank you. We are so lucky. Come at six and I'll show you everything.'

The girl arrives and finds the mother wearing a black cocktail dress, unzipped down the back. The mother's hair is wet. She's in the kitchen ironing her husband's shirt. 'We're running late,' she says, leaving half the story unsaid. They were going at it. Upstairs getting ready, she and he got carried away and now they're late, she's harried. Her face is flushed. She looks at the clock and sprays the husband's shirt. 'He's very picky about wrinkles. Until this year, we had a live-in, it was a luxury. The kids are older now and we've got to save for the big BM.'

'Pardon?'

'Bar mitzvah.'

'Oh.'

She has a little crushlette on my girl. She kisses her for no apparent reason. Kiss hello. Kiss just because. Kiss. Kiss.

The boy. The boy, where is the boy? The girl is distracted wondering where he roams in his father's castle. Why didn't he meet her at the door, greet her with a wink, a whisper, a titty tease? She hopes he has not been taken away, lured out by his friends, bribed with the promise of M&M's and Jujubes.

One after another, the mother opens the kitchen cabinets, showing the girl around. 'Whatever you want, it's here,' she says, gesturing at cans of Campbell's soup mix, mandarin oranges, potato sticks, cake mix. She opens the fridge, the freezer, to show what can be defrosted, done in an oven.

'We won't be home before midnight,' the mother says, 'but I'd like the kids to get to bed at a decent hour. The little one's allergy medicine is here.' She points to a bottle of red syrup near the sink. 'If he seems bothered, give him a spoonful, but not too early. It puts him right to sleep.'

Her boy comes into the kitchen, looks at her, and without a word slinks away. By the way his shorts fit, she can tell he is pleased to see her.

'Matt. Matthew, come here, boy,' the father bellows from the upstairs hallway. The son is taken aside. 'I trust you to behave responsibly. You've been so peculiar lately, I wonder.

You know my position on drugs – take only what the doctor prescribes.'

The boy and girl sit in the den in front of the television making small talk while the parents finish polishing themselves up.

'Do you have G.I. Joe?' she asks.

'Not anymore,' he says.

'What do you play?'

He shrugs.

'How's your forehand coming?' She makes the motion of jerking off. 'Have you been practicing?'

The mother ducks her head into the den. 'We're leaving. See you later. Have a good time.'

'Drive carefully,' the girl says.

The mother gives the girl a quick peck on the lips. 'Thanks.'

Matt ignores it. He lies on the sofa, arm crooked behind his head. He is nothing if not casual. The band of his underwear pokes out of his shorts. She is tempted to yank it, to jerk it, to hike his BVDs high into his bum, pulling his balls tight against his torso. He scratches himself, rubs, digging in, rearranging things, seemingly surprised at her stare.

'What?' he asks, working his hands over his body without the least awareness of what it does to others.

She adores his absent fascination with all that can be picked, plucked, and snacked upon, cuticles, calluses, nails, and of course scabs. He pops pieces of himself into his mouth as though he wishes to eat himself alive. She imagines him twisted into a contortionist's pose, arms and legs braided, his body bent to bring mouth to member, to sample the delicacy forbidden by anatomy's architecture, among other things. She knows the brother of a friend who can do it, who's down on it morning, noon, and night, sucking himself off and shooting high at an archery target mounted on the ceiling, splashing the bull's-eye with the splatter of spunk.

'Arf, arf.' On his hands and knees the baby brother comes to her, playing a dog.

'Are you a dog? A pretty puppy dog?'

He nods. 'Arf, arf.'

Matthew watches television, ignoring them.

'Do you want me to scratch your ears, rub your belly?' She reaches down and pets the little pup.

'Arrfff, Arrrfffff,' he purrs, rubbing against her leg, arching his back, clearly confused about the difference between dog and cat.

Wallace, the real family hound, sits in the corner watching the proceedings, brow raised, perplexed.

'You're a good dog, a cute doggie,' she says.

Wallace's tail thumps the floor.

The dog boy wiggles his butt.

Matthew rolls over. 'I wanna be your dog,' he says to her.

They look down at the baby brother. 'Puppy want to go out?' she asks. The baby boy nods and pants. She gets the leash and collar. Wallace gets up and goes toward the door. 'No,' she says firmly. 'Not you.' She hooks the baby up, fitting him into the collar, attaching Wallace's leash. She takes him out into the yard, hooking his lead to the long chain, the tie-out stake stuck deep in the dirt next to the house. Dog boy crawls around on all fours, sniffing the grass, pretending to dig holes and bury bones. 'If you need anything, just bark,' she says, leaving him there.

'Take off your clothes,' Matt says. 'I need to see what you look like.' He pauses. 'I promise I won't do anything. I just want to look.'

'You don't have to promise anything.'

'Take off your clothes.'

'You.'

'What?'

'Take off my clothes.'

Teaching thick fingers to be nimble is part of the education. She lies on the sofa and lets him unbutton her shirt. For purposes of early education, her bra is front closing. He lets loose the clasp; it springs open. He unzips her pants. She wiggles out, pulling down her panties. For a while, he does nothing, only looks – all the while absentmindedly sucking his own index finger. Finally, he touches his finger to her nipple. It shrivels to a tight knot. He wiggles it back and forth. Ding, dingy. He plays with her titty. He cups a breast in each hand, holding them, molding them as if to divine all he can. He scoops them up, lifting from the sides, instinctively knowing how to get the fullest feel in hand, pushing them together so they might meet and make one, squeezing hard as though a display of strength will win the contest.

She winces but says nothing.

His face is against them, sniffing and licking and then sucking, pulling hard as he would on a soda straw. Nothing comes. He is disappointed, having thought there would be something, a little snack, a single squirt. Still so unfamiliar with the connect-the-dot routine – the simple switches that connect lip, tit, and pussy – he hasn't noticed that all along her hips have been rising and falling, bucking for attention. He has missed the spectacle of her short hairs curling as the humidity increased. And when he finally gets there, when his investigation leads him south, he says, 'Oooohhh, gross, it's all wet. Did you pee in there?'

He peels her apart, asking, 'Is it supposed to be like this?'

'Like what?'

'I don't know, like this?'

'Yes.'

Studying, staring, making what appear to be mental notes, his fingers dip in, slide down the slit and into the hole, feeling around as though by accident he's dropped a penny or a dime and would now like it back. Wiggling fingers. Finding nothing, he pulls out.

'Show me the clip.'

'Clip?'

'You know, your clip. It's supposed to do something.'

She reaches down, exposing the gemstone, the dancing dot of perfect pleasure. 'Clitoris,' she says. 'Clit, not clip.' A short course in pronunciation.

'What's it do?'

He with his great erector set, his bursting birthday toy, the wondrous wand that rises and falls, launching rockets, firing jets of joy, the juiciest jizz of the jungle, he with that magnificent mechanical manhood is not impressed: hers is the wind-up model.

'It feels good when you rub it.'

He doesn't answer, only stares for a moment, then picks up a Matchbox car – an ambulance – from beside the sofa and runs it over her, driving the small black wheels backward and forward over the spot. When nothing happens, he stops. 'Show me,' he says. And she does, illustrating the procedure with her own hand, encouraging him to gently take her titties under tongue while she does the rest, and in seconds there is the shiver, the shudder, and she stops.

'That's it?' he asks.

'Yep.'

'I don't get it.'

She shrugs.

Completely clothed, he lies down on her, rubbing her. There is a barking in the backyard. They go to the window;

dog boy is outside howling, pawing at his bowl.

'Find out what he wants for dinner,' she says. And the boy – the front of his pants stained with a weird wet mark, a secret sloppy kiss that could be either his or hers – goes into the yard and asks the pup, 'Do you want your dinner?' The puppy nods. 'Gaines Burgers or Alpo?'

The pup curls his nose, sits up on his back legs, and speaks. 'People food.'

'You're a spoiled puppy, a bratty boy,' the big brother says. Dog boy whimpers. 'Do you want milk or juice with it?'

'Apple juice,' dog boy says.

'Be right back.'

In the kitchen, the girl opens a can of Beefaroni and spoons the contents into a plastic bowl, adding a serious sip of allergy syrup before slipping the bowl into the microwave. When it is ready, she lays a spoon and a napkin on a tray, pours the kid a cup of apple juice, and lets her boy deliver dinner out into the yard.

While Matt's gone, she feeds Wallace, the real dog, and puts her clothing back on.

I asked Matt what he wanted for dinner. 'Everything,' he said, and so we had it, all of it: egg rolls, cheese puffs, french fries, fried chicken, spinach soufflé, macaroni and cheese, everything out of the freezer. Made pigs of ourselves. Oink, oink. Fun.

Do you get to pick what you eat? Is it like a hospital where you circle your choices? Is the food Oedipal? – a little joke, ha, ha.

Is it Oedipal? I could kill her. I struggle to remember what it is to choose, to decide what you want and then have it. Asparagus. I haven't had asparagus in twenty-three years. I respond with a little history lesson. The FDA allows a higher percentage of hair, mouse shit, whatever evil and vermin you can imagine, into food intended for industrial use as compared to the single-serving cans you open at home – why is there a second standard?

And to drink with that? Wine?

Matt digs deep into the cabinet. 'Only red. Is red okay?'

Yeah.

He pulls out a can of Hawaiian Punch.

She had something else in mind, but punch drunk is punch drunk. Fine.

Because they cannot admit it, cannot even name what it is they desire, their fearful craving encourages them to consume the contents of the cabinets, to sit at the table gorging themselves until they are in pain. And the pain comes as a relief; they push away from the table feeling sated, safely satisfied.

Dinner done, dishes disposed of, she glances out the kitchen window. Baby brother is at the far end of his tether, his pants are down, he's squatting, smiling, pleased with himself, shitting on the grass. He finishes, pulls his pants up, and on all fours comes back across the yard, turns in several circles like a real dog, and lies down in the grass. It is probably good that she gave him the allergy medicine; without it, he would be wheezing.

Brightness evaporates inside the house. It is nearly night. Shadows abound, taking him and her, she and he, the kooky kidlets, down into the dark as if etherizing them, putting them in an odd and uncomfortable twilight sleep. Floorboards creak. In the living room the television talks to itself. Without warning they are two children, alone at home, afraid of the dark. Hear no evil, see no evil, do no evil. They don't speak or move. The presence of something larger than either of them fills the room. (I'd call it guilt.)

Light. The light, turn on the light, one wants to call to them, but they are deaf – the dulling of the senses is part of the darkness.

Outside the yard is bright. Timers sensitive to dusk have automatically turned on the floodlights. Sprinklers kick to a start with a whispering whoosh. The two children hear the water go on, look at each other, and suddenly spared from twilight's sleep run out of the house, pushing down the steps, into the night. The oscillator's sweep sprays water upward against gravity. The water then drops gently down, fooling the grass, the petunias and geraniums. Phlox won't be fooled, my grandmother used to say. Boy and girl fly through the sprinkler's swath; water soaks their clothes. The boy takes off his shirt and throws it onto a bush. The girl slides out of her pants; her shirt is long and covers her ass. Through the water, over the water, under the water, they dash and dance. The spray turns his khaki shorts dark, and the outline of his erection is clear. He takes off his shorts, leaving them on the grass. The thick cotton weave of his BVDs binds his protuberance against his body. She slides off her shirt, stripping down to an intimate bikini, bra and panties. The insects of summer click and clack. Moths circle the floodlights. They chase each other. He plucks the back of her bra, making a melody like she's strung with the strings of a lute. Her breasts bounce keeping time, as do her thighs and buttocks, a wiggle and jiggle that he might find attractive but which slightly rolls my stomach. His member, his aspiring manhood, stretching, growing longer, thicker each time it rises, is now frozen, stiff like something stuffed, aimed up, fixed on God.

He runs after her. He pulls her panties down, pushing her until she falls onto the grass and is down on her hands and knees. He throws himself on her, holding her until his prize is aligned, then pokes her from the back, laying in, bending the bone, riding her as though she's unbroken, his wild mare. He steadies himself by pulling on her bra strap, holding her elastic reins. One arm thrown high into the sky, he rides, hips humping. He slaps the side of her thigh, leaving the muddy mark of his hand – his brand. He rides his fuck until she's bucking violently under him and it is all he can do to keep himself in.

Her brassiere gives way, comes undone, firing him backward, sliding him out and off and into the dirt. For a second his pillar, his pole, lights up the night, red, hot, glowing like molten steel, like the rumored reindeer's nose. But as quickly as it's flashed, she's upon it, bouncing up and down. Shimmy, shimmy, shake. How quickly it is done. She leaves him laid out in the grass and moves over to the sprinkler, spreading herself over it, working the water whip back and forth beneath her. With the tiny teeth, the tickle of a tongue, she water-picks her pussy, sighing under its spray. Both breasts in hand, she tilts her hips back and forth, rocking, coming not just once but in a set, a small series of cataclysmic constrictions. It is something to see, to watch, the work of an artisan. Beneath her, as her hips continue to sway, the water automatically turns itself off.

Nearly finished, she goes to her man, stands above him, and lets go, sprinkling him with a steamy stream, pissing on his privates.

His jaw drops. Only the slightest sound, a sort of an *Oh*, comes out.

'I've been saving up,' she says. 'All day, I've waited for this.'

'Don't ogle,' Mama says without even looking at me.

Dabbed in dirt, dotted in mud, the boy collects the clothing like litter and they cut through the yard. On the far side of the house, dog boy is asleep in the grass. The girl stops, unchains the sleeping boy, and carefully carries him inside. Still speckled with war paint, piss, and mud, they lay the little one out in his bed. While the girl undoes the leash and collar, Matt pulls off his clothing and slides him into his pajamas. Around his neck is an indentation from the harness; not too deep, not too red, it will have faded by the time his mother comes in to check on him.

They shower – thank God it is not a bath. Praise that she does not run the tub, get in it with him, and go rub-a-dub-dubbing, soaping his cock, sliding it up her bum, and again cumming. They shower – I shower as often as I can. And wrapped in his mother's robe, she brings her boy to his bed, tucking him tightly between the sheets. Below the covers, it rises again. She pats it a great good-night. 'Enough for one day. See you soon, my friend. Sleep tight.'

Downstairs, she runs the washer and dryer. The parents' car pulls into the driveway and she dashes to dress. Her clothing is hot. As his father drives her home – her pockets pulsating with pay (the cheap thrill of playing the prostitute, the whore, reverberates) – the metal underwire of her bra leaves burns, two smiling *U*s etched beneath her breasts.

Drunk. The car crosses back and forth over the yellow line like some zigzag stitch on a sewing machine. And I'm thinking I should have walked. But, it's one a.m. and who knows what evil lurks – could be you or one of your friends. Anyway, he goes, 'Thanks. Thanks a lot for, you know, your help with the kids, Matt's lessons and all.'

'Mine, the pleasure is mine,' I say.

'Well,' he says, 'I just want you to know, I appreciate it.'

He squeezes my knee.

Gross, totally gross, no one ever gets enough.

'Well,' he says, repeating himself, 'I just want you to know.'

Impossible! This is not the way it works. And I'm not referring to the scene in the car, which quite frankly I don't even believe, but to what went on before – oh, the tachycardia of the critical heart. Don't you see that her approach, her manner for dealing with the boy, is far too simple, too consciously careless, as though she and he were partners in this subtle crime, when the truth of it is – as you have taken note – she and I are truly the team. Surely, I am skipping beats. How does she know these things? From where does she receive such steamy thoughts? Does she believe these activities have not heretofore been explored, that she has come to them on her own, that she is their inventor? Or is this just sewage spilling, the stew of some imagination – and then the question begs, Is it hers or is it mine?

If only there were someone I could trust, could ask to take a little look-go-see. Surely, she is lying and the story more likely goes that she and he spent the evening sitting on the sofa, their only wrestling over possession of the remote control.

All the same, fact or fiction, her hot air has landed on me like the breath of a bellows, has aroused my flame, made my embers glow. I have come back to life. One wonders exactly what her motive is with this latest move, delivering me the diary of her days. Is the telling of her tale meant to mock and tease or to tempt me with a sticky, sweet treat?

Does she not understand that between us there is a certain agreement and that her foreplay *finalis*, her fucking the boy, has betrayed my trust? Our letters are our contract – clearly and conveniently she seems to have forgotten that.

Admittedly, I found her story somewhat entertaining, and yet had I been invited in and allowed to participate, it might have had a very different end. I don't mean to imply the worst, but all the same . . .

Had I been invited to her party, how differently it would have begun. From the start she would have been bound and gagged, stripped, whipped, shaved with my sharp straight razor. Compared to this, her night with the boy is but an aperitif, whetting the appetite for what turns things take, games a true connoisseur plays.

The examination, the little look-see, would go a little differently. I'd slip her head into a leather mask, hawk's hood, zippers over mouth and eyes. On days such as these when I am already in such misery, it is far too much to meet eye to eye. Were we to peek, to see each other at the wrong moment, I fear what might happen, what surprise would rise, what wrong would be wrought. Be thankful that I keep her blind.

Besides, bound and gagged, she is free to lie back, relax, and enjoy me.

In order that I might get my proper view, the area must be shaved – I abhor pubic hair, it is not a winning thing. Even my own, I keep cut, trimmed to a neat square, groomed like the green around a monument. And to keep my concentration, to do my best work, to avoid being struck by flailing limbs, she must be restrained. Quite routine. Wrists tied behind the head – in older girls this keeps the breasts pulled back and helps the chest look flat. Legs spread. Ankles bound. She should be racked and stretched, no way for the knees to bend, no quick reflex to defend, no accidental injury to the operator – that is, me. An inadvertent knee jerk to the groin is the last thing I need. For the procedure to commence, I sit between her legs, her mound faces fuzz up.

A simple aside: Another reason I dislike girls of significant age is that uncorked, uncovered, they reek of sexual steam, like something long simmering finally released. I hate the smell of cunt ready and waiting. I want it green, before it is ripe, before it has an odor easily discerned.

Fast as I can, I spray the muff with a heavy load of shaving cream. In the past I've doused girls with a chemical defoliant, but they writhed too much, made claim it burned. (Once, some did leak on me and I got a nasty spot through my pants, a raw, oozing sore on my leg.) So, mostly now, I shave. There is something to them watching me while I work the razor, stropping the blade before their eyes – letting them wonder where it will ultimately go. Before I sharpen, I sweep the dull end over their slits, their tits, and into their mouths, and sometimes if I'm feeling frank, I flip it over, cut off a hank of their hair, and tuck it into their mouths – girls like to suck on that, you see them doing it all the time.

With five fast strokes I scrape them down and then real fast do a second round. I slather them with foam, decorate the raunchy rat with Barbasol or the milky white of sweet whipped cream. Again, five fast strokes, I give it the go, taking care on the corners, trying not to nick the lips. Around the anus and close inside there are strays I can't get to with the blade, and so finished with the shave, I come back with a candle and with its flickery flame melt the rest away – the hot wax dripping on the skin an extra thrill, a hint of things to come.

Stripped clean, you are my girl. I fuck you with my fingers. Spit on the spot and, using the salve of my saliva, slip the initial indexer in. The ivory of my nail, my tiny tusk, scrapes your hallowed hall. Pit of pleasure, I patiently explore, knocking my knuckles on your private prison walls, pushing at the boundaries of flesh. I jam in, each time adding extra digits, sure if I work it right, soon I'll find you on my fist.

I am at the center of you.

Flick my thumb against the hidden hood, the most tender morsel in its overcoat. I push back that skin, letting out the little lump, my clam, oysterette, what women call their little prick. I suck that snail, eat escargot. Breath escapes you with your cum. You cum and I do not stop, I go on knowing what comes next, the best is after last, there is always more – always something interesting just the other side of pain.

I kiss. Having always wanted to make out with these sacred spots, I brush your lips with my own, blow you with my breath. I kiss so softly you don't know I'm there. Lip to lip. I kiss this second mouth, part it with my tongue, toothless shark, lots of layers folding and un, becoming quite like tiny tongues. I speak into you, saying things I cannot tell you to your face.

Curl my lip, roll it back, and expose my teeth; fuck you with my face, scraping the liquid of your ecstasy, scraping until your flesh is weak, until you break and begin to bleed. And then I suck that blood, drink you down.

And saving the best for last, I pull out the most favored toy, my precious BB gun – a long-dead father's gift to his only son. I travel with it tucked inside my bag and rarely use it, but today is special because I'm here with you. So I unpack the would-be rifle, pump it up three times, and put it to you. I blast you once and you buck a bit; the second time you seem still surprised as though no one had ever thought of such a thing. I stroke the barrel and am filled with memories; screaming squirrels, broken bottles, bull's-eye pucks in widows' windows. The black paint is chipping. Again, I pull the trigger and then withdraw, leaving you with my ball bearings buried in your walls. You look so perplexed. Oyster, don't you get it? In your shell I have put three grains of sand. Make me a pearl!

12

Random swearing in the hall. Things overheard.

'Walk me down. Walk me down. Why my woman always walk me down? Bitch, whore, fucking cunt. Why you look at me like that? Oh, the humanity. What for lunch?'

'You can't run and you can't hide, where you gonna go, death row? Ha, ha, ha, ha.'

Prison. Bells. Fourth of July. The pyrotechnic plot. Rumor swirls, the rooster crows, something is up, word is passed down, around, we are due for a visitation; a reward or a shakedown? Nervous with anticipation, the men surreptitiously do a late-spring cleaning, disposing of all illicit stock. When the rising timbre, the tidal wave's roar, the fiery flush of industrial-strength toilets becomes so violent, so self-determined as to threaten the septic system, an investigation is instigated. The men, well rehearsed, claim the culprit is something served for dinner the night before, if not the fish sticks, then the tartar sauce. The doctor – the man of my so recent acquaintance – is called, and we are ordered to bare our butts, bend over at the cell door and let his proxy's latex fingers slip us bullets to bind. But as soon as they are gone, the tiny torpedoes of Compazine are fired out the ass, medicating only the toilet water. You can lock us up, but you can't keep us down.

Due to the overload, the water is shut off for several hours. At 4 p.m. we are given the word that despite the surprising epidemic of gastrointestinal upset, our nearly riot level of anxious activity, despite the stoned and sedated state of those men who were not quick enough to squirt their suppositories – the evening's events will go on.

In a grand gesture of community relations, of seemingly self-less sacrifice, the denizens of the town nearby have switched the site of their planned pyrotechnics so that we might passively participate. This year they will fire their fanfare due south so that we behind the walls might have something to see. Snacks will be served. Attendance is required.

Eight p.m. Out of our cages and into the hallway. Men hesitant to leave the luxury of home are pulled from their cells by guards in riot gear. We are handcuffed and hobbled, arms and legs joined in giant ropes of chain. Twelve men form a line. The guards, even though they're getting time and a half for holiday service, aren't happy. Scared shitless is more like it – they've never taken us out at night. Like a conga line we move through the maze, threading through the tunnels and traps, the same old hallways painted battleship gray. With the chink-a-chink-a rhythm of so much chain, the tragic dance of the bound and tied, the shimmying shake of a tambourine, jingle bells, we wind down and around. Right to left, side to side, whatever you do you do it together, in concert with the man in front of you.

The extension of the chain is short, and in order not to be pulled and pained, one has to learn the way. Penguins hop. Synchronous swimmers. June Taylor dancers. Slithering snake. We wrap around the yard and are positioned, stretched out in even lines.

'Sit,' the guard before us barks. And we do, lowering ourselves to the ground. It is a herky-jerky thing.

'They're treating us like dogs, animals, put out for the night,' Kleinman says, scratching himself.

The high carbon arcs of the towers cast a glow over the yard. Bright white. Light, so much light. An opera, a grand opening eve. Ushers-cum-guards work their flashlights like lasers, leading prisoners to their seats. The far stone walls have become a backdrop to the most classical of stage sets – we are the theater.

Through a broken bullhorn, the majordomo addresses us. Only bits and pieces are audible. His cracked address sounds something like this:

'Grateful to the town of ale firing jerks in our face, spiritual if and Owen Overstern, fucking flasher, for aching this onerous gift, the ax you are about to receive, eat candy, men, dentist month. Annoy! Annoy!'

Razor wire glitters, glinting like something hungry. I wonder what else it's caught besides Jerusalem's flesh and the occasional cat who gets its furry throat slit while the bird it chased takes off – the revenge of flight.

'Treats, treats, pass us some sweets,' Frazier begins the chant.

Volunteers, graduate students in criminology, work their way up and down the rows, passing out the party favors, big boxes of Cracker Jacks, past their expiration date, all of them opened and with the prizes removed.

The lights go off. We are dropped into darkness. There is a

steaming hiss, the sudden suck of breath. A hush sweeps the crowd.

It's been more than two decades since I've seen the night. The sky hangs like a velvet curtain. I stare at the stars, picking out Polaris, the Big and Little Dippers, and Cassiopeia, the queen. I offer them the simpleton's prayer, 'Star light, star bright, first star I see tonight, wish I may, wish I might, get the wish I wish tonight.'

In the distance there is a dull thud. We sit in our stone cage, black box, blind and dumb. A few flashlights play over the crowd. The curtain lifts, the first one clears the wall, a fine white burst exploding into a thousand stars. I try quickly naming them before they disappear: Alice and Amy, Barbara and Betty, Cathy and Caroline.

Boom. Boom. Boom. Bombardiers. Chrysanthemums of light.

Sparkles fall like fairy dust and I am doused in memory.

Fourth of July: I set a hundred sparklers in my grandmother's yard – spend the early evening pushing them down into the grass – and when darkness falls, I call my grandmother onto the porch and race to light them one by one, firing them like the magical spill of a domino line.

'Don't use all my Blue Diamonds or you'll be down to fetch me matches come morning,' my grandmother shouts.

'I'm using punk,' I call back. 'Only punk.'

'That's right, you're a punk. Glad you know it.'

'Scorched,' she says the next morning. 'You burned my grass, that was good zoysia I had there.'

Another time, older still, I go off into the woods with my secret stash. In broad daylight of an Independence morn, I fire my works at the rising sun, hold the Roman candle in my hand, light the line, and send off balloons of color, sour balls of light, all of it aimed toward that stronger light. There was something sad about sending up at the height of day, sadder still than in the night. I set my sno-cone in an empty field, lit the fuse, and while it rained, danced around the flames, letting them shower me, dotting my skin with bits of glittering light, stinging me like an insect's bite.

Prison night. Elbow in my side. 'You eating yours?' Frazier asks, pointing at my Cracker Jacks. I shake my head and hand him the box. It is better this way. I used to love Cracker Jacks and caramel corn, but just from having it in hand, I can feel how far gone it is, how passé. After so long an absence, so many years, nothing would be worse than eating stale candy.

Mama is home from the asylum. She takes me to the baths – you remember that – and then to a cheap motel. 'Widow's got to watch her wallet,' she says, pouring herself a glass of gin. 'My medication,' she calls it. 'I am a woman who needs her medication. Here' – she holds out the glass to me – 'take a taste, it won't kill you.'

I shake my head.

She lies down on the bed. 'A little nap,' she says. Her head is down on the pillow and she is asleep.

I wash my hand. Soap and water. I wash my hand and arm up to the elbow. I wash my hand until it is burning red, until the skin can't get any cleaner without being taken off, boiled, and hung out to dry. I scrub myself thoroughly.

My mother lies facedown on the white chenille bedspread, her fingers reading the braille rose, the white relief, the *dit-dit-da* dashing of Morse code like a somnambulist. My eyes grow heavy and I lie next to her. Her arm hooks around me. Mama and her boy in a close knot. My hand beats, pulses, throbs with the memory of her on my fist. Mama fitted around me. And me pushing hard and harder against her, into her. I reach beneath the blankets and touch myself. When I wake up, Mama is gone. The sheets are peeled back, and in the middle of the pit where Mama had lain, there is a bright blush of red, a thick red streak, blood.

I scream. 'Blood. There's blood.'

She is in the bathroom, I can hear the whining of the hot and cold taps. My fault. All my fault.

'My curse,' Mama says through the bathroom door. 'It's my curse.'

And then the door opens and she is dressed, made for the day. 'Did you sleep?' she asks. 'Dream a pleasant dream?' She speaks as if singing, writing herself little lyrics, little lines. She is fine, like herself, like she has always been, exactly as I remember her. Were it not for my hand, my sore hand, I would think it had not happened at all. I would think it was something that had leapt out of me, a bit of my imagination. Me. It must be me. My stomach turns. It is I who's slipped through God's graces and done such a terrible thing. My hand beats, pulses, throbs with the terrible reminder, and yet she seems without these after-effects. I want to lift her dress, snake my fingers, my eyes, into what lies in that lost location, searching to see if beneath its protective costume, its mask, it is truly unaffected, unamused, or whether it is indeed weeping, seeping from the events.

She acts as if everything is as it has always been, as if she is still my mother and I her son.

'You look a little pale, do you need some lipstick?'

Her hand dips under her dress, her legs bow slightly, she pulls out fingers dipped in rust. She paints blood across my lips.

Strontium red stains the sky.

One if by land, two if by sea, you fuck me with your history. Thomas J. and the nation's birthday – it's like Marilyn singing to JFK. I come real close and whisper breathless in your ear, 'Happy birthday to you, happy birthday to you, you merciless fuck, on this the anniversary of your Independence Day.' Seventy-six trombones at the big parade, and the only horn we hear is the farting bleat of the tower tuba when someone tries to escape. We, the captured and convicted, are kept bound and chained so that we might not destroy the fragile foundations of this great society – there is so much subtext between the lofty lines. I have memorized the document my correspondent sent – I have gone over it replaying the words of our most independent declaration:

'When in the course of human events . . .'

A sick trick you play, keeping us jailed on Independence Day. Better it would be if we stayed inside and passed it oh so quietly. Better yet, let's pretend – as we so often do – it never happened.

Revolution! Light flashes against the false horizon, the old stone walls. The ramparts are being bombed while we are held inside, a secret cache, war's prize. Regiments of proud perverts have been rounded up, recruited from every back-room bar, brothel, and jolly house up and down your stinky streets, and they're here now on the distant shore preparing to charge these steely gates. Inside, we rattle our chains, our holy cuffs, and pray aloud that our side wins. Dark victory.

A blue mum explodes in the sky. Clayton, in the row ahead of me, turns and winks. He looks at me and licks his lips. I curl my tongue around a haul of spit and fire it straight at him.

Amber, amber, white. Again, chrysanthemums of light.

She writes: *I'm kind of a romantic, are you? Despite my weirdness, I'm pretty old-fashioned.*

*   *   *

'Alice, darling, dear one, where are you?' A woman's voice calls through the woods.

'I'm hiding,' Alice answers.

'Where are you?'

'I'm hiding.'

'Sweetie, pumpkin, darling, where are you?'

'Hiding.'

'I'm driving into town to pick up a few things. I thought I'd buy you a little something. Do you want to pick it out yourself? Where are you?'

'Coming,' she screams, quickly gathering her quiver, her bow, and remaining supplies.

She takes off up the hill, leaving me naked, tied to the tree. 'See you later,' she calls to me.

The ease with which she abandons me is thrilling. I am naked in the New Hampshire woods, tied to a tree. The rough bark rubs my buttocks raw as I wiggle trying to free myself. I have been bound and tied by a wicked wood nymph. I writhe. My tumescence rises farther still, stimulated by my situation. A breeze stirs the trees, sweeping over, tickling me. I sneeze first, then cum, shooting off aimlessly into the afternoon.

Confused. I am confusing her with another one. I am lost in time. I begged myself not to play this game, she is not that girl but some other one. Are they all the same? How many were there, can my fingers count that high? Memory is such an elusive thing. I had none until the letters arrived, and now I am like a man unleashed. Until these days, this high holy night, it was as if my history had slipped away from me. I remembered nothing – but never told them that, too embarrassing. I played along, quite ashamed at the recalcitrance of my recollection whenever official inquiries were made, a gentle tap, tapping on my mental door, 'Excuse me, sir, we want to ask about one more. Did you do it, yes or no?'

'God, yes,' I'd declare, convinced that their criminal concoctions were quite conservative compared to what crimes I'd convinced myself that I'd committed. 'God, yes,' I'd confess to anything, sure that in fact I'd done far worse. Far, far worse.

And now I wonder . . .

Am I losing my mind or just getting it back? Suddenly, I know too much, can all too well recall the details of my atrocities.

There is an elbow in my rib. 'Stop mumbling,' Frazier says. 'You're talking in your sleep.'

I turn to Frazier, rattle my chains, and say, 'She left a butterfly outside my door. Hoary Elfin is its name.'

A gold report divides the sky.

High, so high. I am the sky, the jet-black night. It is me turned inside out. I am taking this great salute as a tribute to my years, my fine accomplishments. It is so. It is such. Thank you. Thank you so much. Free. Free within myself, unbound, time to spread the word around. Soon I will be out there further still, tap, tapping on your windowsill. It is time for me to take my leave. Here, there is nothing left for me.

That this seems so much like an end is an error, a great mistake. I am at the beginning and about to start again. I resolve to meet her soon.

And where is she on this great night?

Oh, I know all too well she's with him. She spends this liberation day with the boy, the toy, on a pseudodate. He has taken her, or she has taken him – the logistics are no matter, they're both guilty as sin. Fucking in the sand trap at their fathers' country club, while overhead similar pyrotechnics do parade. They are not alone, but with his friends. She fucks him first, their own sideshow, and then she fucks all three, the lardy boy from before and the big one with the beakish nose. She fucks them once, twice, three, and more, and you cringe when I call her a whore. For now I am trapped behind these walls, but she is making do – three scrawny cocks, thirty dirty fingers, sticking something in every orifice, lucky little dicks. God, I hate these chains about my legs.

A manganese of white light explodes against the night.

Mama is dead. The telephone rings. My grandmother answers it, listens, then hangs up, turns to me, and says, 'Gone. She went over, off the road at the Panoramic View, near the steak house. Dead.' Mama is gone. She has left me with a woman who only keeps me because it would be more embarrassing not to. My fault. All my fault. You can't convince me differently. The howling begins. A wail. A siren that never goes off, only grows more distant and more near, a constant warble in my ears. Without trying, without even knowing, without an effort, with only a plea, no, a kind of pathetic begging, no, with nothing but my presence, my person, my love for her, I was drawn in, implicated, involved. And despite my will, the will to remain who I was, as I was, there was confusion, uncertainty, the weakness of my person and then an unknowing of my will. Yes, it did happen, all of it happened. Desire confused itself, and while I once was sure that I had not, I became equally sure that I had – one often gets what one wants. I am her murderer. Believe me.

I try to stand but am pulled down; my steel jewelry prevents me from walking around. Out. I want only to be released, or if nothing else, to be taken back inside. I need to think, to pace. These thick restraints on my arms and legs cripple me, and suddenly I am sure I will spend my life in chains – that is their plan for me. Little do they know, I think differently.

Black-powder bang. Floral fireballs, flowers bloom in the sky.

Fury and frustration. Tremble. Shake. Stomach rises with bile, with the bilge of it all. There is pain.

I know who I am. I dance around it, use my words, my refraction, to obscure what is excruciatingly clear. Were I not to hide, to cloak and clothe myself, it would be unbearable for all – and I include you in this. The reptilian repulsive; even I don't like the look of me.

Where is she when I need her most? Sick, just sick, I am turning on myself.

Something spins in my gut, I don't know what. 'Guard, guard,' I call, but there is no response, save the repetitious report, the final barrage, a billion blasts, a thousand rounds. The sky is bleached pale white. The concussion ricochets off the walls.

Grand finale. I lean forward and vomit into the dirt.

On either side of me, Frazier and Kleinman pull away, tugging at my tired chains, forgetting we are joined. They are stretching me as if to split me. Vivisection. My vomit steams, yellow, red, and green.

There is a great round of applause.

The lights go on. The night disappears. 'It was your goop the other day,' Frazier says as we're getting up.

I shake my head. 'No, not then, just now.'

Going back inside, the chink-a-chink-a walk, shimmying shake, shiver of our synchronicity, becomes a raucous rattle, a rowdy rumble that makes my head ache.

On the wall someone has taped a handmade sign: 'While you were out, your unit was sprayed with an insecticide which kills roaches, fleas, ants, and flies. However, it is not harmful to human beings.'

Extermination. We have been sprayed with a killer cologne, another in their series of experiments. During the night, those of us not quite right will start to twitch and writhe. Chemical warfare. I didn't think it could happen here. Bells ring – a clever death knell.

We cough, choke, and gag.

In ever corner of every room, there's a puddle of the stuff. A squirt of it like someone pissed foul. Again, I vomit.

'Are you okay?' Clayton asks. I have no answers for such stupid questions. 'Did you eat the Cracker Jacks? You could sue for that.'

'I'm fine,' I say. 'Quite fine, better than before.'

Clayton takes me down the hall to the showers and splashes cold water on my face. I rinse out my mouth, sputter, and speak as if I've been drowned. The Declaration she sent still spins in my head:

'Such has been the patient Sufferance of these Colonies; and such is now the Necessity. . . . The History of the present King . . . a History of repeated Injuries and Usurpations, all having in direct Object the Establishment of an absolute Tyranny over . . . thee.'

Clayton throws me against the wall, my face flush to the battleship gray, the texture of the cinder block embossing my cheek.

'I want to fuck you here and now,' he says, pulling at my pants. 'Are you sick enough for that?'

I am spread against the wall as if to be frisked, my legs kicked apart, the pants down. Men walk in and out. From the corner of my eye, I see a few watching. One begins to touch himself.

I am sure this pleases Clayton, reenacts the highlights of his early career. He fucks me. Pummeled, torn from inside out, when he is done, I feel as though a rake has scraped through me. Surely I am bleeding, having a period of my own, oozing from the ass, soon to stain the seams of my shorts a deep and muddy red. It's an inside job.

I don't know whom to hate more, him for doing this to me or me for having let it go on for so long.

'We must, therefore, acquiesce . . . and hold them, as we hold the rest of Mankind, Enemies in War, in Peace, Friends.'

He fucks me and then drops to his knees, buries his head in my ass, and starts to suck my blood/his cum. Again. He's doing it again, rimming me. Last time, I swore that if he tried it once more, I'd kill him. Wasn't this the very act that, although enjoyed, I railed against? Too much, too good. I don't know why, but I get hard.

Flame. I am the flame. I am the fire, the start, the burst of light, that surprising thing.

I wheel around and with strength I didn't know I had, I bang his head against the wall, cracking it on the cinder blocks. He falls. I stun him first and then switch my role, kicking him in the gut. He is down on his hands and knees. I am behind him, stripping him. Force. I force myself against his flesh, until finally it gives way.

'Relax,' I shout into his ear.

I fuck him fiercely up the ass, fuck him like I've never fucked before, with everything I've held for years. I'll not be the pussy anymore. A man, a man again, reclaimed. I have the power. I fuck him, fuck him and a crowd does gather. This is my chance to show them who I really am, the goods I've got. I do it well, do it good, do it like I didn't know I could. I am hard and large. In and out. My loins banging against his bumper. Beneath me now, Clayton is crying. To drown him out I start to sing – it has been that kind of a day. 'What so proudly we hailed at the twilight's last gleaming . . .'

On the last verse, while I'm still riding him, I call for audience participation. 'Everybody join in, sing along,' I say.

'And the rockets' red glare, the bombs bursting in air . . .' And then I really throw myself into it. 'For the land of the free and the home of the brave.'

I let it come, copious amounts, great gallons of jizz, coursing up, out, and into him. I fill him with my most personal touch, a handy high colonic. I've never come so much. Finished, I retreat, zip up. My discharge glistens, an opalescence, like mother-of-pearl shining on his pure white ass. 'Who wants some?' I ask, putting him up for grabs, a gracious giveaway. It's over. It's all over, anyone can have him now. And sure enough, a line forms. Someone steps on the back of his neck, holding him down. I leave with Clayton on the floor, broken, blubbering, finally getting what he wanted all along. I go back to my cell, so pleased, so happy, so relaxed. I go back to my room and begin to pack. After all, I'm leaving soon.

I'm nothing you can catch now. I am black powder, I am singe, I am the bomb that bursts the night.

13

Do all little girls have to die?
  Yes.

The hiss of the aerosol can, the scent of Lemon Pledge. She is awake. Her mother is dusting her room. The Hoover stands upright, ready. 'Finally,' the mother says. 'You're awake. I've been working around you.'

'Don't we have a maid?' the girl asks.

'Once a week,' the mother says. 'But things get dirty every day, don't they?'

The vacuum is on, the white headlight glows against the carpet. 'I worry about you,' the mother says over the din.

'Aren't you more worried about breaking a nail?'

'They're fakes.' The mother taps her nails against the handle of the Hoover. 'If one breaks, I just glue on a new one.' She stops vacuuming, picks up a piece of clothing from the floor, folds it, and puts it on top of the dresser. 'Are you getting up?' she asks. 'It's a brand-new day.'

The girl was awake earlier. She heard her father get up, her mother rising with him. The routine all too familiar. The men work in the city, the city is far away. They get up early, their wives get up with them. While they shower, shave, and dress, the wives make coffee, breakfast. He comes down, she feeds him, he leaves. She eats the leftovers, showers, and begins again when it is time to wake the children.

'Up and at 'em,' the mother says.

'I'm naked,' the daughter says, as though the prospect of seeing such will drive the mother out of the room.

The mother turns away. The girl dresses. The mother talks nonstop. 'With a little effort you could be very attractive. If you want people to pay attention, you have to put out the signal. You have to let them know that you're interested. Are you interested?'

In the bathroom the daughter brushes her teeth. 'You got mail,' the mother says through the door. 'A postcard from France and another of those letters with no return address. You know, the friends you make now will be with you for the rest of your life. Arrange to see them.' The girl comes out of the bathroom. The mother corners her. 'What do you want to do with your life, that's the question. Any ideas?'

'Where's the letter?'

'Downstairs.'

I can tell you anything. No matter what, you listen. You don't pass judgment and that's a good quality.

I have no judgment – and that's a problem.

Before I open the envelope I'm already writing you back. My mother is talking. The whole time she talks, I'm writing to you,

*invisibly in my head. It's a word-for-word exchange. I do it to
drown her out. Downstairs, she has followed me downstairs.
Perhaps I haven't been entirely honest with you.*

I imagine the dining room table set for breakfast. Place mats
instead of a tablecloth. Breakfast dishes, yellow with flowers.

'Can I get you something?' her mother asks, having put on
an apron like a waitress.

'No,' the girl says.

'Eggs, toast, cereal?'

'No.'

'Coffee, tea?'

'No.'

'Eat your grapefruit, it's sectioned, it's easy.'

'No,' the girl says.

The girl goes into the kitchen, boils water, makes herself a
cup of cocoa. She puts a pair of Pop-Tarts into the toaster and
waits. When they're ready, she carries everything back upstairs.

'You know I don't like food wandering around the house,'
the mother says.

The girl closes her bedroom door.

I know who you are and I know what you did.

A pause. A silence. I'm not sure how to respond. I reread.

I know who you are and I know what you did.

Does this come as a big surprise? How could she have
written me if she hadn't picked me on purpose – I thought that
much was implied. Still, there is something about the way she
says it that frightens me.

*I know who you are and I know what you did. Doesn't my
address mean anything?*

Pardon?

Her street. I live on her street.

Oh, God.

How could you not have noticed?

I was never invited to the house.

*Scars*dale, of course, it would have to be there. I could go on but don't. If I were to continue, I'd accidentally and unintentionally reveal the degree to which I've so thoroughly confused the correspondent and the beloved. But now that she's mentioned it, stepped back to say that she is in fact not Alice, clarifying that she is only some lonely neighbor girl, it is all I can do not to ask, Does she have any news, word of Alice's family? Are they still there? The mother? The sisters? That stepfather, who knows anything about him? The one time we met, I didn't like him, didn't like him at all. However, I hold back, feeling that it would be impertinent, even rude, to interrupt at this moment when she is so intent, focused on herself.

*Scars*dale – have you lived there long?

Forever. But don't change the subject, I'm talking now, trying to tell you something. I've known about you all along. Your footsteps are deep and leave tracks like mud prints.

Hers is the false poetry of the overly undereducated, and you wonder why I haven't quoted her more all along? Leaden, forced, falsified. Pretentious though it may be, I remain convinced that my interpretation, my translation, is a more accurate reflection of her state of mind, far exceeding that which she is able to articulate independently. And while putting words in the mouths of others may be my specialty, my naughty narration is fast becoming a tired thing. I'm running out of steam. Perhaps in my advancing age, I have less to say, that or I've lost the strength it takes to wrestle with her. Whatever I suggest the reason to be, the truth is I quote her directly because it's time she spoke for herself, she is in fact insisting on it, asserting herself over me. And without her interpreter, her translator, you – the reader – are free to make of her what you will. Or perhaps I pull back because I know what comes next. However obvious, my retreat is an attempt to extricate myself, to surrender my responsibility – after all, I know how the story ends. Or perhaps all that's at play is the cracked logic of the old adage: If you give them enough rope, they'll hang themselves, literally.

My reason for writing was that I thought it might make me less afraid if I could talk to you, if I could find out who you really are, what makes you tick. What does it mean for a girl like me to write to you? Do you like it? Do you like it a lot? Am I torturing you? I have to be honest with you; plus, there's not a lot to lose. And what are you going to do anyway – come kill me?

She doesn't shut up long enough for me to respond. This is not a conversation, not a dialogue, but her hysterical purge.

Do you even have a clue? My life is completely different because of you. I doubt you realize it, but your influence is everywhere. And it's not only me, it's all the mothers and all the girls. Everyone is afraid.

I wasn't allowed to play in the front yard, 'Out back,' my mother would say. 'Play in the backyard, it's fenced, no one needs to know we have a little girl.' She said it as though my playing on the front lawn was an advertisement for things that might be taken from my parents' house, burgled.

And I couldn't walk to school alone, they were afraid we'd evaporate, disappear right off the sidewalk, that the sidewalk itself was the path that led straight to men like you. 'And never go in the woods alone,' my mother said. I never knew if that was because you'd be there, hiding in your secret headquarters, or if it was for fear of what I'd find – the forest is your burial ground. Once in New Hampshire on a beach by a lake, my father saw something in the sand. 'Look,' he said, pointing at it, 'there's something for you to play with.' The small hand of a Barbie doll was poking up. I pulled it out of the sand and that's all it was, an arm, just an arm, amputated. I screamed. My father laughed. That hand, that arm, could have belonged to someone, could have been part of a real girl, buried in the woods, chopped up and left in pieces, in Dumpsters, in assorted plastic bags, that arm could have been something you did.

Excuse me, but you said New Hampshire? A lake in New Hampshire? Maybe I am not so confused.

Keep an eye out, report anything strange. They say a man like you can be anyone, someone I know, someone I trust, a friend of the family, a relative, even the mailman. How do I know which one is you? What are your distinguishing characteristics? What makes you different from everyone else? Do you walk with a limp? Have scars? Do you leer? Will I feel you coming up behind me? Will your fingers reach around and cover my mouth? How do you pick your girls? Do you look as crazy as you are? And why do you hate me? Or more specifically, why do you hate little girls?

Hate is hardly the word.

There's more. I drive to Sing Sing. I've been going there a lot, hanging out on the hill at State Street by the fire station. From there you can hear the noise inside the prison, you can hear the men.

Jealous, I'm jealous and worried that you're shopping for a new man, a more convenient prisoner, someone with a better location.

Last time I took Matt with me and he totally freaked, he kept saying, 'I don't want to see any people, whatever you do, don't make me see the people.'

There are trailers in the back, weird little Winnebagos where I guess the guards live, and out front there's a parking place reserved for 'The Employee of the Month.' Bet you didn't know that.

Visit me. Let's make a time and date, and in the same place where the tourists press their Nikons through the wrought-iron gates, you'll put your face, pushing your nose, mouth, and tongue through the bars and into my fetid air. At the appointed hour I'll look out my window and you'll do it for me, make a mean little dance, working your hands against yourself. Do as I ask, do as you're told. Come in time for my release. Come so that when I'm let out, you'll be there, ready and waiting to catch me. We can take off in your parents' car for that lake in New Hampshire where finally we'll have our right reunion.

More still. Last week, I drove by myself to the motel in Chatham. I told my mother I was going to visit a friend from school. I slept in the very room you did it in. I asked the housekeeper which one it was and had the manager switch me. There was no hint, no sign that anything had ever happened. And yet, I could feel you, I could feel you everywhere. I live differently because of you, there is no such thing as safety.

Come. Come here. You are coming so close, come a little closer still.

I hope this doesn't turn you off or wreck our relationship – is it fair to call it that? I really like talking to you. Does that make me weird? And what does it mean that I write to you, that I ask your advice? Frankly, I think you owe me something, you owe me a lot.

Silly bug, fly on the wall, our first fight and how quickly we are over it. Of course I don't hate you, dearest, beloved, most cherished, I owe you everything.

'Sweetie,' I imagine her mother calling up the stairs. 'What are you doing? It's a beautiful day, why don't you go outside? Want me to call Matt's mother for you and arrange a tennis date? How would that be? It's not good to just lie around. You get depressed. Lighten up.'

Matt. I don't feel like dealing with Matt. I don't know what I've been doing with Matt. It was an experiment, I needed him, needed someone who didn't scare me. Is it such a terrible thing? Did I hurt him? Will he tell on me? Do I need a psychiatrist? Should I tell someone? Confess? Am I completely crazy? I'm trusting you to let me know. There really is no one else I can ask. Will I do it again? Am I the same as you?

How did you get to be the way you are?

Practice.

When I was growing up, they used to say that we should report anything that made us uncomfortable. Imagine if I went downstairs right now and told my mother. Imagine if I walked into the kitchen and said, 'Mom, I'm fucking Matt.'

What would she say? 'That's wonderful, dear, you've got a little crush. Older women, younger men, it's all the rage. I'm so relieved, your father and I were starting to think you were a lesbian.'

'He's not a man, he's twelve years old.'

'I'm just glad that you've found somebody, that's the important thing. It really doesn't matter who, as long as you're happy. Even if you were a lesbian – which thank God you're not, I really was worried – regardless, your father and I love you. We only want you to be happy – that's what matters most. Are you happy?'

'No.'

'Do you know where my racket is?' the girl calls downstairs.

'You left it in the hall, so I put it away. You know me, always cleaning up after everybody. I can't stand a mess. I'll get it for you. And I bought you a fresh can of balls. Just come downstairs, it's all waiting for you.'

Yesterday they were fucking. Naked in his parents' garage, mixing with the damp, oily smell of cars, the twisted tinge of insecticide, lawn fertilizer, hidden secrets. They were in the backseat of his mother's Volvo, doing it, and Matt's mother came down to get something from the deep freeze. Matt's

157

mother came downstairs and looked right at her. They made eye contact, but the mother's expression never changed. The girl wanted to know if she really didn't notice or if she just didn't care.

The girl wanted the mother to notice, wanted her to think something, to do something, to either fetch a bucket of cold water, douse them with it, and pry them apart like dogs in a yard, or invite them upstairs and offer them the use of her king-size bed. The girl wanted a reaction, but there was nothing, absolutely nothing. She didn't mention it to Matt, who was on top of her, oblivious, hymnal Hendrix seeping out of his headphones.

Sweat collected, forming a pool, a greasy slick dripping off their linked loins. Their bodies were slippery, sloppy, not enough friction, he slid in and out of her too easily, everything had gone loose and lazy, they'd lost their grip.

They were fucking because they were compelled to fuck, because it was free, because it was something they could do themselves, because no one had to take them there, because there was nothing else to do, because it was easy.

She picks up the racket, the fresh balls, and breezes past the mother on her way outside.

'That's the girl,' her mother says.

'Little do you know,' the daughter mumbles.

'Are you getting your period?' the mother asks. 'You must have a little PMS, you're so unpleasant.'

Stop.

She holds up a hand. 'Stop.' She puts her hand on my shoulder and tries to push me away, but my fist is still inside her and I'm doing something wrong. It takes me a minute, more than a minute. I've gone deaf. I don't hear her right away.

'Stop,' she says again loudly. The echo off the tile makes it sound like a shot. 'Stop,' she whispers in my ear. 'It's enough.'

She reaches between her legs, plucks my hand out, and lets it drop like some discarded thing.

She gives me a kiss on the cheek, one on the lips, climbs out of the tub, and lies back on the cot, hand over her eyes, breathing heavily, deeply. 'Don't ogle,' she says without even looking at me.

The sheets are peeled back and in the middle of the bed there is a bright blush of red, a thick streak of blood. My lipstick.

Hey, sorry about the outburst, the rant and rave, forget I ever mentioned it, okay? I don't know what I was thinking.

You know exactly what you were thinking.

She continues. *If I had the strength, I'd run away, pack a bag and be gone. I'd go somewhere where nothing is familiar, where everything is unrecognizable, somewhere where I don't even understand the language, where I can't overhear anything. All I want to do is sleep. Even before I'm really up, I'm ready to lie down again. Nap.*

The streets are empty, a stage set deserted, a diorama. Nothing proves this is real. All of it could be a dream. Everything is so thoroughly familiar that were we – that is, all of us; me, you-reader, and the girl – were we to go blind, we would be able to continue anyway, we'd know how to get there and back, the route is etched in our memory. Maybe we are already blind, maybe this is only a figment of the imagination. A memory.

She passes houses, recalling who used to live where; the set of identical twins, the girl whose father was a spy. All long gone; years ago, they moved away.

Human cuckoo clocks. A front door opens, an elderly woman steps out, dumps the contents of a watering can onto a pot of geraniums, and goes back inside. Farther down the block, it happens again, a minute later, as though they are all set a certain way, the synchronicity is terrifying.

The elementary school, the playground. She slips through a hole in the fence, pops open her can of balls, and starts to play.

I play tennis trying not to think, to keep my mind free from thought. When I do think, it is too awful to even mention. I think the worst things. I think there is no way out. This is permanent. I am permanently like this – does that make sense?

She slams the ball against a brick wall. She went to this school. This was her first school, her home away from home. She slams the ball against the wall.

Do you blame yourself for things that happen in the world, war, crime, starvation?

Yes.

When you were caught, was it a relief?

It is his conscience that puts a man in position to be caught and found guilty.

She hits the ball against the wall and daydreams. She asks herself, What do you want? What do you want? over and over again as though the question itself will bring an answer, revelation, deliverance. She dreams. Nothing. Nothing comes to her. She wants nothing.

The playground. She hits the ball hard, fast, right to the point. Every time the ball hits the wall, there's a sharp echo, a sound that makes it seem as if she's playing harder than she really is.

Aaron, the beaky one from before, the echo of Matt's ego, appears. His hands are jammed deep into his pockets.

'Hi,' he says.

She continues to play.

'That was really fun on the Fourth of July. You, me, Matt, Charlie, on the golf course,' he reiterates the narrative, names and dates, as though the evening's events might have escaped her memory, as though it might not have meant anything to her – he's right. 'I finger-fucked you,' he says. 'I've never done that before.'

She doesn't say anything.

'So, what are you doing?' he asks.

'Practicing,' she says.

'I could use some practice.' He laughs and overtly adjusts himself.

'I'm trying to concentrate,' she says, slamming the ball.

He watches her for a moment, getting her timing down, and when she brings her racket back to swing, he catches her by the wrist. The racket falls to the ground.

He kisses her face, her neck, like a bird pecking. She twists away.

'I've never had it sucked,' he says, pulling at her. He's stronger than you'd imagine. He hooks his leg behind her and knocks her to the ground. With his free hand, he struggles to undo his fly. She looks up at him. His face is covered with large red swellings, more like boils than pimples. His upper lip is coated with thick, dark hair. His legs are coated with the same late lanugo. She is on her knees, the pebbly blacktop has already scraped off a layer of skin.

'Suck it,' he says.

'No.'

'If you won't suck it, then at least touch it.' He swipes the head of his dick against her cheek.

'I'll bite it.'

'I'll knock your teeth out.' He pauses. 'I could have fucked you. Matt would have let me.'

'I doubt it.'

'Bitch,' he says, rubbing his dick back and forth over her face, beating her with it.

'Why don't you call him and ask?'

'Cunt.'

'Fucking asshole,' she says, trying to get up.

He tightens his grip. 'I'm bigger than you and I'm stronger than you.' He is holding both of her arms behind her back.

'I'll get you arrested.'

'I'll kill you,' he says, pulling her across the playground toward a patch of grass beneath a tree.

A station wagon comes around the corner, the window rolled down. 'Aaron,' a woman's voice calls. 'Aaron, it's not even funny. You're in such trouble, you don't even know.' He lets go of her arms. 'Get over here right now,' his mother screams. 'For thirty minutes I've been driving around looking for you. Did you forget you have an orthodontist appointment?'

He sneers at the girl, then walks across the parking lot, squeezes through a hole in the fence, and gets into his mother's car.

The girl sits on the blacktop. She doesn't want to go home. There's no reason to go home. There's nothing at home. She goes to Matt's house. She sneaks in. It's not difficult, the kitchen door is always unlocked. She opens the door, tiptoes down the hallway, goes stealthily up the steps and into his room. The shades are down. It is cool, dark. Having just come in from outside, she can't really see. A figure is in the bed, under the sheets; she reaches for the sheet, pulls it back, and starts to crawl in. The figure turns toward her and speaks. 'Help me.' It is Matt's father. Matt's father is in Matt's bed, masturbating between Matt's Batman sheets. Her eyes are adjusting. He is covered in sweat. He's purple all over, his entire being is engorged, as if he's been at it for hours. 'Help me,' he says. Her jaw drops, her mouth hangs open in a slack *O*. He reaches for her, puts his hand on the back of her neck, and pulls her to him.

'They've gone to the pool to join the swim team,' the father says.

Her mouth still hangs open. He pulls her toward him, positions her over him, her head at his crotch.

Warm, sweaty, hard but without conviction, his penis is flavored with dirt from the palm of his hand. In her mouth it becomes firm, full of promise. Her nose is in his underbrush, he smells like an old sneaker. Her concentration isn't what it should be, this isn't what she was expecting. She's been caught off guard. His fingers dig into her hair, scratching her scalp. He holds her head close to him and fucks her deeply. She gags. Her tonsils knock against the head of his cock. His thrusts are in counterpoint to her choking. She feels as if she can't breathe, as if she's suffocating, she tries to back up a bit, to get some distance. He holds on tight.

'Put your finger up my ass,' he says, tilting up so she can reach behind him. 'Up my ass.'

She fingers his asshole and then pokes a digit in.

'More,' he says. 'More fingers.'

She sticks two fingers up his ass and he starts to groan. Vaguely disgusted, she slides her fingers in and out, each time going deeper. He grips her head in both hands and slams into her throat. Her jaw aches, his pubic hair scratches her face. Thinking it will bring things to a quicker end, she shoves a third finger up his ass.

He bellows, 'I knew it was more than tennis lessons,' then ejaculates, splashing her face, her hair, with cum.

This is what my life is really like. I think you tend to romanticize me, but this is reality. P.S.: Am I supposed to feel sorry for you or think you're grotesque?

A bit of both would be about right.

Back at her house, the girl, the child, assumes the position, the only possible position, supine on the sofa.

'You were such a happy little girl,' the mother says.

'Things change.'

The black hole, the pit, the bridge over the river Adulescens.

'Nothing ever seems to be enough for you,' the mother says. 'Whatever it is, it's not enough. What do you want?'

'More. I want more. Didn't you ever want more?'

'What more is there? I have a beautiful home, filled with beautiful things. A husband, a daughter who could be beautiful if she wanted to be. What else is there? What do you think about, dear? You can tell me. Tell me anything, I promise not to be shocked, no matter how awful it is.'

'I hate you.'

The mother begins to cry. The daughter, who in the past would have felt remorse, would have forgotten herself and comforted the mother, gets up and walks away. 'Why?' the mother cries. 'Why? What have I done to create such a monster, a girl who hates her own mother?'

The daughter cannot get far enough away. 'If it makes you feel any better,' she screams, 'I hate everybody. And I hate myself even more than I hate you.' She runs upstairs and slams her bedroom door.

The father comes home from work. He sits in the living room waiting for dinner.

'Your mother is very worried about you,' he says to the girl, who has resumed her position on the sofa.

'Do I even know you?'

'What does that mean?'

'It's not like you have a habit of talking to me. I just wonder, why now?'

'I told you, your mother is worried.'

'Oh,' the girl says. 'Just checking.'

'I'm your father. I pay the bills around here. I bought the clothes on your back. Your mother, my wife, is very upset. She asked me to speak to you. She said there's no talking to you.

And you know what?' He pauses. 'She's right.'

The mother comes into the room. 'What do you want to do with your life?' the parents ask.

There is no answer.

'A lot of people your age go to Europe for the summer, don't they?' the father asks. 'It's not too late for you to go away, I'll buy the tickets.'

'Dinner is ready,' the mother says. 'Lamb chops.'

Her throat is sore. The flavor of Matt's father mingles with the blood of the lamb and drips down her throat. The string beans go down like razor blades.

As soon as dinner is done, without a beat, as though she doesn't have to stop and think about it for even a minute, as though it were decided long ago, she goes straight upstairs into the bathroom and starts emptying the pill containers. The medicine chest is well stocked. Both parents dose themselves daily, depending on their mood, on the weather, on their pain. She swallows anything and everything, popping pills by the fistful. She swallows everything and washes it down with bottles of NyQuil, Hycodan, and Robitussin.

Ill. She feels ill. Maybe it's the combination of the cough syrups, maybe it's the lamb, maybe it's Matt's father. There's a bad taste in her mouth. She rinses with Listerine and spits.

She's over the bowl. Everything is coming up, violently rising.

The mother, as if psychically summoned, opens the bathroom door, goes to the girl, and holds her forehead. Fortunately, the mother doesn't look in the bowl, doesn't examine what's coming up and out, the thick mix of red and green syrups, pills, capsules, caplets, tablets, all of it in various states of dissolve. This mix and match has made the girl not only nauseated but very tired.

When there's a pause in the puking, the girl sticks her fingers down her throat and starts it again voluntarily. All of it has to come out.

The mother seems confused. 'Hope it wasn't something I cooked.'

The girl cannot bring herself to confess. It is too embarrassing, too humiliating, too telling. She is too old for this. This is how she should have felt at fourteen, at fifteen, but now, at her age, nineteen, nearly twenty, it's ridiculous. It's worse. Like certain childhood diseases that become more dangerous the later they are contracted, this one has the potential to be fatal.

Suddenly, she doesn't want to die. She has no real reason not to, no sudden revelation, except that it's equally pointless to die as not to die. Why doesn't she die? She lives because she's meant to live, because she's already alive and it's comparatively easy to stay that way. She lives because, even though she doesn't know what it is, there must be a reason she's here in the first place. She lives because either she's not as brave as all the dead girls who've gone before her, or she's actually braver – it's hard to tell.

The daughter continues to vomit, flushing the toilet again and again, until the father comes upstairs and stands outside the bathroom door.

'Is something broken?' he asks. 'Are you breaking something in there? Plumbers get a hundred dollars an hour. You have no respect for machinery.'

'She's throwing up,' the mother says, cracking open the door. 'She must have eaten some *chozzerai* this afternoon that didn't agree with her.'

'Oh,' the father says, backing off. 'Hope it wasn't something you cooked.' He stands in the hallway for a minute, listening to the waterfall, the whoosh and roar of the best American Standard. 'Well, maybe she doesn't have to flush so much, so violently. Could you just ask her to flush less?'

*   *   *

We are quite different, she and I. She is not who I thought she was, who I presented her to be, and so it goes for all of us, for all of this. Things are never quite what they seem. Her time with Matt was not what I had hoped. It was not the discovery of a drive, the awakening of an ambition, the development of a discerning palate for nature's delicacies, the start of a brilliant career. Clearly, she is not a careerist. If she were, she would have been invigorated by this interlude, her appetite only whetted. She'd be ready, willing, rushing to begin again, to cultivate a fresh one. Instead, she wants out.

No, it's apparent that I was wrong. This was a onetime thing, a rite of passage, a kind of bridging of the gap between childhood and adult life – however developmentally delayed. And despite her depression, her despondency, she is actually galloping right along, catching up, catching on. By the time school starts again, she'll be ready to have an affair with either the melancholic professor of Russian literature or the lucky lady adviser living down the hall. I daren't conjecture which way she'll go – some things must remain a mystery. But she has been playing both ends against the middle, hoping to work something out. Is she there yet? She is en route.

Despite my best efforts, I am always the one who gets fucked. It won't ever be any different, some things don't change – I suppose I have to learn to enjoy it.

14

Prison. Morning. The tintinnabulation of the bells. I stand at the door, the gate to my cell. I hear the calling of the names. I hear the names, I know the crimes.

'Jerusalem Stole,' the sergeant calls.

'It's a mistake, call me Jerry.'

'Frazier,' the sergeant says. 'Frazier.'

'What do you want, blood?' Frazier bellows.

I stand ready. But when my name is called, I am strangely silent.

Again the sergeant calls. He presses against the bars of my cell, his keys jingle. He asks, 'Everything all right?'

'What time is it?'

'Almost time.'

Prison. Morning. Breakfast doesn't come.

*　　　*　　　*

Legi Rupa, breaker of the law.

I am calmer now, resting, readying myself for what comes next. I prepare, I pack.

You worry.

You worry because I act as if I've forgotten what happened – Clayton – as if it were nothing, no matter. You find my lack of commentary, my dulled demeanor, disconcerting as though I have too easily dismissed the day. The violence is not what counts. That's expected of us. In fact I probably wouldn't have even mentioned the scene with Clayton except that I knew you were waiting for it, wanting it, had been wanting it all along.

I aim to please.

Predetermined, predestined, fantasy cum reality. What kind of prison would it be if the men did not prey on each other? And is it really so different in here than it is out there with you? What value is there in dwelling on that sour moment when before us there is something more, something better? What's done is done. Let's put it behind us and move on.

'What do you want, blood?' Frazier screams unbidden down the hall and begins to blow his harmonica.

I am getting ready to go, done here. Finished. If I seem rushed, hurried, and harassed, it is because time is of the essence. Suddenly, after twenty-three years, another day is too much. I have received note and notice that momentarily I am to go before the committee.

When I leave, I will take with me only one thing, my archive.

In the smallest of storage spaces my treasure is buried, hidden in the hollowed-out shell of my foam pillow. Years ago I plucked out the spongy stuffing and little by little flushed it down the toilet mixed with my daily droppings. I constructed for myself a sort of safe-deposit box, a container for the bits and pieces, slivers of society. I carefully packed them in and restitched the ticking's edge. Were I ever to be found out, to have the contents confiscated, a second set, a more complete compilation – including early versions of my own letters, letters I've sent – is kept under similar circumstances in a slit in my mattress. The items stored in this second safe are of slightly less value, the feather bed at my age seeming a more precarious repository – there always being the possibility that I might lose myself in the night, might wake to find myself swimming in something other than a wet dream, a flood, an incontinent's nightmare. Piss-stained pages, paper tinged yellow shimmering with the mineral crystals, the crustation of evaporated excrete – a conservator's conundrum, not the kind of compilation collectors would kvell over. In such condition a collection would surely suffer a serious drop in value, making it less than salable at Christie's despite the interest of both serious collectors and that damned new museum – therefore it is my policy not to take liquids after 8 p.m.

I cannot give you the details of my archival activity; such specificity would leave me a target for theft and blackest mail. But let me drop you a few hints. I have your letters, all of them, the ones you wrote and should never have sent. Along with those, I possess the ruminations of a noted novelist, a man of strong opinions who for quite some time considered me his confidant, until I said something sharp about his wife and abruptly he broke off. In my file is the record of a series of exchanges between a prominent – pompous – film director and myself, the declaration of his desire to adapt my life to the silver screen. I indicated interest, specifying of course I would have to write the screenplay. Hasty letters hurried back and forth from coast to coast. I saw it as a love story, he as a horror flick. Sadly, there was a parting of the ways. *C'est la vie.* I have the detailed plans of psychiatrists who wished to take my case, not to cure me, but to pursue the publication of my musings on morality and criminality, notes on the nature of the beast, rounded out by forewords and afterwords, crude critical commentaries they would fashion themselves. I refused. *Intellectus insanus.* Fuck off, I said.

I have all that and more. I am the keeper of man's mind, the chronicler of his fate, I make maps of the things he thinks but doesn't dare admit. I carry confessions, stories of fathers who pass little girls walking to school and feel compelled to tackle one, mothers who purposely make their children cry, only to be called on to comfort them. I have the details, the pathetic outpourings of those who open their coats and flash that fang of flesh at whatever eye they can catch and then feel flush, thrilled – more fulfilled and productive at the office.

I have my files, a compendium of all persuasion and perversion. A literal library of man's fate, every derivation, deviation, and despicable desire I keep squirreled away, stitched into my headrest – it's no wonder I don't sleep nights.

Kleinman passes my door. 'No mail today.'

'Holiday?'

'Gaff. Just thought you should know. I've written a letter of complaint, but even it won't go out until Wednesday.' He walks on. 'No mail today,' he tells Frazier.

'What do you want, blood?' Frazier screams again, the phrase now stuck in his head.

Today's the day. The clock is ticking. I have been summoned to speak. I go before the committee with a chance to exonerate myself, to extricate, or at least explain the debacle that has become my life.

A statement, a simple speech, a song and dance that will set them straight, an incandescent incantation, a charming presentation, a show of sorts, the show of shows, it's the only chance I've got. My appeal must be appealing, not entirely revealing, tucking in the tendency to be argumentative, artfully augmenting my audacity with the acuity of my observation and the alarming accuracy of my action. What can I possibly say or do? Act normal.

Everything is different from what it was before – before summer, before she arrived. I am alive again, unfettered in the head. Captivity is killing me, stifling even my sentences, my speech, confining my consciousness to this crappy cell. I'm coming undone. Enough is enough. I am chomping at the bit, dying to be released, but I cannot let them know that. My anxious arousal would only exacerbate their aggravation, their elaborate argument that I am not fit for society. Dispassion is the name of the game; flat as a pancake, dull as a board.

And before I go on, while we're having this moment of privacy, there's something I need to talk to you about, something that needs settling between you and me. Direct address: I'm talking to you, Herr Reader, realizing that it's not the usual thing, knowing I'm not supposed to disassemble the invisible scrim that separates us. My apologies for suddenly aggressing. But it's time we had it out, the two of us, alone, without interference. Concentrate, pay close attention, this is the last flash of lightning lucidity, before my rigor turns to rigor mortis.

I feel the need to reassure you – don't respond, don't answer, just listen, do with it what you will, and I promise not to mention this again.

I am fully aware of what you've been doing while you've been reading this – these are my pages you're staining with your spunky splash. Your arousal, the woody in your woods, tickle in your twitty-twat, the fact that as you've read my mental monologue you fished out the familiar friend, rubbed it raw, stroked yourself, hello, pussy, sweet kitty cat – let the tiny tongue between your legs lick your fingers, giving them a sticky bath – and despite the depths to which it disturbed, you were released.

To is a preposition. *Come* is a verb. See Lenny Bruce for the rest of this routine.

To cum and then be disgusted, wholly horrified, is nothing to worry about – it happens to me all the time. That my speech makes your Suzie go silly and slick, your Walter whine, doesn't mean you will turn into something as twisted as me – we all have our fantasies. But if I've struck a deeper cord and caused your randy raper to be reborn, to twitch and tingle, I would advise that as much as possible you avoid stress. And should great upheaval visit your life – it is in those moments a man might react and unwittingly take his daughter onto his lap – I suggest that to diffuse your imprudent impulses, you discuss as much as possible with your wife, and perhaps when you sleep, leave on the light.

Just be sure when settling down to go to bed that you leave the book open to these pages and let the ghostly air of eve draw the moisture from the paper magically, taking what's damp and smutty and making it fresh, clean, and crispy for when we pick up again.

Some might believe that I blither just to shock, but what is shock if not some ancient identification, meaning that I have touched a sore spot, hit a nerve – think on it, will you – and some might believe that I blither to get a rise, and admittedly I've done that, too, but it is hardly my goal. True, I get trapped in my tirade, but would assume, would trust, that you – being who you are, where you are, out there and not in here – have sense enough not to get caught up in it. I would assume that you are bright enough not to buy the surface of my grotesque but know how to push it aside in order to see what's really there. Me. I am here. Buried beneath these unspeakable things. A boy, a man, a person quite like yourself. Even if that makes it worse, even if it makes it harder, don't forget: I am no better or worse than you. A conspiracy, a social construct supported by judge, jury, and tattletales, has put me away because I threaten them. I implore you not to be such a scaredy-cat.

You see me like this, so desperate – how do you think I feel, so permanently undressed?

Prison. Bells. Commotion in the corridor. I think they're coming for me, but instead it's an emergency house call for my neighbor. Frazier has attempted to kill himself. He has swallowed his harmonica. The doctor is with him now, working on it. It's stuck, lodged in his throat. When he inhales, he blows a note, a sharp, squawky E. Exhaling, it's flat B.

Prison, here, now, this is the moment I've been waiting for. After things have moved so slowly for so long, they happen quick, quickly now. Beside myself with joy, I bounce up and down on my bed, accidentally knocking my head against the wall. Momentarily I will be released. How will it go? What will be the protocol?

Am I to be taken to the door and unceremoniously turned out? Or perhaps they'll want me to stick around and sign some autographs? My stomach gurgles and growls. Asparagus. The first thing I'll eat will be asparagus. I haven't had any in years.

Henry, my private pharmacist, has left me a few tablets, something he made himself, hand-pressed. I take two, hoping they'll head off a soon-to-be headache.

I begin to prepare, ripping open my pillow, pulling out the archive. Same with the mattress, I take it entirely apart. The room is strewn with material debris, the aged tick, ticking of my bedding, cotton pad turned to cotton balls. Suddenly, my cell, my cage, is every bit the chicken coop, feathers flying.

My archive, my autobiography, is in hand.

It comes as no surprise that I haven't got a carrying case, no nice leather luggage for my loot. I empty my shelves, my wanna-be drawers, wrapping everything in a sheet. On top of it all I carefully place the last of her six Schmitt boxes – the butterflies I have so carefully saved to preserve a piece of history, no small memory.

I ponder my parts, asking myself, How should I go? What should they see?

My costume, classic criminal couturier. For my exit, I will wear the very outfit I entered in: the white shirt and mouse gray suit that has been lying in wait all of these years, permanently pressed under the weight of my library books, awaiting my triumphant return to society. Dry with disuse, the shirt cracks as I unfold it, comes apart at the seams – it's not what you wear, but the way you wear it, I tell myself. All too easily, I can justify anything. Though it is early, the temperature is up. A layer of sweat coats my skin, making me a little greasy. When was the last time I bathed? The pants, winter wool, are too tight – the jacket, I remember, was traded away years ago for an extra blanket. A thin roll of flesh seeps over the waistband, I try to suck it in, it doesn't respond.

Underwear or not? I try it both ways. With, it bunches up, looking like a diaper. Without, everything is obvious, perfectly clear. I go without. The anxiety of anticipation.

Before I zip, I piss a bit – a single squirt – into my hands and run my fingers through my hair, slicking back what few threads I've still got. The high mineral content of first morning urine gives this homemade hairspray extra hold. Inhaling the sweet stink of my own perfume, I comb everything into place, including the pubes.

My shoes are impossibly tight and with broken, knotted laces.

Checking myself in the mirror, I am dapper if dilapidated, the effects of time are evident.

There's something else; another thing I've not said – for days I've had an erection, or part of an erection. I've been pulling at myself, whacking and waxing it with spittle, with

Chap Stick, with anything I can find. I've not been able to get it to go off or just go away. Permanently demanding and yet will only get a little stiff. And now it hurts, actually aches, is rubbed raw as though I've taken it back and forth over a cheese grater. Regardless of the level of my injury, I cannot let it alone. I take to leaving it out. The last three buttons of my fly are undone. I fish it out, balls and all, and let it sit, plumped and promising in the air.

I want only that it should rise again and shoot off once more. I cannot leave myself like this; tail between my legs, hangdog, limp dick. My mind goes everywhere trying to find something that would appeal. Butter. I squeeze the pats of the oleo they brought me with my supper and stroke myself, creaming my corn, making the mighty man into a lightly salted sweet thing. I butter up and still it hangs only at half, a greased and shiny rod, looking as if it's already been dipped, pulled fresh from the hole, and is now settling down, going back to sleep. Again, I try and imagine the graciousness of a girl, her spacious slit, the womanly wound that can swallow me whole. How odd it must be to have at your center a great gap, a poisonous pit.

Nothing works. It lies limp. No longer fascinated.

Henry arrives on his morning rounds. 'I have your shot,' he whispers through the slot in the door. The metal door frame acts like a microphone and amplifies his voice. 'It's cooked and ready to go. Open up.'

The door is locked. I am in prison, in jail, and my door is locked! Panic upon panic. Ordinarily we are unlocked from 8 a.m. until 9 p.m.; unlocked and encouraged to circulate.

'Open the door,' Henry says.

I have fast developed a voracious appetite for Henry's potions, although I've no idea what exactly the elements of his elixirs are. Regardless, the poison is perfect. Not surprisingly now, I need that shot more than anything.

'Open the door,' Henry says.

My heart beats fast. It is frightening to feel you can't get out. 'It's locked,' I say breathlessly. All morning. I didn't know it until now – how could I have been such a fool? It never occurred to me. 'It's locked,' I scream, suddenly scared out of my wits. What are they planning for me?

'Calm down,' Henry says. 'We can work with it. I'm a professional, don't forget. I know whereof I speak. I know what to do. Put your mouth on the hole,' Henry says, referring to the slot in the door. 'I'll shoot you through the hole.'

Carefully casting my corporeal container into the curves of a contortionist, I fit my mouth into the slot in the door.

Henry's needle pokes my cheek. 'You'll have to guide it in. I can't see anything.'

I feel the needle in my mouth; a drop of poison drips onto my tongue.

'Ready?' he asks.

I curl my lickety licker around the needle, rolling it around until the prickly pointer is aimed down, under my tongue. A guttural *aha* indicates that the position is perfect, and Henry plunges the needle in. Flesh pierced, drug in, needle out. My head swims. The flavor of blood swirls in my mouth. I fall to the floor, slipping into something like sleep, like a dream. I travel back in time, living my life in reverse until I'm back at the beginning. The rest of my journey is a travelogue.

What makes a man become a man become a murderer? This is the story you've been waiting for. What makes a man become a man become a murderer? A girl. Ruby Diamond Pearl. Call her Jewel; ruby of my heart, Alice.

I have rented a small cabin in New Hampshire, the farthest part of a fallen family compound as advertised in the pages of the *New York Times*, May 7, 1971: 'Contemplation? Quaint summer retreat, secluded, perfect for single person, near lake, no smoking, no small children.'

(The now yellowed clipping, the one-half inch of typesetting that changed my life – remember that her family paid to have it placed – I keep mounted for conservation considerations on a three-by-five, acid-free index card. Its presence is a cornerstone of my archive.)

I have come away, leaving life behind in an effort to escape the power of my predilections.

In Philadelphia I frightened myself.

Fitting feet in a children's shoe parlor, having for the tenth time sold myself short, accepting a position thoroughly beneath and below me only to be closer to the objects of my obsession. I made my on-the-job entertainment my methodology for testing to see whether or not the shoe fit. Pulling close to the kinder who sat safely next to their maters, or the mater's maid – the baby-sitter – I spread my legs and drew the foot toward my crotch. Tenderly cupping the heel, I slipped off the walking shoe and pressed the besocked pedalis against the bulge of my balls, then asked, 'Can you wiggle your toes?'

And while Mummy watched, the little puellae gracefully gave me a sweet minimassage. No one ever said anything, stopped me, or even indicated they thought it anything out of the ordinary. 'Go tell Aunt Rhody.'

'Good. Good. Now the other one.'

Massage completed – the immediate need satiated – I set the footie on the floor, picked up the old shoe, and directed my attention to the mother, the old gray goose.

'Were you thinking of something special? Anything particular come to mind? Do you see something on the wall?'

And so the shoes were sold, the deal was done, again and again, day in, day out. But on that particular afternoon my frustration had peaked, and looking for something new, some fresher and more furious relief, I insisted on walking home a girl whose mother had sent her for Mary Janes. Using the odd excuse that the delicacy of her feet, their fine contours, shape, and delectability, made it absolutely essential for me to test the fit of all the shoes in her closet, I led her home, hinting that if the rest of her footwear was as ill fitting as those she'd walked in with, she'd quickly become deformed, defective, would suffer strange bony protrusions and other assorted crippling, crusty deformities. Within months she'd be walking like an old woman, if walking at all.

All too easily she took me to her parents' house, a hideous modern monstrosity. I should add a brief description of the girl; she was absolutely nothing out of the ordinary. In fact, my selecting her was part of the scare I gave myself. My standards were slipping. She could quite honestly be described as bovine-to-be, a cow in the future if not immediately. My only excuse my boredom, my deepening depression.

I imposed, inviting myself to her home, having become so practiced, so recently slick, that I believed I could get a girl to do anything. One quickly learns to detect the perfect princesses who will, all too willingly, say yes. In this case the illustration of interest, mounting desire, however unconscious, was extreme – played out in the pink puff of her lip. When she spoke, this thick lip rolled back exposing an enormous amount of gum, the lips themselves slightly swollen – and all ye men will understand this – quite clearly giving the impression of the lock they could form on one's privatest parts. In other words, her mouth screamed blow job, forgive my crudity.

She led me to her room. Her chamber was painted Pepto-Bismol pink and featured matching plush carpeting, heavy wooden white lacquer furniture decorated with golden trim, and a canopied virgin bed – a twin – all of it implying I had entered the lair where an angel would sleep. I sat on a red-tufted chair that fit snugly under her vanity and tried not to spy myself in her mirror. She threw open the double doors of her closet. Laid out neatly on the floor were at least a dozen pairs of shoes. I smiled, pleased with the cache – this would take hours. To slow my excitement, to distract myself, I glanced around the room. Fixed on the wall were the theatrical masks of comedy and tragedy. On the nightstand, a pink diary lay open. I had no desire to read it, I knew it would only inflame, enrage my current condition.

'And what do you wear with those?' I asked, pointing to a pair of patent pumps.

A black velvet dress was extracted from the closet and waved back and forth in front of me.

'Show me,' I said.

She stepped into the closet, which was not really constructed as a fitting room, but she walked into it anyway, displaying a modicum of modesty. If she were truly genteel, she might have excused herself or me and made her changes in the bathroom down the hall. However, she stepped into the closet and pulled the louvered doors closed behind her. There was the sound of a bitty battle raging, crash and clang, hangers falling, thump, thump, elbows banging, so on, so forth, all of it fast and furious. Clearly she was rushing, working fast, hoping I wouldn't lose interest.

Finally, she flung the door open and stood before me transformed.

I played dumb. Bending to my knees, I crawled toward her, felt her feet, squeezed her toes, all the while resting my left hand on the cool, smooth, silken skin of her bare white thigh. Sigh.

'What else have you got?' I asked, my eyes slowly rolling up from the floor, first sweeping under her dress, catching sight of the tender plump of her inner thighs, then traveling higher still, over the latent breast, ultimately catching her eye, smiling. 'Let's try something else,' I said.

And as she dipped back into her costume closet, closing the door behind her, I unzipped my own trapdoor, took wild Willy out, and let him get a feel for the room. Stroking myself, still sniffing the sweet stink of her, I wax and wonder and Willy grows strong and hard. As I hear her making final adjustments, banging against the doors, I tuck the mighty member away.

She has put on her pink tutu, her little leotard, her entrance is a dance she does for me. And while I am supposed to be admiring her technique, her ability to be en pointe on the Pepto-pink carpet, as she makes her jetés across the room, I am watching the breast buds bloom seemingly before my very eyes. The same goes for her crotch; through the cling of her tights I swear I can see the labia lips thickening, dousing the nasty nylon with something sweeter than sweat.

I massage myself through my trousers, pausing to applaud the great performance. 'Encore, encore,' I shout, adding to my cry the question, 'What time does your mother get home?'

'Not until eight-thirty or nine.'

'And your father?'

'Tuesday.'

'What other roles can you perform?' I ask, standing to stretch, to flip through the remaining outfits, to consider what I'd like to see her in. 'Have you got any uniforms?' The truth is, as I glide over the rack, parting the hangers, sending some off to the right, some to the left, with my free hand I'm re-arranging matters in my pants.

I rummage through and find a blue satin dress.

'From my sister's wedding,' she says.

'Matching shoes?'

Nodding, she retrieves a pair of silk pumps hidden beneath her bed – what other goodies might be buried there? She hurries into her cramped cabana, sensing my mounting impatience. In truth I am already hopelessly bored, my air of annoyance is just an affectation, a demonstration of my affliction. I look out the window. It is coming close to seven; my stomach growls. No mention has been made of dinner. And while I'm sure I could all too easily have her whip up something for me, it's better not to bother. I want to do this and then depart to dine alone, feasting on the memory, on further fantasy, on what I imagine might have happened, if only, if only.

My ruminations, my dubious daydreams, have left me not paying attention, and while I was out to lunch, she must have popped out of the closet, and unfortunately, this time the bovine beast forgot to duck and has knocked her head against the low interior wall with an unbelievably loud *ka-thunk*, like the metal-on-metal cacophony of a car crash. She has again captured my attention. I snap to and find her falling backward, her legs collapsing beneath her, head landing with a thud on the pink carpet. Out cold. I rush to her side, am instantly upon her. The blue satin dress is hiked up a bit; I raise it farther still, pulling down the panties, exposing the gemstone, which is clearly glowing, beckoning me.

She makes no move, no sound but a soft moan, the result of the blow or my touch?

Alone with such a thing, free to do with it as I please, no watching, no waiting. First, I open it and have a long, slow look, working my eyes more closely, less romantically than I would otherwise be able to do; this is the clinical view. I examine it, amazed, ever in awe, then poke at it with my tongue, paving the way.

It is all about me, my desire.

I fuck her every which way, pulling out just in time to leave my squirt, my hot sealing wax splashed over her lips, gracing her face. When she wakes, she will think it is heavy drool; she has slobbered or seized in her artificial sleep.

A warm rag doll. A living, loving thing, laid back in complete compliance.

I dance around the room, paint my face with her lipstick, and leave strange kisses on her cheeks, which I then rub in, giving her a false blush. I fuck her again, can't help myself. It is the first time I've stolen sex, taken something without asking.

There is no desire other than my own. I think only of myself and it is incredibly liberating.

Truly done, going home, I pull up her underwear, taking the time to tuck her hand down under the band, to spread things so her finger is between those lucky lips – if someone finds her first, she herself will be the prime suspect.

'What were you thinking, dear?' her mother will ask.

Feigned innocence. She'll shake her head, it will throb from the concussion. She has no idea.

I leave her, soundlessly sneaking down the carpeted steps, darting out of the house, disappearing into the twilight of a spring night. Fireflies blink at me, flashing yellow like caution lights. I pay heed and upon returning to my home, telephone my employer and offer condolences on the occasion of my early and unexpected retirement. I must leave town immediately.

'Sorry to see you go. You were a hit with the customers, never saw a salesman bend balloons the way you did,' he said, referring to my apparently unique ability to twist inflated wands of rubber into sculptural objects to be given to the boys and girls as rewards for good behavior. 'Are you sure there's no circus in your blood? The only people I ever saw who could make rubber curl like that were circus folk.'

'No circus,' I said. 'Just practice, much practice. Well, I should be going. Thanks. Thanks again,' I said, hanging up – he could go on for hours.

In my shame, my fear, my deep consternation as regards my apparent loss of control, I respond to the advertisement in the previous Sunday's *Times*.

I've been to New Hampshire once before with my mother and father when I was three or four. I have no memory of it. I have nothing except a small black-and-white photograph; the three of us in a rowboat. My mother, porcelain and milky glass, fragile, not yet cracked. My father, even seated, towers over everything, as if the picture were a bit of trickery, playing perspective games, making the man look bigger than the boat, larger than the lake he's floating on. He wears a white shirt. He holds me up, high above his head. I am hanging, hovering, flying. In a striped T-shirt, I am a human bumblebee.

I have come to New Hampshire to repair myself – if such a thing is possible – to piece together the puzzle that is me.

In Philadelphia the girl has come to or worse yet has been found on the floor still disarranged, the box containing her Mary Janes spilled beside her. Someone has called the police. My clever craftiness has caught up with me.

Prison. *Captivus interruptus.* An enormous clattering, rolling wheels. They have fetched a stretcher and are taking Frazier away. He wheezes his way off-key through an entirely new version of 'Mary Had a Little Lamb.'

The sergeant stops at my door.

'Busy day,' I say.

'Either it happens all at once or not at all.'

'What time is it?'

'Haven't got time,' he says. 'Are you dressed? Pull yourself together, it's not a pajama party. They're coming for you, they're on their way.'

'Okay, okay,' I say, resenting that he won't take a moment to tell me the time, resenting his intrusion into my daydream.

In New Hampshire, I start a diary, a kind of daybook,

charting my moods, the measure of my madness. On page one I print the plan, the rudiments of my regime. Everything I do will be mandated, part of a prescription: eat, drink, exercise, smoke, etcetera, etcetera. A personal treatment plan. Five times a day I will be required to touch myself, whether I want to or not. Desire no longer has a destiny, the idea being that if I approach it before it arrives, force arousal using only the stuff of my imagination, I will eventually exhaust myself, causing my condition to come under control. The plan is this. Mornings at seven-thirty, reveille. I touch till eight, then the room is tidied. Breakfast is taken, followed by a brisk walk through the woods and twenty minutes of calisthenics. I boil water for tea, read for an hour, and break for a cigarette. At eleven I release myself again, this time dipping into the farthest reaches of my imagination. It takes the full hour. Noon is lunch. One o'clock, swim. Then nap and bath, the order of which is reversible. At three-thirty, the hour when, in the right season, school is typically let out, I am permitted to make an escape, to drive into town and run what errands I must. At six, cocktails are served, and I allow the liberating effects of the libations to lift my libido again, furiously frigging, while the dinner meat marinates. Dinner is served at seven, and at eight, dishes done, I listen to the radio or read until ten, when I prepare for bed, waxing myself once again before dropping off to dream.

For four days I have been the world's best boy.

It is morning, I am reading, my virtue is high; however, the mind wanders, I daydream. Before my eyes is Philadelphia, her dress pulled up. I see a splash of hair that I didn't remember until now. It comes off as quite charming, really rather endearing, a furry dot that marks the spot. My thoughts disconcert me. I don't like hair. I know I don't like hair.

Read.

I will myself back to the words.

Something dashes by.

Bam! Bam! Bam! I wonder how long that's been going on. A heavy knock, a pounding at the door. And I notice that I've buttoned my shirt wrong. I hurry to do it again. Uncoordinated – it's been a long time since I worked anything into such small holes.

'Assume the position,' a muffled voice commands me. 'Hands behind your back, legs spread, back to the door. Freeze.'

Prison.

A flash like the explosion of a photo cube, the blue dot left in front of the eye. I see a girl. A girl. I blink. Again. The girl is still there. I am being tempted, teased.

Concentrate. The silence of the first few days, the extremity of being alone, is excruciating. All I hear is myself, louder and louder, faster and faster, until I surrender, until I can bear to hear nothing at all. Silence.

A rare memory: my father's undershirt, white ribbed, sleeveless, rests on the chair. I put it on, it hangs to the floor. My mother laughs. 'Your dress,' she says, and we dance around the room. 'Your ball gown is sweeping the floor.'

I cannot escape myself.

The lake. I swim in the lake. It is the one place I go where I cannot think, nothing enters my head except the sensation, the pain of the cold water. Forcing myself to swim, I go round and round in circles, praying I do not have a cramp or a heart attack. Although the water is not deep, one could easily drown. I swim naked, buck naked: my nakedness is proof I have nothing to hide.

I wish to thoroughly reveal myself.

A fever. My thoughts are filled with the odd imaginings of a heated head.

My mother's face changes with her mood, dissolving while she sleeps. She is beautiful in her dreams. Awake, a streak of bright red lipstick splits her mouth, splashes her teeth. She kisses me and I go outside stained, the impression of her mouth everywhere.

There are noises in the woods. Something is out there watching me. They are watching me and I am writing it down. Hidden in my words are confessions. They are closing in. I feel the cold eye of a magnifying glass, a scope. I am writing down the very words I should destroy.

Ollie Ollie Oxen Free.

Dinner. Fish. A bit of flounder. String beans almondine, baked potato.

A pinch of marjoram.

Again the heavy knock, pounding at the door. 'Follow the instructions. Assume the position,' a muffled voice commands me. Where is the sergeant, my friend? I struggle to stand, to do what they ask.

I think I see something. I will catch them at their game, get them watching me. On the windowpane is the wet press, the mark from where a nose was all too recently laid.

I'm not sure if I'm seeing this or dreaming it; she stares at me. There is war paint on her face.

Hearing something, I call, 'Hello, hello, is anybody out there?'

There is no answer.

The fever becomes a summer cold, my head aches, I am sneezing constantly. I take aspirin and Scotch and continue with the routine.

They are up there in the hills, a camouflaged commando with a bullhorn and a bullet. I wait for the sound, the amplified bellow of a human bark. 'We know you're in there. Come out with your hands up. The building is surrounded. There is no way out. I repeat, there is no way out. You have until the count of ten.'

One, two, three, what will I do? Will I give up graciously, be led away screaming, or do I attempt an escape?

What excuse could I give, what feeble apology might I offer? I am what I am.

The day comes and goes.

I keep to my routine. The imagery of my eleven o'clock session is thoroughly depleting.

Promptly at one, I take my towel to the lake, stripping near the water, neatly draping my clothing over the low branch of a tree. I force myself in. It is cold, it is bitter cold, painfully cold, so cold that all one can think of is the cold. I swim in circles until I am numb, until there is nothing left. It is torture. Sheer hell. I love it. Breathless, I walk out of the water, my body shriveled, pulled tight against the bones.

Naked by the lake is how she found me. She is there on the beach, standing between me and my clothing. I turn away, overcome with false modesty. She watches. She wears war paint and carries a quiver filled with white arrows ending in blue suction cups and a bow to match. She giggles and makes a gesture that points to my shriveled self down below.

She finds me amusing.

Her amusement I find humiliating, arousing.

I instantly want to do something – to silence that stupid giggling.

She collapses, beside herself with glee.

I say something sharp like, 'Quiet, you little fool.' Followed by this interdiction: 'Have you no manners? When you come upon someone in their nakedness, you should pretend you have seen no such thing. You act as if you have come upon someone dressed in white tails. And if you are compelled to comment, you address the person by saying something along the lines of, "My, you're looking well today."'

'You're my captive, my prisoner,' she says, still half-laughing.

If only she knew how true it was.

She points to a hearty oak tree. 'I must tie you up. Will you go easily?'

What choice do I have, she has won my heart instantly. I pretend to play along.

'You mustn't come so close. Perhaps on my person I have a hidden gun, you might get shot, wounded by my release.'

'And where would you hide such a weapon?'

'You never know.'

'Then that's the price I pay,' she says, yanking my arms behind my back, exposing me. She produces a coil of rope – the tickling touch of her small, clammy hands causes blood to rush from my head. My knees buckle beneath me.

'Your totem pole rises,' she says, referring to the state of my nakedness. I am thawing from the freeze.

So it does.

She jerks my arms tighter behind my back, showing herself to be surprisingly strong and quite adept, if not practiced, at the art of knot tying. 'You're a trespasser on my land,' she says. 'This is my great-grandfather's forest.'

'But I've taken a summer's rental.' She is bent at my feet, binding my ankles to the tree. 'One of your relatives has taken five hundred dollars from me so that I might enjoy myself until Labor Day.'

'I've heard nothing about it,' she says, wrapping the length of rope around my ankles.

'Is this the way you win your friends?'

'Yes.'

'Well, then, I take it you're a popular girl?'

She looks at me. 'Have you any goods you might buy your freedom with?'

I shake my head.

'Ruby, darling, gemstone, littlest one, where are you?' A woman's voice echoes through the woods.

'I'm hiding,' she calls back.

'Where are you?'

'I'm hiding.'

'I'm driving into town to buy you a little something, do you want to pick it out yourself? Where are you?'

'Coming,' she screams, and quickly rounds up quiver, her bow, her remaining supplies, and takes off up the hill, leaving me tied to the tree. 'See you later,' she calls to me.

The ease with which she abandons me is thrilling, as is the seriousness of her game. I am naked in the New Hampshire woods thoroughly tied to a tree. She is not joking. My shoulders are stretched in their sockets, my wrists aching. The rough bark rubs my buttocks raw as I wiggle trying to free myself. I have been bound and tied by a wicked wood nymph. I writhe. My tumescence rises farther still, stimulated by my situation. A breeze stirs the trees, sweeping over, tickling, like tonguing me right there. I sneeze first, then cum, shooting off aimlessly into the afternoon.

Ruined. Stained. This unplanned eruption has wrecked my routine.

Heavy knock, pounding at the door. 'Can you hear me,' the sergeant shouts. He is back, he must have gone off to run an errand.

'Yes,' I say. 'Of course I can hear you. I'm not deaf, you know. No need to yell.'

'Assume the position,' a second muffled voice commands me.

'It's time,' the sergeant says. 'Are you ready?'

I am. I am so excited I can hardly contain myself. With my legs spread, my back to the door, arms extended up over my head, I stand ready.

The door opens. The room fills with guards. They grab me roughly. I smile. I try to turn my head to see who's there. My jailers are not in their usual attire but in riot gear, flak jackets, helmets with the visors pulled down. They, too, realize it's a special occasion. I can't tell who is who.

'Is that you, Jenkins, Smith, Williams?' I ask.

They don't answer.

They kick the debris of my packing process out of the way. Accidentally, and I forgot to mention this before, my haste, my hurry, caused the television set to fall to the floor. Parts of it are now scattered around the room.

I am cuffed, shackled, belly-chained.

I try to play along. When I speak, my words come out with a spray. 'Spectacular sunrise,' I say, speech suddenly sloppy, sloshy with superfluous saliva, my s's surprisingly sibilant.

'Did he spit? I just saw him spit. He spit at us,' one of the guards says.

'Don't worry, we're covered,' another adds.

I nod in the direction of my bed, my belongings neatly piled, wrapped in white linen. 'My luggage,' I say – l's lazy, elongated with loads of lugubrious loogies. 'Shall I take my luggage with me now or do I get it later?'

They are pulling me out of the room. I try to joke, to break the ice. 'Why couldn't the milkmaid milk the cow? She had no regard for the feelings of udders.'

I am taken through corridors I've not seen before, though it's difficult to know for sure. Rat maze, a monkey house for men. The noise, the constant tremulous roar, the echoes of the caged, is deafening.

The committee room. Rumor, rampant, rife, rarely accurate, paints a portrait of it as a limbo land of three doors, the one through which the prisoner is led, one through which the committee walks, and a third that supposedly opens onto a long road, a broad and uncrowded street. The reputation of the room presents a place where persecution persists, performance is primary, and punctuality is preferred. And I have heard that the prisoner is kept chained like some wildebeest supposedly for the protection of the furniture, which on occasion has taken flight, split the air, and splintered, cracking committee heads and ruining the antiquities – desks and chairs made of that rare upstate governmental wood known as Oh, Albany.

We're buzzed in. All in all, it's not what you'd expect; no spotlights, no proscenium, no bleachers or orchestra pit, none of the stuff of an extravaganza. I am unimpressed.

There is a table covered in white cloth, four chairs, a small stenographer's desk, and a single seat set apart.

I take the single seat and scope out the room. I am looking for the three doors. There is the one behind me, the one through which I passed. On that same wall is a second one, and the third on the opposite side of the room is clearly marked, labeled with a red and white sign that says Exit.

Door number three. I'm banking on it. Let's make a deal.

The three committee members enter through the second door. One is a youngish man who looks vaguely familiar – is this what they mean by a jury of one's peers? And there are two women, one black and middle-aged and the other an old white woman with white hair – I find her the most frightening.

I stand.

Guards tackle me from behind, slamming me down. 'Oh,' I say, expressing my surprise as they pin me to the floor, forcibly causing my breath to escape. Their boots are pressed into my neck, my back – leaving prints, I'm sure, on the back of my clean white shirt – and I'd tried so hard to put myself together, to make a pleasant appearance. Their disregard for my outfit is most distressing. Chains are produced and wrapped round and round me in a display of metallurgical madness. I'm then lifted back into the chair and my links are locked to the floor. A leather strap not unlike a seat belt is fastened around my gut, holding me in proper posture. I am incredibly secure. I don't resist.

The members take their seats and arrange the high stacks of paper that are before them on the table.

A secretary appears with a pot of coffee and a tray of Danish. Coffee is poured and each of the panelists picks a Danish. A pitcher of cream is passed around.

'There seems to be a problem,' the woman with white hair says, licking her fingers.

'Yes,' the man says, looking, I assume, for the sugar. He glares at me.

I nod.

'Is there any Sweet'n Low, saccharin, or Equal?' the black woman asks.

The secretary shakes her head, sits down, and stenos everything they've said so far with the world's fastest fingers.

'Let's start with the simple things,' the black woman says, turning her attention to me. 'Do you know why you're here?'

I nod.

'You've been held in this facility for twenty-three years?'

'Yes.'

'And how has that been?'

'Fine. Good. Well.'

'How do you spend your days?'

I pause a moment to think.

She continues, on my behalf, 'You read. You've checked out four thousand one hundred sixty books from our library since you arrived, implying, given our inventory, that on several occasions you've read the same thing twice?' She raises her eyebrows; they appear to turn into fully formed question marks.

Terrified, I nod.

'You write,' she says. 'You've mailed fourteen thousand five hundred sixty-four letters; if nothing else, you're prolific.' I think of the unmailed letter tucked into my luggage, fourteen thousand five hundred sixty-five letters. 'And,' she continues, 'you exercise. You've been in the outside yard two thousand eighty-two times.' She pauses. 'And yet we don't seem to be able to keep you entertained.' Again she stops. 'I'm referring to the incident on the Fourth of July.'

She is wearing a red blouse, a red silk blouse, with red flowers – it's the first time in years that I've seen such bright color. I can't keep my eyes off it. Red flowers. Sunlight. My grandmother's geraniums. Mama is home, she comes into the yard.

'We have taken possession of you,' the old woman says, scaring me. 'As though you were our own, we have kept and cared for you. How do you think we feel to have failed so miserably?'

'You make us look bad,' the man says. 'It's embarrassing.' He pauses. 'We must put our feet down.'

Boom! A stack of files, a pile of notebooks, falls to the floor. The sound is heart stopping.

'Is this some mock execution?' I blurt. 'Am I supposed to find this arousing?' I rattle my chains, loud as I can. 'A perverse and pornographic plethysmograph? Are you measuring me? Do I measure up? Are you jerking me off with your chain-link routine? I can tell you I'm not amused. I am limp as a lady.'

Fear has eaten my sanity.

'Let's just get on with it, shall we,' the man says, his voice shaking.

There are big windows in the room. Lots of light. Bright. White. A shade flaps in a breeze, knocking against the window frame.

'Columbia County case No. 71-124,' the secretary reads aloud.

'August 1971. Defendant aged thirty-one, white male, single. No record of previous arrests. Personal file. Born Richmond, Virginia, on March eleventh, 1940. Father, employee Commonwealth Bank, suffered giantness, deceased as of 1945. Mother, mentally disordered, manic-depressive type, alcoholic, frequently hospitalized, committed vehicular suicide July 1949. Defendant raised by maternal grandmother, deceased, natural causes, September 1970.

'Defendant graduated University of Virginia, Charlottesville, May 1961. Pursued menial jobs, moving frequently. Relocated Philadelphia, PA, 1969, last employment prior to arrest, Phil's Foot Parlor, a children's shoe store, employed eighteen months – no difficulties.'

As they begin to tell the tale, I realize it is my story they're telling. They're telling my story and they're getting it wrong. That or twisting it on purpose, forcing me to correct them, to add to their file, filling in the bits and pieces they didn't have before. Like a fairy tale, a myth, or the game of telephone, each time it's repeated, it changes. The exception being that I know what really happened, I was there, witness and participant. This is the story of my life.

'It belongs to me,' I shout. 'Me. Mine. It's not yours to tell. You've got it all wrong.'

A guard comes forward, hissing in my ear, 'Didn't you see *Bambi*? Don't you remember when Thumper says: "If you don't have anything nice to say, then don't say anything at all"? It's not necessary to comment.'

A pain cuts through my chest and into my arm.

'Defendant departed Philadelphia in white Rambler station wagon, Pennsylvania plate MJB 464, proceeding to the state of New Hampshire, where through an advertisement in the *New*

York Times he arranged to rent a cabin from the Somerfield family. Defendant took possession of the cabin on May twenty-first, 1971. A short time later defendant meets Alice Somerfield, the twelve-and-a-half-year-old granddaughter of his landlord, at a nearby lake.'

Yes. Yes, I met her at the lake. I told you this before. She appeared out of nowhere on the pebbly beach by the lake in madras shorts, cinched at the waist with a length of rope, an old hunting knife hanging off her hip, white Keds, no socks, red nail polish – half picked off – blond hair, blue eyes, like Pippi Longstocking gone awry. She tied me to a tree and then disappeared. There and gone, like a figment of my imagination.

Later, I hear a noise in the woods and am drawn to the window hoping to see her. Every day, I swim in the lake with my eyes on the shore, watching. Once, I see her high on a hill, chasing after something with her butterfly net.

June 18, I return from the lake and find at my door a dead butterfly affixed to a piece of yellow construction paper. Its name, 'Hoary Elfin,' is printed neatly below. Around the border, scrawled in the waxy calligraphy of Crayola, is an invitation: *Tea tomorrow, 4 p.m.* The invite is accompanied by a small separate map consisting of a squiggly line – I take to be illustrative of a path through the woods – and two X marks, one labeled 'you are here' and the other 'I am here.'

Everything is crystal clear. The same size and shape as some missing part of me. She is the piece that completes the puzzle.

She lives alone in a small cabin that was once her grandmother's playhouse – hardly bigger than a bread box – but with cold running water and an old camping stove. Her tea set is chipped crockery, china from England. 'Gram's,' she says. 'But I'm glad she can't make it out anymore. The chips would bother her.'

Her costume for the event is an antique lace and linen blouse

– clearly a cherished thing – now several sizes too small, pulling across the chest, binding under the arms, neatly tucked into a blue and green plaid skirt like the uniform from Our Lady of Pompei.

'A girl's got to live, doesn't she?' she asks, banging the dishes around, setting her table. 'What's the use of having something if you can't break it.'

My sentiments exactly.

When I am overstimulated, all of life becomes more extreme, my senses heighten, colors saturate, turning into the high hysterical hues of shock, horror, and ecstasy.

Nothing could be more perfect. She has a certain *je ne sais quoi*, call it a kind of charm. A lucky charm. Magically delicious.

We settle down to tea: I sit perched precariously on a three-legged stool and behave politely. She serves cookies she's been saving since last Christmas.

'Haven't opened the tin since December twenty-sixth. I was hoarding them for an occasion.'

'Surprisingly crisp,' I say, biting the head off a snowman.

She crosses one leg over the other and I can't help but notice, not the skinned knee, not the bruised shin, but the writing on the bottom of her shoe, neat print.

'Tell me about your sneakers,' I say, children's feet of course being my area of expertise.

'On the right is Emily Dickinson, 712, and on the left, the one you're looking at, is Sylvia Plath, "Lady Lazarus." "Out of the ash I rise with my red hair and I eat men like air."'

Disturbingly disarming. I nod appreciatively.

She smiles. 'It drives Mother crazy, especially when I put Ferlinghetti on my patent leathers. She hates modern poetry.'

'And who is your favorite poet?' I ask, admittedly conde-scending.

'I have no favorite,' she says. 'A person my age should have many poets.'

The conversation pauses. I take a sip of tea and eat the whole of an old iced Christmas stocking. The ancient icing shatters between my teeth.

'And how long have you been interested in lepidoptera?'

She jumps up and shows me her supplies, her net, killing jar, spreading board, insect pins, etc. 'My sister's boyfriend taught me everything last summer. I've got quite a collection.' She digs out a set of Schmitt display boxes from under the daybed. 'But she's broken up with him now, so I guess I'll have to get a new hobby.'

'Why?'

'It's just how it goes,' she says, shrugging and again taking her place at the tea table. She pours me a fresh cup and I eat another cookie, this time faintly detecting the air of rancidity.

'I almost had a hysterestimy this year,' she says. 'But I decided against it.'

'Oh, really?'

'It seemed unnecessary. I resolved it could wait.'

'One always should get a second opinion with serious conditions.'

She nods gravely. 'Let's not discuss it anymore. Do you play jacks?'

'As often as I am asked.'

We move to the floor, taking with us our cracked teacups – she has brewed a bold Darjeeling. We work our way through twosies, threesies, and fours. I win twice and wonder if she is intentionally throwing me the games.

'In your whole life, what's the most awful thing you ever did?'

Without knowing anything, she knows too much. On the first date she has cut to the core; I have nothing but the deepest respect for a girl like this.

'Would you mind if we switched to Parcheesi?' I ask.

She takes out the game and sets up the board.

'The worst thing you ever did to anyone?' she quizzes again.

We roll for first.

'I killed my mother,' I say – with no choice but to answer honestly.

'Really?'

'Really.' (Definitely.)

'Really?' she asks again, almost gleeful in her disbelief, as if she finds it humorous or otherwise entertaining.

'Yes.'

'Are you sure?'

'That's how I remember it.'

'Did anyone try and stop you?'

'They encouraged me, but I didn't know it at the time.'

'Really?' She has won the roll. She shakes the dice and sends them across the board. 'Five and three. Really?'

'You're starting to sound like a stuck record.' I take my turn.

'What did your father say?'

'He died when I was five. And what about your father?' I ask, turning the table.

She shrugs. 'I saw him once – well, saw a picture of him. Mother says I took it from her and tore it to pieces. Mother says that's all there was, there isn't any more. A short marriage.' She holds up her cup, indicating I should refill it. 'Why'd you kill her?'

'Didn't mean to. I didn't mean it at all. It was an accident, all an accident. I loved her very much.'

'Have you loved anyone else?'

'Only you.'

She nods gravely. The game is over. Nobody has won.

In the distance a cowbell rings, not naturally but as if it's being struck, banged on purpose.

'My dinner,' she says.

I check my watch, 7 p.m., they're calling her home.

I don't want to leave. I want to stay, to busy myself in this place until she returns, and then I never want her to go again. I can't be without her.

'You can stay,' she says. 'I'll be back later.'

'I must go.' If I don't leave now, I will stay forever. I will spread myself out on the floor playing games forever and ever, making up imaginary and arbitrary rules as I go along.

The bell is banged again. 'Dressie's bell,' she says.

'Gram's cow?'

She nods. 'I have to go. But before I leave, I have a favor to ask.' She looks at me and waits.

'Yes?'

'Let me see it again.' I know what she is referring to and instantly blush.

'Oh, don't be a dolt. Show me. I just need to see.'

I have no desire to flash her my manhood, am in fact embarrassed by it – suddenly it is far too ungainly and grotesque a thing, huge, hanging dark and long. Afraid of frightening her, instead I slip one of my hands into my waistband and, with the other, unzip my fly and poke my index finger out through the fabric door, wiggling the digit. Her eyes fix on my pseudopart with such intensity that regardless of the fact that it is only my finger I'm flashing, the juice in my veins pools in my crotch, pushing the finger up a bit, giving it altogether a different pulse. She giggles and bends closer, examining my indexer. 'You bite your nails,' she says, and then runs off, out of the cabin and up to the big house.

I return home and lie in bed lingering over the sensation of the afternoon and the repeating flavor of tea and old cookies. I belch and I'm in heaven.

During the night there is a tap-tapping at the door. Hearing it, I am sure they've finally come for me. I go to them, ready to turn myself in. Open the door, no one is there, it is night, only night, black all around me. I return to bed. The window is open. She is there between the sheets, pulling my blanket to her chin. 'Couldn't sleep,' she says. 'Strange dreams, like nightmares, only my eyes were open.'

A stranger is shaking me. 'Hey, hey, are you all right?' I try to raise my arms, to brush him away, but I am all tied up. I'm in chains. Prison. Guards.

The sergeant is there, trying to rouse me. 'You must have fallen asleep. You must have dropped off.'

'What time is it?' I ask.

'Time.'

The sergeant steps aside, the members of the committee are looking out over the table at me. 'Would you like something to drink?' the black woman asks.

'Another cup of tea would be lovely.'

The black woman nods and in a minute the sergeant is holding a cup of tea. How can I drink all tied up? The sergeant brings the cup to my lips. I sip. Hot tea.

'Heaven,' I say. 'Thank you.'

'Can we continue?' the black woman asks.

'Pardon, I beg your pardon.'

'We were talking about New Hampshire. New Hampshire and Alice Somerfield,' the black woman says.

The man adds, 'The family has written a letter, asking that you not be released. Are you aware of the letter?'

'No.' I had no idea they'd written. 'Are they still in Scarsdale?'

No one responds.

The sergeant gives me another sip of tea.

'It is June,' the black woman says. 'You have rented the cabin, you meet Alice Somerfield at the lake.'

Close the window, lock the door, all too easily she fits herself around me.

Awake before dawn, it is my plan to wake her and send her on her way. I shake the bed a bit. She sleeps soundly. Across her lips is a faint grin.

'This may seem odd,' I say aloud, 'but I don't know your name.'

The sweet breeze of her breath sweeps my chest, teasing the hairs like wind through trees.

'Ruby Diamond Pearl,' she says groggily. 'The jewels of my mother's marriages.' She pauses. 'But Gram calls me Alice.' And then she is back in her dream.

'Won't you be missed at breakfast?'

Eyes still closed, she mumbles, 'I never eat so early in the day.'

We are in bed. I am attempting to make idle conversation.

'Where do you usually live?'

'In Scarsdale now, Mum's just married a Jew. I hate him. He wants to send me away to school.'

'Tell me more about your family.'

'I'm trying to sleep.'

'We could go swimming.'

'No one swims anymore. Uncle George drowned in the lake when he was almost twelve – exactly my age now – so did Cousin Douglas and his friend Lizbeth. Everyone hates water.'

'Do you?'

She doesn't answer.

'Tell me about your accent. It's vaguely . . .'

'Don't bother,' she says, swinging her legs out from under cover, getting up. 'It's an affectation.'

Her nightgown, as with much of her wardrobe, is poorly fitting, too small. It's torn at the neck to keep her from choking and again at the cuffs – the sleeves are so short they almost begin at the elbow.

'I've grown two inches this year,' she says, noticing my concern. 'Headed for the world record.'

I want to do with her as one would a proper lover, fuck her ferociously, working up an appetite for a beast's breakfast and then returning to bed, to do it again, finally rousing at two or three, to snack, feeding each other in bed like baby birds still in the nest, fucking again, then sleeping until supper with the comfort of newfound familiarity.

I want to feel the suddenness of being a couple.

She knows nothing of it. Instead she is out the door, the screen slamming behind her. 'Thanks, that was fun,' she screams as she runs up the hill, in her flowered nightgown, in broad daylight.

I sit by the door panicked, queasy, convinced I will never see her again – someone will see to that.

I wait. I wait, thinking that if I leave the house, she will come back, find me gone, and not return.

I wait for hours and then find myself preparing to go out, now equally sure that only if I'm gone will she return.

A ride in the car. It's good to get out of the house. Gifts. I will buy her gifts. I find myself in an antique store, rounding up a treasonist's trousseau, an ancient white nightgown – yellow butterflies finely embroidered around the collar – and a diamond ring. I have no idea what brings this on, but it seems unavoidable. I am compelled to make my intentions clear.

Returning to the house, there is still no sign of her. Unable to stand it any longer, I set off, charging up the hill toward the big house, not knowing what I'll do.

Hidden in the woods, leaning back against a tree, one knee bent, is a woman smoking a dark cigarette. In her free hand she holds a drink, all of it quite posed as if she's standing for a photograph. I am almost literally upon her before she has any sense of me.

'You frightened me,' she says, completely cool, dropping her cigarette in the leaves, crushing it with the toe of her espadrille.

'Pardon,' I say, attempting to disguise my own surprise at coming upon the mater of my babe.

She is tall, nearly six feet, built like a boy, flat as a board, thin as a reed.

'The renter?' she asks, lighting a fresh cigarette.

I nod.

She exhales. 'Gram doesn't like smoke in the house. It's my nasty habit.'

'I suppose,' I say. 'But a delicious one.' She offers me a cigarette. I decline, pulling out my own pack. She smiles.

'I thought I heard something in the woods,' I say.

'What did it sound like?'

'I don't know, I'm not used to the country. A wild boar possibly.'

'My daughter,' she says, finishing her drink. 'You're probably hearing my daughter. She's out there somewhere.'

I make no acknowledgment.

'I hate this place,' the mother says spontaneously. 'Damned greedy lake.'

A striking but buxom young woman opens the back door. We see her through the trees. 'Mother,' she calls into the woods. 'Mother, I'm leaving now, see you on the weekend.'

'Be right there,' the mother shouts, grinding out her second cigarette. 'My middle one, Gwendolyn. Just graduated Emma Willard and very anxious to see the world.'

'Up near Troy.'

'Yes. You'll come to dinner one night. Gram doesn't get out much, she's starved for company.'

'Thank you.'

I am lost without her, thoroughly depraved. I spend the afternoon alone in my hut, masturbating endlessly, failing to find relief. Near dark, I go and jump in the lake. For dinner I take toast and three shirred eggs. At twenty past nine, I go to bed.

Again in the night she comes. Pretending to sleep through her arrival, the clumsy, clunking clattering of her small paws prying the window open, the grunts and groans as she hoists herself in, through it all I snore sonorously.

In the morning while she's aslumber, I slip the ring on her finger. She wakes looking at it as if it were nothing out of the ordinary. Going to the window, she scrapes the stone across the glass and asks, 'Is it real?'

'Of course.'

'Are we engaged?'

'Apparently.'

'Gwen and Penelope will be so jealous.'

I struggle to find the words. 'Darling, sweetheart, dainty dumpling . . .'

'Get to the point.'

'Our arrangement is best kept between us. The ring, a private gift from me to you; something your sisters might easily misunderstand.'

'You mean, you don't really love me.'

'Oh, but I do.' I pause. 'But my age. I'm so much older than you.'

She cuts me off. 'How old?'

'Halfway through thirty-one.'

'That's nothing,' she says. And that's the end of it.

It occurs to me that if she does turn rat, if anyone ever asks, I can easily suggest that the ring once belonged to my mother and Alice so reminded me of her that I made a gift of it.

'And what should I offer you in return?' she asks. 'Is the pleasure of my company enough?'

I cannot even bring myself to answer. So pious, so holy, still so sure this is entirely a fix. Secretly she is wearing a wire, a microscopic camera has been implanted beneath her skin, they are there somewhere, watching me, maybe even staring out from inside her titties.

And despite my priestly guise of apparent abstention I excuse myself frequently, furiously frigging in the bathroom eight or nine times a day if only to relieve the pressure, so steady is the need. At some point, too, I abandon all efforts at concealing my interest and she sees it bobbing excitedly beneath my worsteds.

'Does it have a name?' she asks.

'I call it Walter, after my father.'

Her calves are the loveliest, longest, and most subtle shape. Thin ankles, delicate feet, long toes.

Her armpits are dappled with fuzz, a thing about to bloom yet oblivious to any notions of what it means to finally blossom.

Again and always I wish I were a photographer, could master the light, could make a picture that would illustrate, with all clarity, the effect she has on me.

Later I will ask myself what made me break my Philadelphia vows; was it a particular event or simply, stupidly, the path of least resistance?

What you should know is that in this rare case, it was she who took me. A seduction somewhere between a romance and a rape. I have no explanation for behavior such as this except a few theorems hinting at a sad and sordid explanation for her apparent, if addled, understanding of adult desire. I'm hinting at the possibility of some previous acquaintance with goings-on such as this – perhaps we had that in common as well. I wouldn't doubt it. Details and the like, admittedly, I didn't want to know.

'I'm sorry, what did you say?' the old woman asks. 'I couldn't make it out. You mumble. Speak more clearly. Enunciate.'

Again, they are annoying me.

My speech is slurred, *s*s sibilant, *l*s lazy, my mouth is sore from Henry's injection. And there's this damned pain splitting my cheek, my neck, shooting down into my left arm.

'I was saying that I think perhaps she's been abused as a child. If they write you another letter, you might want to write back and ask them that.'

'Are you speaking now of yourself or her? I'm not clear what you're getting at,' the old woman says.

Why do they take everything and turn it, make one thing into something else? In trying to help her, I've just made it worse for myself, I've said something they don't want to hear.

'Explain yourself,' the old woman demands.

I shake my head. 'Everything is not autobiography.'

'We're losing our focus,' the black woman says. 'We were talking about the events that occurred in New Hampshire.'

'Yes.'

'Is there anything you'd like to add, to clarify.'

I'm thinking about how the story goes – I wake to find myself tied to the bed, wrists, ankles, bound and even a rope around my neck.

Dressed only in cowboy boots and a skirt, Alice dances around the room, grabbing at her chest, pinching her nips. Hopelessly hard beneath the cover of a stale sheet, I watch the devil parade.

'God, I hope I don't get big boobs,' she says, looking at me.

My heart races.

She plays with her breasts, having named them Mildred and Maureen.

On an earlier occasion she has told me that she paints narratives around them with watercolor and then jumps in the bath and watches her stories disappear.

At the time I offered to buy her paper, but she said it would defeat the purpose, suggesting instead that I might take a Polaroid of each painting as she finishes.

I decline, not wanting to create evidence.

Now, she dances half-naked singing a little song about Mildred, Maureen, and the man they've got strapped to the bed.

She hoists herself onto the mattress and straddles me.

I distract myself by asking what poem she has on the bottom of her boot.

'"The Cowboy's Lament."'

She crouches over me, drawing on my chest with a pink Magic Marker. Simultaneously I'm straining toward her, wanting more and recoiling in horror.

'You might want to think about cutting off this hair, it's kind of disgusting,' she says, making pictures of horses jumping fences. 'If Mother's new husband wasn't such an arse, I might be able to have a pony.'

She begins to post as if she's riding me, the motion of her sliding, bouncing on the bed, works to pull the sheet down. Quite unexpectedly I feel her flesh against me.

'You're not wearing underwear!' I scream.

'I like to catch the breezes.'

With no warning she is down upon me, unforgivably on me, riding me like an experienced equestrian.

My eyes are closed. I'm in heaven. I'm in hell.

It is the tightest fit. Despite her apparent experience, she hasn't done exactly this before. She pushes herself down, taking her time, clearly struggling. Yet she makes no exclamation, her face merely curls into a scowl.

My stomach turns, I'm sure I'm feeling the bones of her ribs against the top of my prick.

'You're my precious pony,' she says, stroking my skull. 'My best horse.' She slaps my flank and keeps on with her ride.

When she finally crawls off, she makes the strangest comment: 'I'd keep going, but I think I'm out of quarters.'

She pops off my prick with a thick sound like a suction cup released.

I'm drenched in sweat. She releases my restraints.

She goes into the other room, talking to herself all the while. 'First, I'll sponge you down, and then you'll get a big bucket of oats and, if you're good, maybe an apple.'

Delicately, I use the sheet to clean the mess and then rearrange things to cover myself.

She comes back and begins dabbing at my chest and neck with a kitchen sponge. 'Doesn't that feel good? What do you like on your oats, butter or sugar?'

I don't answer.

She leaves again, returning with two steaming bowls of oatmeal. She climbs into the bed. We eat.

'Isn't this fun?'

I feel nothing but fond of her. Although undoubtedly I've not said it before, I do firmly believe it is up to an adult to ignore the attempted flirtations of the young, to allow the child to express her powers of persuasion in a seemingly safe setting. She is asking for it, if only to learn, to practice such; it doesn't necessarily mean that she really wants it or even knows what *it* is. She is in fact compelled by the culture. For the first time in my life I feel vaguely paternal.

But soon I am brought, nearly forced, to the conclusion that if it hadn't been me, it would have been someone else. And quite frankly it's lucky it was me. I loved her. It should always be one who loves you who is given such a thing; that greatest gift best goes to someone who can truly treasure and appreciate, someone for whom it continues to accrue meaning.

I know whereof I speak. My sweet concubine.

'Do you find me attractive?' she asks.

'Undeniably.'

'Do you desire me?'

'Indefatigably.'

'What part do you like best?'

'The entirety.'

'My breasts?'

She aims the buds at me and all I can think of are those flowers that squirt water into a fool's eye. Instinctively I duck.

'No,' I say.

'But don't I have beautiful breasts?'

'Your question was what part I like best.'

She nods.

'Your hidden smile.' I aim my finger at the spot – cracked slit.

She preens, kisses my cheek, and asks, 'How do you make a hickey?'

'How do you know the word *hickey*?'

She doesn't answer. 'Give me a hickey,' she says.

I shake my head, refusing.

'You're mean.'

'No, I'm not.'

'Yes, you are. I want to know what a hickey is.'

I pick up her foot and suck on her toes. 'That's a hickey.'

She laughs and shakes her head. 'No, it's not.'

I kiss my way up her leg. She squeals, 'You're tickling me.' She grabs my hair. I am in her thighs, long muscle and soft skin, no fat, nothing extra here. I flick at her with my tongue. She stops squealing; I continue. She looks dreamily out the window and lifts one leg so it hangs over the edge of the bed. She is the most lovely thing.

When we fuck – and we do fuck, frequently – there is something so familiar about her skin, about the way we fit into each other, that it is as if I'm inside out, touching myself. There is something between us not made on earth.

'No matter what happens,' she says later, handing me her six Schmitt boxes, her butterfly collection, 'I want you to have these. Don't forget, every now and then change the paradichlorobenzene crystals, otherwise they decay.'

'I'll treasure them always,' I say entirely honestly.

'They claim you kidnapped Alice on more than one occasion.'

Again they're at me with annoying questions, sonorous statements.

I shake my head. They have no idea.

For a break, a bit of an escape, we go on excursions, dainty day trips. I drive us in increasingly large circles round and round the state of New Hampshire – sightseeing.

'Clam rolls,' she calls to me as I leave the car. 'Two clam rolls and some coleslaw.'

We have stopped at a roadside stand modeled in the shape of an ice cream cone.

'And don't forget my soda,' Alice bellows as I reach the ordering window. 'And maybe some french fries. Suddenly, I'm starving.'

Darling Alice, gone despicable, wolfs down everything in arm's reach, including half my sandwich, my fries, and finally a large ice cream cone, of which she doesn't even offer me a lick.

When she's nearly finished, having indelicately dripped her melting sweets over my interior upholstery, she smiles, flashing clots of clam roll and cake cone pressed between her teeth. And although momentarily she disgusts me – I believe she does it on purpose – I remain in love, still plotting at summer's end to marry her.

'Here's to Labor Day,' I say, making a toast.

She raises her cone into the air and dabs what's left of the ice cream onto my nose.

'How laborious,' she says, licking my face.

I shrug and have a close look at her. Her skin has gone shiny, become a massive oil slick, a sea of sebaceous secretion. One must blot it before kissing.

As I back out of the parking lot all too quickly, an oncoming car swerves and hits its horn.

'Sweet Jesus, be careful,' she says.

'Pardon me, I was distracted,' I say, wiping the remnants of her ice cream and lick off my nose.

We stop to shop. I buy her things, not so much what she desires but what I decide she should have, mostly books. Recently she's been asked to surrender her library card. The matron of the town facility had reached the end of her rope when apparently every book Alice borrowed was returned with its pages heavily marked with bright red pistachio stains.

While I peruse the Book Worm's stacks, she excuses herself to the five-and-dime, saying, 'I just need something.' Whips and chains and coils of rope, no doubt.

When she's gone, I ask the owner for a volume of Ovid's love poems, thinking they would be more appropriate than Ferlinghetti for dear one's patent leathers.

'Finally, a true bibliophile,' he cries, coming out from behind the counter, slapping me on the back.

I blush. 'Hardly that,' I say, and am quickly out of the store.

Having fast abandoned my professorial pursuits, I find

my way to Woolworth's and unintentionally observe her shoplifting.

'Don't you get an allowance?' I whisper in her ear.

She has pocketed, of all things, a thick padlock. I daren't ask for what.

'The new husband doesn't believe in allowances,' she says, slipping a bottle of nail polish remover under the band of her skirt.

'What about baby-sitting? Don't most young women make pin money baby-sitting?'

'I hate little children. Can't stand them.' She picks up a Mars bar, peels the wrapper back, and eats it on the spot.

'You've already had lunch.'

'So?'

'And dessert.'

'Well, I'm starving, absolutely famished.' She pops the whole of an Almond Joy between her lips.

I am beside myself with frustration and attempting to shield her from the eye of the woman working the luncheonette, who seems quite drawn to our argument.

'If you get caught, you'll be in trouble,' I hiss.

'No, I won't. I'll say you made me do it.' She turns away, tucking a Chinese jump rope into her shirt. 'You put it in my pocket and made me walk out of the store.'

'I'll be waiting in the car,' I say, fuming.

She takes ten minutes more. I'm hardly surprised when she comes out carrying an all-too-new red-plaid overnight case.

'You lifted that?'

'Nope. Paid cold cash for it.'

'Planning a trip?'

'Shouldn't we be getting back?' she asks, checking the time on her new watch, having filched a fresh Cinderella whose arms are time's hands, making the passage of the minutes a slow-motion version of the Mexican hat dance.

'Do I ask where you've left your beloved Mickey M.?'

She shakes her head. 'No.'

Back at the cabin, our quirky campground, she unzips her new bag and feigns surprise to find it filled with little things, 'gifts' she calls them.

'What makes you do a thing like that?' I ask, appalled.

'Leave me alone,' she says, opening a jar of Noxzema, smearing a thick layer, a mask, over her face. 'Do you have to know every thought in my head?'

'Yes.'

'Come here then.' She beckons to me with a finger coated in cold cream – if only it were frosting, I'd suck it off. She digs a hole through the muck on her face. 'My first pimple,' she says, showing me a hivey swelling.

'It's a mosquito bite.'

'Zit.'

Crabby, she goes into the kitchen, opening and closing every cabinet. 'There's nothing to eat.'

'You've been eating all day.'

She moans.

'There's a bowl of fruit on the table, a perfect still life I arranged myself.'

'Something sweet,' she cries. 'I crave sugar.'

'Wash your face,' I say, forced to surrender my reading. I find her on her knees rummaging through the lower kitchen cupboards, a dust mouse clinging to her cheek.

I make her a cup of cocoa, which temporarily calms her. She sits sipping it, legs splayed akimbo on a chair.

All too easily I am able to look up her dress. Her mound is dappled with down, a disgusting dusting of hair, imparting the impression of a milk mustache, something you'd be inclined to wipe away.

'You know, dear,' I say, 'one day you'll have to begin wearing underwear.'

'I doubt it,' she answers, draining her cup. 'More?'

I shake my head. 'That was the last of the milk.'

She picks herself up, puts her cup in the sink, and goes into the bedroom.

I decline to follow, temporarily glad to have her gone, to have a moment's rest.

'Yoo-hoo,' she calls after a while. 'What're you doing?'

'Enjoying my book.'

'Oh.' There is a pause. 'I'm bored.'

Closing my text, taking care to mark my spot with a slip of paper, I find her in the bedroom.

With her hair, her long locks, she has tied herself to the bed, dividing her tresses into two pigtails, wrapping the ropes around the frame, establishing herself as quite racked out.

I kiss her titties, which are beginning to grow like globes, and sit beside her on the bed.

'I want you to hurt me,' she says.

'It's against my inclination.'

'Please, don't make me beg. I need you to hurt me.' She pauses. 'Make an exception.'

'What do you have in mind?'

She glances at her hunting knife resting in its sheath on the table by the bed. 'That.'

'No.'

She nods. 'Yes,' she says quite firmly.

I shake my head. 'I have no interest in causing you pain,' I say, walking away. 'In fact I have the idea that perhaps you've already had too much.'

'What about the others? Did you care so much about them? There were others before me, weren't there? Surely this isn't the first time?'

'Stop it. Just be quiet.'

'Make me.'

I am silent.

She wiggles her foot. 'Tie it up.'

Using the clothesline that's hanging off the bed, I bind her ankle. She wiggles the other one. I do the same again.

'There,' I say. 'That's all.'

She shakes her head.

I look at her spread out, gorgeous wine stain on her thigh.

It is not her desire that fails, but my heart. It cannot summon itself to pump blood to the necessary places. I am left to fuck her with my fingers.

'More,' she says. Already I've got two in, but I manage to fit a third.

'More,' she says again.

My pinky pokes at the edge of her ass. I'm so unhappy. I'm doing it entirely dispassionately.

In the last weeks, she has added some extra flesh, a fast seven or eight pounds, her fresh breasts jiggle, like pudding not quite set.

Transcending the limits of skin – there are moments in sex when you flash upon the idea that she might give herself to you, make the sacrifice of complete surrender, the prospect of death seems quite possible, acceptable, even desired. The most extreme and rare of sensations, true intimacy, something to aspire to.

I glance down and notice her foot has turned blue.

'Wiggle your foot,' I shout, penetrating our daze. 'Wiggle your foot.'

She doesn't respond except to lift her head and blurrily ask, 'What?'

There isn't time to undo the knot. Reaching for the hunting knife, I cut the rope away. The foot is purple. A thick line shows where the rope was laid. I gently massage the part. 'Does it hurt? Can you feel anything?'

'Who cares,' she says, lying back. 'Just keep going.' She raises her hips up and down. 'Just fuck me. Is that asking too much?'

My fingers slide in, one, two, three. . . . My hand is inside her, her heartbeat on my fist.

She sleeps soundly until seven when the cowbell is banged.

'How's your ankle?' I ask as she gets ready to go.

She looks at me as though she has no idea what I'm talking about. I say no more.

While she's away, I sneak off to the store and stock the larder, purchasing all the makings of a picnic and more, a wide variety of cakes and cookies, two or three of everything. I can't afford to lose her over the triviality of sweets.

During the evening I venture out, filling a jar with fireflies. Awake, waiting for her, my heart beats erratically, part broken. She doesn't return until nearly eleven, as always preferring the window to the door. I've fixed a little ladder to make her entrances easier. 'Gram wasn't feeling well,' she says, slipping into bed. 'I had to sit with her for a while.'

We make up tenderly, my heart well primed for the occasion. The green glow of glitterbugs fills the cabin.

'It's more than half over,' she says in the middle of the night.

'Shhh. You're talking in your sleep.'

'Obviously.'

In the morning I pack a picnic lunch and we set off toward the lake. I pull the rowboat out of the scrub and into the water. In the middle of the lake she undresses. 'I love to sunbathe,' she says, easing out of her shorts. The boat rocks unevenly.

My eyes spin along the shore, worried someone will see, still convinced this is a setup.

She reaches into the basket for a sandwich; a roll of flesh protrudes from her belly. It wasn't there before. There was nothing extra when this started. 'Why are you here for the whole summer?' she asks, biting into a ham salad, pink meat squirting out of the corners of her mouth. I look away. 'Why don't you have a job? Don't most men work?'

'I quit my job,' I say, thoroughly distracted.

'And in the fall what will you do?'

'Marry you,' I offer softly.

She eats a fistful of potato chips. 'I'll be in school.'

I can't look at her. 'We'll run away,' I say, staring at a distant dock.

'Where to?'

'Anywhere you want to go.'

'To hell in a handcart,' she says.

I glance at her feet, there's a mean bruise on her ankle. I ask again, 'How's your ankle?'

'Oh, I must have banged it.'

'It's bruised.'

'Things happen.' She opens another sandwich. 'I forgot to tell you, you were supposed to come for dinner night before last. Gram was looking forward to meeting you.'

My ire, my powerlessness, pulsates. I'm at the mercy of a master. 'Pity you forgot.'

'Actually, I told them you must have forgotten. "Do we give second chances?" Gram asked me. "Rarely," I said.'

There's no way I can win.

She continues to eat. When she's done she suddenly stands. 'I hate water,' she says. 'It terrifies me.' And then she is in. She's jumped naked into the lake and I haven't the slightest idea of what to do. Is this her idea of an afternoon swim, another of her juvenile jokes, a devilish game of cat and mouse? Am I supposed to go after her, make a mad dash into the water? Or did she go to escape me, to prove she couldn't be possessed?

I take off my shoes. She still hasn't come up. There is a thunk on the underside of the boat, a knocking that could only be her. I throw myself over. I am under. In the bracing cold, I see nothing but murk. I come up for breath, gasping, fearing it is me who might drown. I draw air and go under again, feeling with arms and legs, deep as I can go. I brush against her, grab, but she slips through my grip. I shoot to the surface, break for air, and go back again, this time finding her, fetching her, hauling her up.

Unconscious, unbreathing. I raise her torso, hoist her into the boat – which pulls away from me. Taking great care not to capsize the small ship, I then pull myself in. Luck, only luck, and a burst of physical fitness let me do this.

Establish an airway, chin up, head back. My mouth sealed over hers in total desperation. I fear she's made me her murderer, chosen me intentionally. I will not settle for this. I am an innocent man. You must know that. Furiously, I blow into her lungs, willing to trade my life for hers. With the full weight of my anger I breathe, I blow, I beat at the breast, and row, row, row, fast as I can, back toward shore. She coughs, sputters, and comes back to life. I wrap her in the tablecloth of our picnic and climb out, splashing through the last few feet of water, crashing barefoot through the woods toward her house.

I am bringing her home, giving her back. I don't know what else to do. Breathless when I reach the porch, I kick at the back door until finally Gwendolyn, in curlers, answers.

'The boat, the lake, her head banged,' I blurt.

'Mother,' Gwendolyn bleats. 'Mother, come quick.'

I lay little Alice across the backseat of their car.

Gwen raises the edge of the tablecloth and covers Alice's exposed breast. 'She looks too old to be skinny-dipping.'

'I've brought her back,' I say as the mother comes running out. She looks at her daughter and flies fast into the front seat.

'Do you need a doctor as well?' the mother asks. I shake my head, oblivious to the fact that my feet are bleeding.

I could have taken her home, kept her for myself, but I brought her back to them, is that what she would have wanted? 'She banged her head on the bottom of the boat.'

'Damned lake,' the mother says, turning the ignition. The engine grinds, is slow to turn over. 'Damn it to hell.' Gwendolyn pulls the door closed. I am out on the side of the road. The car backs away.

I don't know what to do. I go back to the lake, the boat has disappeared, the current has carried it off along with the remains of lunch, her clothing, all of it evidence.

A bath, a drink, another drink, dry clothes, bandages for the feet, and I drive into town, parking at a pay phone across from the hospital.

'Good condition,' the nurse says.

'Good?' I say.

'Yes, that's right. Admitted for observation, concussion.'

'Yes, she bumped her head. But she's in good condition?'

'Yes, that's right. And you say you're the father?'

'Yes, that's wonderful,' I say, hanging up. Good is like better or best, it's hopeful, promising. It means everything will be all right.

Alone at night, I don't sleep at all. I lie on her side of the bed, my head against the pillow where she usually rests. I turn my face into the pillow and breathe the scent of a little girl who bathes infrequently, sweet dirty sweat. Still hooked to the bed frame are strands of her hair; I take them into my mouth, sucking them. What to do? What to do?

Pain. Pain wakes me. My arm. My chest.

'Breathe,' the sergeant is telling me. 'Breathe.'

I am being divided, cleaved in half, a sharp searing pain splits my chest.

Salts are passed under my nose. I am at the sea, I am at the shore. I am in a doctor's office, there is the smell of a doctor's office.

'Breathe.'

I am awake, upright. I am in the chair, still in the chair, in the committee room. The members of the committee have disappeared. I see their backs as they are leaving, passing through the second door. Guards surround me. My chains are undone.

'Are we finished? What happened? Did I scare them away?'

No one answers me. Did they hear the question? Did I even ask it out loud?

'Are you all right?' the sergeant asks.

'I think so.'

'You must have fainted. These hearings can be very stressful, and at your age . . .'

I am lifted to standing and then led, half-carried, through the very door through which I arrived. No door number three today.

The key doesn't unlock the cell. The sergeant goes halfway around his chain, trying to find the right key. The guards, my escorts, pass me back and forth between them, taking turns fiddling with the keys.

'What time is it?' I ask.

Growing increasingly nervous, the escort guards ask, 'Is this the right room?'

'Ah,' the sergeant says, fitting the key into the lock, opening the door.

It is my cell, my same old cell. Home.

Everything is as it was. Deeply relieved, the guards push me in, undo the belly chain, the shackles, the handcuffs.

'Is that all? Is there more?'

'Tomorrow,' someone says. 'It'll be finished tomorrow.' And

then the door is closed, locked, and I am left on the shreds of my mattress.

My belongings are still on the bed frame, ready to go. Seeing them there still waiting is an insult. It is as though my own things have turned on me. The glass on the Schmitt box is broken. When I left this morning, I could have sworn it was intact. But it is broken now, pressing in on my ancient butterflies. I lift the lid, the glass falls away.

From my sewing kit, I take a spool of thread and tie thin white lines around the bodies of my butterflies. Holding them high above my head, I fly them like kites, whipping them through the air, whirling round. Hoary Elfin, Painted Lady, Common Blue. Old and infirm, they break apart, the wings easily come away from the head. Between my fingers, they crumble to dust.

Dinner comes, a tray slipped through the slot in the door, Henry's hole.

'There must be a mistake,' I call to the guard, pushing the tray back through the slot.

The guard pushes the tray through the hole again.

'No,' I say, pushing it back once more. 'A mistake, there must have been a mistake.'

'Think again,' he says, keeping the tray, moving off down the hall. 'Fucking lunatic,' I hear him mumble.

Not to worry, I tell myself, not to worry.

My room is a mess, dotted with debris, remnants of my packing party. Pushing everything off to the side, I find paper and pen. I write a letter, a letter to my love, a precious poem, pouring it on, syrupy thick. This is it. I'm begging, pleading that she come back.

Henry beckons me to the door. 'I have something for you. A gift, a little nightcap.'

'Oh, I don't know,' I say, suddenly depressed, worried about my budding addiction.

'I cooked it just for you, it's special,' Henry says. 'You didn't eat your dinner, so try my little concoction. Taste, just take a taste.'

And again I cast myself into the curves of a contortionist and fit my mouth into the slot in the door. Henry's old glass works go through the hole, the needle pokes my cheek. 'Raise your tongue.'

'Is it sterilized?'

'I clean it with Clorox every time.'

I lift my lickety licker. 'Hold it,' Henry says. The needle is in position under my tongue. Drug in, needle out. I pitch forward, instantly asleep.

In my dream I drive a yellow truck.

15

Despite my best efforts I'm always the one who gets fucked.

Going, going, gone. She lies in bed. Yesterday, she tried to kill herself, today she is a little tired, groggy, under the weather.

Her mother carries in a breakfast tray, bowl of farina, burned toast, cup of tea.

'Are you all right? It's after noon. You slept like a log. How do you feel?'

The girl doesn't speak.

The mother sits on the edge of the bed, sprinkles brown sugar on the cereal, and stirs it around. 'When you were a little girl, sometimes I used to bring you breakfast in bed for no reason.'

A fresh flower is on the tray. The mother tries hard.

'Butter or jelly?' the mother asks, picking up a piece of toast.

The girl makes a face. The mother hands her the bread, dry. 'I spoiled you. Maybe that's what I did wrong. That's what this is all about, you've had it too easy. But what could I do, you're my only girl, you're all I've got.' The mother dips the spoon into the cereal and holds it up to the girl.

'You're not going to feed me?'

'Of course not,' the mother says, putting down the spoon. 'You're perfectly capable of feeding yourself.' Getting up off the bed, she picks up clothing from the floor, folds it, and puts it away. 'Eat your toast. I burned it on purpose, the charcoal is good for you, very absorbent.'

The girl's passport is on the breakfast tray. 'That's the thing about Mommy,' the girl's father said late last night. 'She keeps the details in order. She's always got us ready to go at the drop of a hat.'

The girl gets out of bed, dresses. She feels thin like paper. Her head is hollow.

'If we hurry, the hairdresser can squeeze you in,' her mother says. 'Mush, mush, let's go.'

Theirs is an uneasy peace, a reconciliation based on near tragedy.

At the beauty parlor the girl puts a pink robe on over her clothing. The shampoo woman turns on the water, tilts her head back, and massages shampoo through her hair. On the shelf in front of the girl are glass vials, serums, special treatments.

'How come I never get one of those?'

'You're not damaged enough,' the shampoo woman says. 'Just a little dry. This'll straighten you out.' She pumps a few squirts of conditioner into her hands, smooths her fingers through the girl's hair, then brings the girl to the hairdresser's chair.

'She's going to Europe tomorrow,' the mother says to the hairdresser.

'So, you want something easy that you don't have to think about?' the hairdresser says.

The girl nods. The hairdresser begins to cut. Chunks of hair fall to the floor.

'You're being made over,' the mother says. 'How do you feel? Do you feel all right?'

The girl feels dulled, as if she's been hit in the head with a brick. She secretly wonders if she doesn't have a little bit of brain damage. 'Tired,' the girl says.

'I forgot to tell you, Matt called this morning. He wanted to make a tennis date. I didn't think you'd be in the mood for tennis today. I told him you'd call him later.' Her mother continues to talk. She is able to talk for hours about nothing at all.

The hairdresser turns on the blower, momentarily drowning the mother out.

'Much improved,' the mother says when the dryer is off. 'A good cut, it brings out your face, and you have such a pretty face.' The mother hands the girl two dollars and says, 'Go, give them to the shampoo lady.'

All down her shirt she can feel little sharp pieces of hair, a hair shirt; she squirms.

'You'll need a few things,' the mother says, talking as she drives. Motion. The girl must be in motion. Moving against the world, it is the only thing that's calming now, soothing. She doesn't care where she's going, just as long as she keeps moving.

The mall is nine stories. 'We'll just do a little bit,' the mother says. 'I know you're tired from all that vomiting last night, but you absolutely need a suitcase.'

A single bag. She will pour herself into a single bag.

'Something light,' the mother says. 'You don't want to be

carrying lots of heavy baggage all over the world.'

It is ninety-two degrees outside and the stores are filled with fall clothing. Sweaters are on display.

'A suit,' her mother says. 'Every young woman needs a beautiful suit.'

Her mother picks things out and she tries them on. She sits in the dressing room while her mother and the saleslady run back and forth, hunting and gathering, collecting clothing like nuts and berries, bringing it all back to the dressing room, the den.

'Oh, that's it,' the mother says, clasping her hands together. 'That's it, that's it.'

In the shoe department, the mother picks out a pair of pumps, the girl tries them on.

'How are they?' the mother asks.

'Crippling. I've had them on two minutes and already my heels are bleeding.' The girl turns to the salesman. 'Do other people's feet bleed from their shoes?'

The salesman looks at her.

'Who knows anything about what happens to other people,' the mother says.

'I just wonder.'

'Shoes aren't supposed to be comfortable. You look grown-up, that's what counts. People will take you seriously. That's what all this is about, isn't it?'

'Do you want them?' the salesman asks.

'Whatever makes her happy,' the mother says. 'I want her to have whatever makes her happy.'

The shoes won't make her happy. Just the idea that they're supposed to make her happy makes her hate them. She takes them off and hands them back to the salesman.

'I'll think on it,' she says, knowing she doesn't want them, but thinking it impolite to say so.

Her mother buys her a camera, ten rolls of film, a folding alarm clock, two travel books, and an empty journal.

'For your thoughts.'

My head is banging, my brain knocking against the walls, all the padding is gone.

'Daddy's picking up your tickets,' the mother says when they are home. 'It's so exciting, isn't it?' The mother is in her room packing the girl's bag. 'I'm excited, aren't you?'

The girl shakes her head.

'It'll be such fun. I wish I could go.'

'You can,' the girl says. 'Just go.'

'I can't. Who would take care of your father?'

'There's something I need to do,' the girl says after dinner. 'An errand I have to run.'

Matt. She goes to Matt's house. As she walks up the driveway, she instinctively, reflexively gags. She spits bile into the bushes. Matt is upstairs in his room. His mother is in the kitchen, cleaning up. His father, working late.

'I called you,' Matt says.

'I'm leaving.'

'What does that mean?'

'I'm going to Europe and then back to school. My father bought me a ticket.'

'I love you,' he says. 'I didn't say it before because I thought it would gross you out.'

'We all love something once,' she says, her first effort at being philosophical. 'That's how it starts.'

'Will you come home at Christmas?'

'Too soon to tell.'

She has brought her new camera and a roll of film. She photographs him.

He gives her a small white jewelry box. 'I've been saving this for you. It's from my elbow.'

She smiles.

'Should we fuck farewell?'

'I should go,' she says, getting up to leave.

'Stay.'

'I can't.'

Her parents drive her to the airport.

'Do you have enough money?' her mother asks. 'Whatever you want, just put it on the card. Enjoy yourself. You only live once.'

'Don't encourage her,' the father says. 'It's very expensive over there.'

'Call us, let us know you've arrived.'

'We hope you feel better,' her father says, kissing her good-bye.

She passes through the metal detector. She has three weeks, twenty-one days, to reinvent herself, to metamorphose.

Harrods. Victoria and Albert. Madame Tussaud's. She is on a red bus riding down High Street. Sweaters for Mom and Dad at Marks and Sparks. Westminster, the Bloody Tower, the Florence Nightingale Museum. She has been drinking Orange Squash for six days straight, morning, noon, and night. Orange Squash and Kit Kat bars. The changing of the guard.

Rome. The Teatro di Pompeo, Venice at the Serenissima, in Florence at the Morandi alla Crocetta. Everywhere she goes, she gives her camera to a strange man and asks him to photograph her, there, like that. At the Il Campanile di Giotto, a girl she knows from school sees her. 'Big world,' the girl says. 'How funny. Last week I saw Sally Wilkens at the zoo in Prague.'

In Portofino, she is at the Splendido, looking out over the sea.

I am with her, too, she carries me in her pocket, in her suit-case. She carries me wherever she goes.

In her hotel rooms she makes notes, she writes, but doesn't

mail the letters. It is a journal now, hers, hers alone, private, personal, I have no idea what she's really thinking.

Once, she calls home once.

'I didn't tell you this before, but your father accidentally opened one of those letters,' her mother says. 'I don't know what you've gotten yourself into, I'm not sure I want to know. Your father and I are very concerned. When you get home, you're going to have to talk to someone about this.'

Her heart stops for a minute, and then because she is young, because she is strong, it starts itself again.

'Let's not dwell on it now,' her mother says. 'We'll deal with it when you get back.'

She doesn't call again.

She borrows a car and drives. In a town in Tuscany, a madwoman runs down a street, grabs the girl, and kisses her. 'A kiss is a kiss,' the woman says in English.

The girl is tired. Sometimes she just stays in the hotel. The thought of going out, of figuring out where she is, where she wants to go, is exhausting. Sometimes she is perfectly content to sit in the room and look out the window.

In the hotel in Paris, a blind man sits in the lobby with a dog. She befriends the dog. One night, she leads the man and his dog up to her room. When the girl brings the man to her bed, the dog grows excited and jumps up, joining them. 'Couche,' the man orders the hound. 'Couche,' he says, and the dog waits for his master on the floor.

It is August. Paris is on vacation. She rides the boat on the Bateaux Mouches, shops for school clothes in the St-Germain, eats bouillabaisse, escargots, and blood sausages. Walking the Rue de Rivoli, Tuileries, the Bois de Boulogne, she is always moving, in motion. She has the quality of seeming to know where she is going. People come to her and ask directions.

Oddly, she is able to tell them where to go. She makes gestures and draws diagrams. She has no language.

There are no more letters. There is nothing to say.

She is at the airport now. She is coming home.

P.S. I'm not afraid of you anymore, I'm more afraid of myself.

16

Prison. Bells. Morning. The names are called; attendance is taken.

'You have to eat a peck of dirt before you die,' the sergeant says, checking on Frazier, who was returned to his cell late last night.

'My Hohner is gone,' Frazier says, his voice raspy and weak. 'My Hohner is gone.' Apparently in the effort to remove his harmonica from his larynx, the instrument was destroyed.

'It's not so easy to kill yourself,' the sergeant says. 'The body resists.'

Sometimes.

The sergeant is at my door. I hear no jingling keys. 'There's a continuation,' he says. 'It won't be long. Get dressed. Get ready.'

Round two.

Again breakfast doesn't come. Budget cuts?

My pants are fitting better now that I've lost a few pounds.

Henry arrives on his morning rounds.

'Thank you for last night. It was lovely. Just what I needed. In due time your good works will be rewarded.'

'I hope so. You're running up a real tab.'

'What exactly is in your mix?' I ask the recipe only to distract him from the subject of my bill.

'A bit of this and that,' he says, tapping his needle against my door.

Again, I've been locked in, a box within a box, how degrading. Where do they think I'd go?

I mount my mouth against the hole. There is a dull pain in my jaw and all down my neck. My left side in general seems not to be working well. I slump to the floor and arrange to have Henry shoot me on the right.

'Can you do it?' I ask.

'I am a magician, a sorcerer, I can do anything.'

The needle is in. I am out. Henry is gone.

Pounding, pounding, just like yesterday, there's a pounding at the door.

'Is that you?' I ask.

Guards: cuffs, shackles, belly chain. Again I am on parade, led limping through the corridors, my left leg dragging languid, lazy behind me.

'Sorry I'm so slow,' I say, apologizing for my sluggishness. My speech is slurred.

The day has a certain clarity, an absence of aggravation, of anxiety.

A clock on the wall of the committee room reads ten of ten. I sit. The members of the committee file in, get their coffee orders straight. For some reason I'm surprised to see the same three people again today. I don't know why, but I imagined that each time it was different.

'Are you feeling well?' the black woman asks.

'Better,' I say.

'Did you sleep last night?' the white-haired lady adds.

'Did you sleep well?' Mama says. 'Dream a pleasant dream?'

I smile. Fumes escape my mouth. I didn't brush my teeth. I run my tongue over my incisors and bicuspids. They have the texture of moss, the flavor of mold, of fungus run amok. In fact, I don't remember when I last brushed my teeth. I don't remember ever having a toothbrush in this place.

'Yesterday, we were reviewing the events.'

'And then you lost it,' the old woman says, as if she's required to remind me.

'We need to discuss the options,' the man says, speaking softly. And then I think I hear him say medication, castration, and I mean to ask if that's really in their repertoire, but a flash of internal lightning, a pain, divides my chest.

'Tell us about Alice,' the black woman asks.

'What more can I say?'

'How did you feel about her?'

'Fond. Very fond.'

'In a letter to the court, her family claims you tried to kill her, to drown her in the lake,' the little old lady says – and I hate her.

'I saved her.'

The lake, the boat, why do you make me repeat myself?

I bring her home, give her back. Breathless when I reach the porch, I kick at the back door, until finally Gwendolyn, in curlers, answers.

'The boat, the lake, her head banged.'

'Mother,' Gwendolyn bleats. 'Mother, come quick.'

I lay little Alice across the backseat of their car.

Gwen raises the edge of the tablecloth and covers Alice's exposed breast. 'She looks too old to be skinny-dipping.'

'I've brought her back,' I say as the mother comes running out. She looks at her daughter and flies fast into the front seat.

I could have taken her home, kept her for myself, but I brought her back – is that what she would have wanted?

'She banged her head on the bottom of the boat.'

'Damned lake,' the mother says, turning the ignition. The engine grinds, is slow to turn over. 'Damn it to hell.' Gwendolyn pulls the car door closed. I am out on the side of the road. The car backs away.

Alone at night, I don't sleep at all. I lie on her side of the bed, my head against the pillow where she usually rests. I turn my face into the pillow and breathe the scent of a little girl who bathes infrequently, sweet dirty sweat. Still hooked to the bed frame are strands of her hair; I take them into my mouth, sucking them. What to do? What to do?

In the morning I pack. If nothing else, they will want me gone. If I'm lucky, they will simply send someone to say that given the circumstances I should leave. I take my boxes from the storage shed and fill them carelessly with the exception of the gifted butterfly collection, which I wrap carefully, using my summer clothes as padding.

I hate this place. This damned lake.

Before dawn, I have filled the trunk with all but the essentials. And then I begin to wait. I cannot leave before I've been given the signal, before someone says go. If I jump the gun, it will seem as though I'm running, as though I have something to hide.

For four days I sit in the house waiting for word. No one comes. House arrest. I sit, I stand, I walk from bed to chair, to table, to desk, imploding, exploding, going entirely insane.

Finally, there's a knock on the door.

'Yes,' I call from inside the house. The moment has come, and although I've been waiting, suddenly it's unexpected.

'It's Gwen,' a voice says through the door. 'Sorry to interrupt.'

I open the door. 'How is she?' I ask, fearing that I seem all a fraud.

'It's Gram,' she says. 'Gram's not well. The doctor thinks she's had a stroke. We're flying her to New York. They're taking her to the airport in an ambulance, but our car's not starting and, well, could you give us a lift?'

'Of course. Right now?'

'Yes.'

'Let me just get my wallet.'

At the house they're already loading the beloved Gram. She's propped up on a stretcher, a green plastic oxygen mask over her mouth, well tended, tucked in with many blankets, her gray hair wrapped like a crown around her head.

'They're taking her to Columbia Presbyterian,' Gwen says, jumping out of the car, running to help Penelope with the bags.

I get out and open the back doors, nodding in the direction of the mother, who's talking with the attendants. She ignores me.

'The trunk is full,' I tell the girls, who then pile their bags into the back. I look around for my beloved, but she's nowhere to be seen, there's not even a hint of her. And then finally she comes out the back door, overnight bag in hand, restrained, even sheepish. I'm flooded with a rush of affection. My blood swirls, races to hot spots.

'I did it,' she whispers as she's getting in the car. 'I told her about you and it killed her. Now, I'm a murderer, too.'

Fear that she's really spoken such grips my chest, grabs my

heart, nearly stopping it. My knees buckle. I lean against the car.

'Alice dear,' her mother says, 'don't cause trouble.'

We follow the ambulance out.

'Sorry you weren't able to meet Gram,' Gwendolyn says to me.

'She's not dead yet,' Penelope adds.

'Well, she can't last forever,' Gwen says.

'If you don't mind,' the mother adds. 'She is, after all, my mother.'

'Sorry.'

They are quiet. The mother turns to Alice. 'While we're in New York, maybe we'll have you checked. Make sure there's no real damage.'

'My head still hurts,' Alice says.

'They said it would for at least ten days.'

In my rearview mirror Alice seems small again, a girl, not a monster. She clutches the overnight bag on her lap as if it holds something precious.

At the airport, the plane is waiting. The grandmother's stretcher is carried up the steps. The two older girls and the mother follow. Alice refuses to go.

'I can't,' she screams, suddenly stricken. 'Just go without me.'

'There isn't time for this,' the mother says, coming back down the steps, taking Alice's hand. 'Get on the plane.'

'No,' Alice shouts, pulling away, throwing herself down on the tarmac and having a tantrum befitting a two-year-old.

'Watch your head,' her mother says. 'Don't bang your head again.'

Alice kicks and screams most embarrassingly – not only for herself but for all of us.

'I'm going to have to call a psychiatrist,' the mother says. 'But

I can't right now, so just pick yourself up and get on that plane. Gram's inside and we have to go.'

The engine starts. The propeller spins. There's wind in the air. Gwen and Penelope stand at the top of the steps. The mother starts to cry.

'Would you like me to carry her up?' I ask.

'Is that what you want?' her mother says. 'To be carried like an infant?'

Alice weeps and shakes her head.

'Ridiculous,' the mother shouts. She pulls at Alice, who's made herself into cement.

'I can't fly,' Alice howls. 'I can't fly.'

Although I'm trying to stay out of it, I feel responsible. 'I could drive her to New York,' I say. 'We could leave immediately and meet you there this evening.'

A man from the airport comes and speaks to the mother. 'We have to go,' the mother says to Alice. 'Are you coming with us?'

Alice shakes her head. 'No.' Snot is running down her face, her hair hangs down past her chin.

'Then will you go with him in the car to New York?' the mother asks, gesturing toward me suspiciously.

Alice nods. I'm surprised, but secretly pleased.

'No shenanigans?' the mother says.

Alice nods again.

'I trust you to behave.' The mother says to me, 'Columbia Presbyterian. And if you're not there by ten o'clock, I'll call the police.' She is up the steps, the door is sealed. Alice stands aside and the plane pulls away.

We're alone on the tarmac.

'Well, it's good to see you,' I say.

She doesn't speak, but climbs into the car, claiming the back-seat for her own. I'm her chauffeur, servant, slave. I drive her away.

'I lost the ring,' she says after a while. 'In the lake. It must have fallen off.' She stops. 'Does that mean we're divorced?'

I shake my head.

'You must hate me.'

'No.'

'Well, I hate you.' And then she is silent. Hours pass. I stop for coffee, she declines to get out. I stop and buy myself a fresh shirt, a new toothbrush. I ask her if there's anything she needs. She pats her case. 'I have everything.'

Every time I leave the car, I watch her out of the corner of my eye, afraid she will bolt, run away, and leave me in deeper trouble.

Near North Chelmsford, we stop at a roadside stand.

'What'll it be?'

'I'm not hungry.' She's in the backseat, doing her nails. The sedan stinks of polish.

'Yes, but you should have something anyway.'

'Then just bring me the usual. And a vanilla milk shake.'

'We're a little south for clam rolls.'

'Hot dogs then. With relish.'

I'm so glad to see her, so terrified and terrorized.

'Don't ever leave me again,' she says when I get back in the car.

'Why?' I ask, meaning Why did you jump in the lake, why did you try to leave me, why can't I leave you? Why?

'I have no one else.'

'Your mother, the sisters, Gram.'

'It's not the same.'

At every turn, every cash register we pass, I buy her something: postcards, comic books, candy. All the while she stays in the car, except twice to pee, asking me then to take her to the ladies' room, to wait just outside.

'My head,' she says. 'It's not all right.'

'You seem more or less like yourself.'

'Less,' she says. 'Less all the time. Everything is changing. I'm changing. It's awful, disgusting, and I can't make it stop.'

Despite the fact that visiting hours are over when we arrive at the hospital, they let us go up. The pale hues of the walls, the silence, cling like a death mask. The grandmother is tucked in, the girls and the mother are saying good-night. The stepfather from Scarsdale stands in the corner.

'Who's that now?' Gram asks, her speech slightly impeded.

'Alice,' Gwen says. 'And the man from the cabin.'

'Send them in.' And although we're already in the room, we step closer.

The grandmother looks at me, her eyes still piercing beneath their cataracts. I smile feebly. She knows. It is as if my fly is open, my member out and aimed like a directional arrow at her granddaughter.

'You missed dinner,' she says.

'I'm terribly sorry. I had the date wrong. But when you're better, I'll cook a meal for you. What's your favorite food?'

She makes a face shooing me away, then bends a bony finger and beckons the young one near. 'Once I had a friend,' she says in a papery voice. 'He soon died.'

'Gram, we have to say good-night,' the mother says, interrupting. 'Rest now. Sleep tight.'

Alice holds my hand. She slips her palm into mine. No one says anything. To tame a child, to take and train her, is to charm a snake. The music of the seduction is the um-pa-pa of a carousel, the twist of a fairy tale, everything is in the believing.

'We've taken rooms at the Plaza for the night,' the mother says. 'It was all I could get. I took the liberty of making you a reservation. Tomorrow, we'll go back to Scarsdale. I've no idea what your plans are.'

We are walking down the hospital corridors. It is close

to midnight. The shift is preparing to change.

'I have no plans.'

'Perhaps then you'll go back up to the cabin.'

The guard opens the front door and we are out in the New York night.

'Frankly,' she continues, 'if I never see that damned lake again, it'll be too soon.'

The feeling is mutual.

We're out on the street. The air, hot and tired, has nothing to offer. I drive the six of us to the hotel and am deeply relieved to watch little Alice being led off to bed in her mother's company. 'Night,' Alice calls.

'Night.' I go down the hall to my room, wanting nothing more than to be left alone.

Fitful sleep. I prepare to depart before dawn. Leaving the mother a note at the front desk, I say how sorry I am about the circumstances and how much I'm wishing Gram a speedy recovery. I pay the bill and arrange to leave the car parked until evening.

Seven-thirty a.m. I'm in Central Park. My mind races, skips from thing to thing. Giddy. I break into a run, anxious to get as far away as I possibly can. At the center of the meadow, I stop to catch my breath. Around me pass dog walkers, standard poodles and the odd Great Dane, nannies with baby carriages, and the party boy who hasn't quite gotten home. The world is filled with possibilities. I can begin again. Start fresh.

Bethesda Fountain. The shallow boating lake. Carousel. I am all over the place, wandering drunkenly. In a diner on the Upper West Side I have breakfast: juice, eggs, bacon, toast, coffee, all of it delicious. My tongue tingles from the salt. I sit back and read the *New York Times* and the waitress refills my coffee cup.

Later, I go to the Metropolitan Museum. There is calm in

there, a certain fixedness. Making my way down Fifth Avenue, the film *Bonnie and Clyde* is playing. A matinee. A dark theater. Killing time. Escaping the heat, I sink into a cushioned seat.

Near dusk, I return to the hotel for the car, stealthily sneaking through the lobby, making every effort not to be seen.

I drive north, upstate, knowing I'm not going back to New Hampshire. I drive north knowing I should be going south. Tomorrow I'll turn around and go back the other way, but for now I'm just driving.

It begins to thunder, to lightning. An hour out, the traffic is thinning. Two hours, I'm hungry, haven't eaten since breakfast. A red neon sign, a great white structure, a place for the night. 'Motel.'

'Checking in?'

I nod. 'A room, please.'

'You and your family?'

'Just me.'

'Funny,' he says, pulling out the paperwork. 'I thought I just saw a little girl go by.'

My breath catches. I smile, checking the impulse to whirl around, to look behind me. He must be imagining things or seeing someone else. The world is filled with little girls.

I fill out the registration card, giving New Hampshire as my permanent address, and ask the clerk to recommend a restaurant.

He tells me the name of a place and sketches a map on the back of a postcard.

'Thanks,' I say, taking the room key. I walk across the parking lot. The air is filled with humidity. It is almost dark, the trees stand out against the night.

Opening the door to the room, a wave of inexplicable depression sweeps over me. The room is regulation, ugly, orange plaid. I don't go inside. I close the door and tell myself that once I have something to eat, I will feel better and then it will be only for a night.

Light evaporates from the sky. The air is heavy. Every breath is taken with hesitation and great suspicion. One tries not to move too quickly. The early promise of the day has faded. I'm tired now and a little bit afraid. I have no idea what I'm doing. I'm traveling without knowing where I'm going, or what my future will be. I'm going, knowing only that it must be different.

'Could we see the photographs?' the man asks.

'I don't need to see anything so explicit,' the white-haired woman says.

'They document the event,' the man says.

'I feel like I already know what happened,' the old woman says.

'It is our job to review everything,' the black woman says. 'Let's have the photographs.'

The secretary opens a big brown envelope. 'There are two sets,' she says.

'The three of us can share one. Let him look at the other.' The man nods in my direction. The secretary hands the guard a pile of eight by tens. He holds them up in front of me. Glossy.

'This is Alice,' the man says.

Instinctively, I turn away.

The restaurant. Booth. Menu.

'What'll it be?'

'Meat loaf.' There can be nothing better than a thick slice of meat loaf, with mashed potatoes, carrots, and peas.

'To drink?'

'Black coffee,' I say, and feel relaxed. I leave my jacket at the table and go to the men's room. I splash my face and the back of my neck with cold water, blotting dry with a wad of brown paper towels.

When I return, my food has arrived, a steaming plate is waiting on the table.

'God, I'm starving,' she says. 'I'm so hungry I could faint.' She has my silverware in hand and is digging in.

I slip into the vacant seat.

'You're a liar,' she says, eating my dinner. 'You promised not to leave me. Luckily, I knew you were a fake. I knew it all along.'

'Your mother will call the police.'

She gestures toward the food, offering me some.

I decline. My appetite is gone. 'How did you get here?'

'In your car,' she says. 'I lay in the back of the car, all day. I couldn't let you just escape. You're unbelievably oblivious and' – she pauses – 'a speed demon.'

She hands me a spoon. 'Take it. Under the table, put it in me.'

She spreads her legs, her knees knock against mine. A fork clatters to the floor. I bend to get it; the waitress beats me there. 'I'll get you a clean one,' she says, picking it up.

'Come on,' Alice says.

I shake my head. 'No.'

'Yes.'

'No. I can't do it. I can't do it anymore.'

'Yes,' she says intently.

The spoon is old, soft around the edges, it fits in easily.

'This is awful,' I say, on the verge of tears. 'I feel awful.'

'Awful is awful. I feel awful, too. Everything hurts. My head hurts, my face is covered in bumps that I'm driven to touch until they're raw, even my tits ache.'

The volume of her speech escalates, reaching peak when she spits the word *tits* across the table. 'And I'm in a foul mood, always in a foul mood.'

'How's Gram?'

She hands me the fork.

'Let's not play this game. I can't.'

'Of course you can. What, are you crippled?'

The waitress interrupts. 'Can I get you anything else?'

'Pie,' Alice says. 'Hot apple pie, à la mode. And a cup of tea.'

'Nothing for me,' I say, and the waitress disappears.

'Fork,' Alice says.

'No.'

'Where there's a will, there's a way.' She slips the fork into my hand.

I pray the tablecloth is really as long as it seems.

I did love. The details I can't give, they only diminish it, force too many comparisons. She was the one, one in a million.

'Go ahead,' she says.

'I'm not your slave.'

'Then what are you? A dirty old man? Just because no one says anything, because they're oblivious, doesn't mean I am. I wasn't born yesterday.' She is pleased with her tirade. 'What you're doing is illegal.'

'Do you plan to turn me in?'

'No.'

'Why not?'

'I can't let you get away that easily.'

I hold the fork and imagine the four tongs poking her, each one piercing. The pie arrives. Using the fork, I take a bite. The apples are hot. I scald my tongue.

She scrapes a dinner knife back and forth over the tablecloth. 'This,' she says, tapping it. 'I want you to do it with this.'

I'm sweating, beading up. I put the fork down. I can't eat any more. 'Please,' I say, signaling for the check. 'Let's go.'

'We can't. I'm not done.' She drinks her tea, slaps the knife in my hand. I refuse and let it fall to the floor. Constant clattering. The other patrons must notice how clumsy we are.

The waitress brings the check. Under the table Alice

removes the spoon. She uses it to stir her tea. 'Want a sip?'

'Let's go.'

'I'm turning into a circus act,' she says in the car. 'A regular freak show.'

It thunders. A wide swath of lightning divides the sky. I drive back to the motel.

'Now what?' she asks.

I pace the room unable to rest.

Again thunder and lightning. I close the drapes.

She disappears into the bathroom and is gone for a long time.

I worry what she's doing in there, some god-awful thing, cutting herself with razor blades, eating broken glass, the mood is right for something like that.

'Everything all right?' I ask through the door.

The toilet flushes. She comes out, her face bleached pale white.

'I'm bleeding.'

'Let me see.'

She puts her hand under her dress and then shows me her fingers, tainted red. 'It's blood. You've done something awful to me.'

I shake my head. 'I didn't use the knife.'

'I don't feel well. I don't feel well at all. My back hurts, my head aches, even my tits are sore.'

Something occurs to me. I reach for her, fit my hand into her, against her will. I pull my fingers out, sniff them, bring them to my mouth. I taste the blood. I have tasted such blood only once before. The flavor is thick, metallic, stale, like something that has built up for a long time. It is missing the tang, the sweet afterbite, of fresh-flowing injury. She is no longer fresh. Her body is expelling itself. I smear the sample onto the white motel notepad.

'A little lesson,' I say, tapping my bloody fingers on the paper. 'You're menstruating.'

'You did this to me,' she cries.

'Is what I'm saying so thoroughly unfamiliar? Didn't anyone ever talk to you about it?'

She shakes her head.

'Penelope? Gwen? Don't they tell you anything?'

'You cut me with the knife.'

'How could you not know?'

'You cut me.'

'I didn't,' I say, although admittedly I'm worried. There was the spoon and of course there is always the possibility of injury, one can easily tear or puncture something.

'You're a disgusting and dirty old man, a horrible thing. Don't even talk to me. I don't want to hear you. Your words get in my head. I don't want to think like you. I don't want to be anything like you. I hate you.'

'I can explain everything.'

'This is Alice,' the man says.

Eight by ten. Glossy. The photographs are presented as though they're proof.

In a way I saved her, I hope you can understand that. I spared her a situation that would only get worse. She was a girl, unfit to become a woman.

'This is Alice,' the committeeman says. 'Can we have your attention. Can I ask you to take a look?'

I look. I do. I look. I close my eyes. My mind unwinds like a spool, spilling thoughts. Photographs.

'Don't try and humor me.' She begins to cry. 'I want my . . . I want my. . . .' She bellows, unable to fill in the blank. 'I want my . . . ,' she repeats, unable to name her desire. 'I need a doctor,' she concludes.

'You don't need a doctor.'

'Don't tell me what I need.'

Her overnight bag is open, she's rummaging through it. It's filled with things, books, toys, parts of her tea set, the strangest assortment of stuff. Her hunting knife is in her hand. It's out of its sheath. She's flashing it at me, all the while holding her stomach. 'I'm in pain.'

I move toward her.

This is Alice. The guard puts a photograph in front of my eyes.

Images explode like fireworks. I feel the heat in my head, the rupture, the rapture, the warm rush of release.

'He's wet his pants.'

'Disgusting.'

I forgot to go. This morning I forgot to go.

'Pissed his pants.'

'This is Alice,' they say, and another photograph is in front of me.

The end of Alice.

'Don't come near me or I'll kill you. I swear I will.'

'Put it down,' I say. 'It's perfectly normal. Every month from now on, you'll bleed like this for a few days, and then it will be over. That's the way it goes.'

'I don't believe you. You're making excuses for yourself, for what you've done to me. Stop. Stop lying.'

I shake my head.

She cries, puts her hand over the spot, clutching herself, as if she can hold it in, push it back inside her.

'It's perfectly normal. In your underwear you wear a napkin to catch it.' I say this realizing that she has no idea of what I'm talking about, realizing that I sound insane. How does one explain a napkin, as if to dab at one's face, to place a heavy bandage between the legs. I can't bring myself to say more. It doesn't matter anyway. She is inconsolable.

'This is Alice,' the committeeman says again and again, and each time the guard shows me another photograph.

'Tell us what you see.'

A Rorschach in reverse. Red, lots of red, like geraniums, dark red like autumn leaves. Red and brown and black. Trees, the leaves of trees, wind through the leaves, the texture of bark.

'Look again, what do you see?' the black woman asks.

'Flowers, trees, a path through the woods, a woman disappearing.' I refuse to see what they want me to see. I will see only what I want to see, my desire, my vision. I see myself as above them. The pain builds in my chest, spreads, stealing my breath. Something is happening to me. I don't remember to forget.

'This is Alice,' they say.

I nod. I know Alice. I know all about Alice.

'The end of Alice.'

The storm. Lightning crashes. The lights go off, then on again, punctuating our dialogue.

'You cut me,' she howls. 'I'll bleed until I'm drained. My heart will grow fainter and fainter and then it will stop. It will just stop. You've killed me,' she screams.

'Shhh. The neighbors will complain.' I don't know why, but I reach for the knife, take it away.

'Give it back,' she says. 'Give it back.' She comes toward me.

'I didn't touch you with it,' I say. 'I didn't touch you. *This* is touching you,' I say, touching her with the knife. 'This is fucking touching you. I didn't touch you here.' I poke at her skirt with the blade. 'Don't you understand? I don't want to hurt you.'

'Then why did you do this to me?'

I have no answer.

'Why did you do this?'

'Why do you make me?' I'm crying. 'Don't make me.'

The first time it plunges in, there is resistance, but I'm angry, full of fire. I force it into her gut. The next one goes into her neck, a bigger splash, bright spray, the hiss of an artery. A hot, sticky fountain of blood douses everything. She makes a face and falls back on the bed, gurgling like a little girl, a baby with her rattle. Again I plunge in. She looks surprised. Again and again. I can't stop myself. I have in mind only the beginning and the end.

She's in pieces, splattered around the room. Rivers of blood form small tidal pools. I don't know which blood is which, from whence it came. The scent is meaty, the putrid stink of slaughter. I'm embarrassed by the vigor, the extent of my outburst. It is as if I've lost myself, broken away.

Have I made my point?

I go outside. Blood is caked under my fingernails, leaving rust stains on my skin, dried flakes of it fall off my face. There is blood everywhere. The lights dim and stay that way. Sheets of rain move across the parking lot. A distant pop. A transformer blows and the lights go out completely. The red neon title of the place and the orange vacancy sign are gone.

On a night like this, one gets the false feeling that the rules have been waived, certainty is suspended. I am wet, cold, soaked. My bare feet are on the cement sidewalk. There is dark blood on my instep; I stick my foot out into the rain, it washes off, runs away. My cigarette sputters, burns unevenly. I spit twigs of tobacco. Far off, lightning flashes like someone flicking a switch in a house, wanting only to check something for a second, to look in and then turn the light off again and pretend it never happened.

It never happened.

It is morning. I am still outside. The cleaning lady comes.

'Can I go in?' she asks.

I don't answer. Her cart is filled with everything she'll need, towels, soap, deodorizer. She'll make everything all right again. It will be clean and neat as if it never happened. She wears a mustard uniform, white apron, and yellow rubber gloves. She looks at me. I nod. Frankly, I'm glad to see her.

The end has arrived. I make a noise, a scream, a cry. There is no real word for the sound I make, but it is large and loud and from the bottom of this pit, an open throat. Startling myself, as if awakened from a nightmare, I'm back in the room, but not out of the woods.

They are at the heart of things. The heart. A painful squeeze in my chest.

'Are you all right?' the black woman asks.

I remember everything.

'We really should get on with it,' the man says, looking at me carefully. 'We're running out of time.'

'Go on then, read the rest,' the white-haired lady says. 'Cut to the quick.'

The secretary reads aloud: August 9, 1971, Chatham, New York, twelve-and-a-half-year-old Alice Somerfield is found dead in a motel room. Cause of death: multiple stab wounds – coroner counts sixty-four. Initial five on upper torso, jagged, indicative of struggle; remaining fifty-nine, smooth cuts, most likely occurring after death. Victim decapitated, her head positioned between her legs, weapon recovered at the scene – jammed in victim's vagina. Buck hunting knife. Fingerprints on handle match accused. Lab identifies menstrual blood and semen in vagina, anus, and mouth of deceased. Accused apparently continued relations with victim after her death. Victim's face and body covered in kisses. Accused dipped his lips in victim's blood and then kissed deceased repeatedly. Victim's blood found on accused's clothing, hair, fingernails, ears, painted over his lower torso and genitals. Photographs and samples taken. End note: Accused oddly calm at time of his arrest, expressing gratitude to arresting officers.

It is enough now, more than enough.

To you alone I've told the tale, do with it what you will. That's all there is, there isn't any more. I'm out of breath.

The deal is done. I'm taken out, carried, permitted to pass. Finally free. It is summer, the end of summer now. I feel the tired heat that comes in August. There is sky and trees, a high wire fence, a long road, and at the end of it you are there, waiting for me.

So glad to see you, I say. Missed you so much, thought about you every day.

The author would like to thank Karl Willers, Amy Hempel, Jill Ciment, R. S. Jones, and JL – who listened so attentively from the pay phone – along with The Corporation of Yaddo and William Sofield/Thomas O'Brien and Aero Studios for the desk and title of Writer in Residence. And for their support along the way, the author thanks Sarah Chalfant, Andrew Wylie, and Nan Graham.

Also by A. M. Homes
and available from Granta Books
www.grantabooks.com

THINGS YOU SHOULD KNOW

'This prose has teeth . . . you cannot shake a Homes story
off your mind, you cannot rid yourself of the creeping
unease it brings to your bedside table' Zadie Smith

'An extraordinary collection of stories . . . these are
stories you should read' *Sunday Times*

'Like Fitzgerald Homes is a sublime short-fiction
writer whose stories are like sharp and luminous rips in
the social fabric she so acutely describes. The collection is
funny and glinting and masterful, light as air, strange as a
dream. Monstrous as truth: the real; and classic thing'
Ali Smith, *Guardian*

'The stand-out, indeed knock-out, story here forces you
to admire Homes's cleverness, makes you laugh out loud,
then finally breaks your heart. That's why she has and
deserves her A-list status' *Independent*

Also by A. M. Homes
and available from Granta Books
www.grantabooks.com

JACK

'Honest, uncompromising and savagely funny – likely to work its magnetic attraction on anyone who picks it up'
Madison Smartt Bell

'A moving novel, and a very refreshing one. Jack is such an engaging, attractive human being, it's a pleasure to believe in him' David Foster Wallace

In *Jack*, A. M. Homes gives us a teenager who wants nothing more than to be normal – even if being normal means having divorced parents and a rather strange best friend. But when Jack's father takes him out in a rowboat on Lake Watchmayoyo and tells his son he's gay, nothing will ever be normal again.

Also by A. M. Homes
and available from Granta Books
www.grantbooks.com

IN A COUNTRY OF MOTHERS

'Very few writers push the envelope with such
style and confidence' Mark Haddon

For Claire Roth, an established psychotherapist with an adoring husband and children, her new patient Jody Goodman – a witty and attractive young filmmaker – is a welcome diversion from her predictable life. Jody, successful yet uncertain about recent developments in her life, is at first disarmed by Claire's interest and approval. Gradually, however, the lines between friendship and family, love and compulsion, begin to lose their focus – especially when one of them starts to believe fanatically that some things simply cannot be coincidences – and that what they share, in fact, is the deepest bond of all.

In a Country of Mothers is a transfixing psychological thriller. A. M. Homes forces us to confront our own judgements about sanity, danger and desire.